PRAISE FOR THE LINGERING

"... the best of the series to date! ... twists and turns that kept me captiva
ted... I loved the "following the rail lines" aspect of this book! ... the end
totally took me by surprise! I cannot wait until the next book!"
  - D. Alaniz

"...was absolutely soooo relatable! Gives you total Stand by Me vibes...
Super Presh! ... didn't everyone go out to the woods/cornfields and drink
trash beer, and smoke cigarettes while rocking out to 80s tunes?"
  - Abbyxrd, caffeinatedbabbles.com

"... pulls you in and doesn't let go. This series is addictively HORRI-
FYING and I can't get enough! ...couldn't be more "IN" the story, I can
literally see, feel, and sometimes smell the story."
  - A. Marczal

"For fans of adventure and 80's nostalgia! ...a story of friendship that
will move even the toughest reader."
  - Kelly, Review Cat 86

"... a fun journey spent bonding with friends turns into a nightmare.
...the supernatural encounter made my skin crawl. Getting lost in the
woods is creepy enough when you don't run into any monsters..."
  - E. Teutsch

PRAISE FOR THE RELICT

"...knows how to write around the action of the story... not just bare bones... expressive quotes throughout the book... adds so much life to the book. Hard to believe this is a debut novel..."
  - Kelly-Review Cat 86

"This book was quite the page turner, very well written, a bit creepy and a bit gory and I kept trying to guess what was going to happen at the end! I'll definitely continue on with this series..."
  - Christina-Amazon

"...powerful occult thriller... a gripping blend of horror, thriller, and investigative mystery..."
  - D. Donovan, Senior Reviewer, Midwest Book Review

"... a fun book with plenty of action, a fair share of gore, and spice that made me blush up to my ears!"
  - Tersie, Amazon

"Mixing Norse mythology/history with Native American folklore was brilliant. Everything was done respectfully... This is definitely a mystery, horror, thriller and I highly recommend reading this!"
  - Erin, Amazon

PRAISE FOR THE QUARRY

"Dark and terrifying. I loved every minute of the book and felt so many emotions while reading."
  - Brandy, Goodreads

"If The Descent was a book, it would be this."
  - Gavin, Amazon

"...an extraordinarily disturbing story emanating from a dark subterranean maze... From old wives tales to a very real unimaginable evil ...combines gods, monsters and myths... an advanced level of scariness."
  - Mike Rankin, Horror Bookworm Reviews

"...edge of your seat reading, so be sure to plan a good stretch of time as you won't want to put it down."
  - Cindy, Amazon

"I loved how dark, somewhat psychological this book was. I also would like to note, I no longer want to explore in any kind of caves... like... ever..."
  - Autumn, Goodreads

THE LINGERING

SKULLDIGGERY BOOK 3

DM GRITZMACHER

PIQUED PUBLISHING

CONTENT WARNING

The Lingering contains graphic depictions of violence and gore that may not be suitable for some readers.

LINGER

Linger-1: To stay in a place or be slow in leaving it, often out of reluctance. 2. To continue or persist: To remain feebly alive for some time before dying. 3. To proceed slowly; saunter

ARBELLA, MISSOURI
AUGUST 3RD, 1910

HIS SHADOW WAVERED UNDER the luminous moonlight as the railcars lumbered slowly past. The ground underfoot trembled and, on every side of him, tall cornstalks swayed leisurely back and forth. Their green leaves, stiff and coarse like sandpaper, whispered amongst themselves as they rustled in the passing breeze of the train. He stayed motionless, patient. Hunched down and hidden where the groaning steel and wooden railway bordered the farmer's field. Careful to keep his head below the tops of the corn as the burdened locomotive and its endless line of freight cars rolled unhurriedly past. Dark smoke billowed from the top of the train's stack, the industrial aroma of burning coal and oil briefly filling the air as the steam engine labored under the load. The clickety-clack of its steel wheels running across the rails soothing and eerily hypnotic. Filling the stillness in the surrounding fields and countryside with their familiar clatter.

The railcars slowed, just as he knew they would, when the steam engine approached the small town of Arbella a half mile down the line. Though the freight train wouldn't stop in the dead of night, its slow approach in and out of the farming community ahead was as regular as clockwork.

The shadow split the green sea of cornstalks hiding him. Eyes narrowing, searching for an unoccupied and empty boxcar to hop into. Careful to avoid any random hobo or enterprising railroad dick hitching on the same rail line. But this night, as usual, there were many deserted cars to choose from. He left the leaves of corn behind him slick with blood, and a small pool of the same seeping into the dark soil where he'd lain in wait. As he clambered up the side of the moving freight car, the locomotive's shrill whistle screamed. Alerting the tiny town ahead it was about to cross its path. Not realizing the warning was far too late. The train's newest cargo having already visited one unlucky family that crossed his path.

Without a warning...

CHAPTER ONE

"FLACCID!"

"You can't be serious..."

"What do you mean? That is the perfect name." Stander gave Secrist his best mock indignation look. "I am thinking we can do some Air Supply, Christopher Cross, John Denver... maybe Simon and Garfunkel?" Stander took one hand off the wheel and ran it through his longish grey locks. "Does anyone remember the group Bread anymore? Maybe do a couple of their hits?"

"Did they have hits?" Tom Secrist, having recently retired after a long career in law enforcement, looked across the black interior of the Jeep at Russell Stander who was ten years his junior. "I can't think of even one."

"What? Oh, come on! 'Make it with you?' Or how about 'Baby I'm-a Want You?' Those are classics right up there with 'Close to You' from the Carpenters. Or 'Muskrat Love' from Captain and Tennille. I'm talking the AM radio standards of our youth!"

"Oh, okay Mr. Long-Hair-Heavy-Metal guy. How could I have possibly doubted your vast knowledge and love of lame soft rock music?" Secrist, to make his point, spun the volume dial on the Jeep's satellite radio. The base thumped loudly and someone was screaming about running to the hills before he twisted the dial back down. "This is the only kind of crap I ever hear you listening to," he said, pointing to Stander's black Motorhead t-shirt. "What makes you think you'd be happy playing folk-like music in some acoustic group?"

"Not a group, really. Just me and Lucas strumming our guitars and harmonizing. I was thinking we could do some shows at my bar starting out. You know, until we get wildly popular. And we'll call ourselves 'Flaccid.' It's the perfect name for a soft rock group." Stander, his face dominated by a white bushy moustache, brushed a couple strands of hair away from his blue eyes and scrunched his features up in thought. "Or, since we're a duo, maybe 'Scrotum' would be more appropriate? There would be a 'pair' of us..." He pulled both hands off the steering wheel and made air quotes as he spoke, smiling broadly and winking.

"Jesus, Stander. You can't be serious. Just... just quit talking about this. Please!" Secrist, dressed in khakis and a blue polo shirt, put both palms up to his eyes and shook his head. "Anyway, last I knew Lucas can't play the guitar. And I know for damn sure you couldn't carry a tune even if you packed it in one of your bags back there." The long-time detective thrust one thumb over his shoulder. Both he and Stander's belongings for the week were piled on the backseat in a couple of carrying cases and duffle bags. "Besides, Lucas is still in France, right?" Stander nodded begrudgingly. "Any idea how much longer he'll be working at the site?"

"Can't really say until he gets a handle on whatever we found buried alongside the quarry pit. I'm actually hoping he sent me an email with an update when we get to the hotel. I haven't heard from him yet this week." Stander reached up with one hand and tweaked the tilt of the rearview mirror. His full sleeve of colorful tattoos, bright in the streaming sunlight. A moment later he flipped one turn signal on before sliding over to the left lane of the interstate. His newer Jeep Wrangler roaring past a semi-truck full of doe-eyed cattle likely bound for slaughter.

"Where are we anyway? How much longer until we get to Davenport?" From the passenger seat, Secrist stretched his feet out in front of him. "These long drives are murder on my legs anymore."

"Quit being such a fucking baby. It's only an eight-hour drive from Marquette, and we just passed Sterling. So, it's only like another hour now. When we get there, we'll check in and grab some dinner. In the morning we can head down to Almore and check out my great aunt's old place. I haven't been back there since I was a kid." Stander kept his eyes on the highway. A sign declaring a toll booth upcoming one mile ahead caused the surrounding cars to switch lanes, seeming without rhyme or reason, jockeying for phantom positioning. He reached one thickly muscled arm over to the cup holder filled with loose change, thumbing the coins before pulling a small handful out.

"And you think what you saw around there as a kid somehow ties into whatever we experienced in that cave in Michigan, huh?"

"Yeah. I mean, I'm not sure. But, unless it is just some cosmic coincidence, I'm pretty certain I've seen what we found up on Mount Arvon before. Not as a big maybe, but made of the same substance..."

"Well," started the veteran police detective of 25 years, "I don't believe in coincidences."

"Me neither, man. Me neither." Stander looked over at his good friend of the last twenty some odd years. Outside of Frazier, his dog back home, Secrist was the closest friend he had. Easily his best friend since he was a kid. "What we saw kind of makes you doubt everything we 'think' we know, huh?" Stander again pulling his hands off the wheel to make air quotes when he spoke the word think. The black Jeep now stuck crawling bumper to bumper at the only toll booth with an actual operator working inside.

"Yup. And after what we witnessed, it kind of made the idea of staying retired seem like a waste of time. I just hope we can figure out what happened. Still kind of hard to believe." Secrist shook his head back and forth.

"You only retired from the police force. Now you work in the private sector, Tommy. I mean, unless you don't want me to pay you anymore..." Stander smirked at Secrist before dumping the loose change into the outstretched hand of the toll booth attendant and getting a nickel back.

"Hey, you offered me the job, remember? Help you research your family's history and what you found over in France. If, on top of that, I can get my head around what we saw while getting paid? I mean, how could I say no, right?" Stander nodded along, this conversation a small repeat of topics they'd already discussed in detail previously. "The pay is ridiculously generous, you know."

"Yeah, yeah, yeah. Don't sweat it. I think I can afford it now." Stander looked away, slightly embarrassed. Though his father had been a physician with a successful private practice near Chicago when he was growing up, as an adult, Russell Stander had always refused any financial help from him. Fiercely proud, he'd turned to professional boxing as a young man at one point when struggling to make ends meet rather than take a handout. Though his success in the ring was modest at best, he'd taken his meager winnings and spun them into several flourishing businesses over the years. Before eventually selling them all off to open a tavern back in Marquette, Michigan, where both he and Tom Secrist lived. Stander was most comfortable behind his bar pouring drinks and spinning stories that made his patrons laugh.

But now, as Secrist was well aware, Stander had unexpectedly inherited a vast fortune in wealth, assorted business holdings, and property. The entire array is still being sorted out by a team of lawyers back in Chicago. His father's recent death bequeathing everything to him. The single heir of a family with ties, he'd only now learned, apparently stretching across oceans and back generations. "Besides, you and Lucas have turned out to be model employees so far."

Secrist grunted and turned to face the passenger window, lost in his own thoughts. Stander accelerated and switched lanes on the interstate once more. Swerving back into traffic and continuing their drive south towards the border of Illinois and Iowa. He reached over and turned the music back up. "Duality" by Slipknot coming out of the speakers. Smiling, Stander's head begins to bob up and down as he sings along.

"I push my fingers into my eyes
It's the only thing that slowly stops the ache..."

CHAPTER TWO
1980

Doubt began to slowly creep in. For the first time the ten-year-old boy finally admitting he may be lost.

The blond kid, Russell Stander, or Rusty as his friends knew him, had been doggedly hiking all day and, when he first left, was very sure of himself. But now, some four hours later, with all the snacks he'd packed already eaten and his canteen hollowing out, he no longer felt certain of anything. He wondered if his aunt even realized he wasn't at the house right now. Rusty started to think he should just turn around and retrace his steps. Maybe the gardener, Harold, was wrong. Or, worse yet, playing a trick on him.

Rusty had crossed countless fields holding small herds of brown or black and white cows with brightly colored tags hanging from their ears. He had carefully skirted the edges of those trampled meadows so he wouldn't draw any unwanted attention to himself. Cautiously stepping over or ducking under rusting barbwire fences and ignoring the various "No Trespassing" or "Private Property" signs posted. At other times, quickly hurdling rows of planted beans or plunging deep into towering cornfields. Hoping to remain unseen but staying the course he'd set out on.

Why hadn't he reached the river yet?

Rusty was big for a soon-to-be 5th grader. Born ten years earlier in 1969 and now almost eleven, he was long and lanky and had been the tallest boy in Mrs. Pepper's fourth grade class last year. Although several girls in his grade were still taller than him.

Not that girls really mattered...

The lone boy walked gloomily over to a large, knobby oak tree at the edge of the woods he'd just emerged from. His favorite Star Wars t-shirt was damp with sweat, and one knee on his bellbottom blue jeans was caked with drying clay after he'd slipped on some leaves trying to scramble up the side of a creek bed earlier. He slid a dirty white canvas bag off his shoulder and let it tumble to the ground at his feet before sitting under the shade of the tall, thick tree. The old bag – found in one of his great Aunt Madeleine's many closets that morning – was now empty of food but still held a flashlight, his slingshot, a baseball cap, and a hooded grey sweatshirt. Rusty leaned against the rough bark of the oak and dejectedly kicked his tired legs out in front of him. He looked out across the sprawling but empty cow pasture in front of him. Flies buzzed lazily in the air over the dried-out cow patties dotting the flattened field.

He wondered what time it was.

Though he knew there had to be farms somewhere nearby, Rusty hadn't spotted anybody or even a single house in over an hour. The last person he'd seen had been a girl he didn't know swimming all alone in the small lake that bordered his great aunt's property. The girl, who must have been about the same age as him, had said her name was Izzy and asked if he wanted to swim with her. But Rusty had been so eager to continue his hike that he'd barely stopped and spoken with her. The blonde girl calling after him that maybe she'd see him around later. At the time Rusty had thought to himself, *not if I see you coming first*. He had no interest in playing dolls, Barbies, or whatever it was girls liked to play together.

They all had cooties anyway.

After that, to help pass the time, he'd pretended he was a spy on a dangerous, top-secret mission. Sometimes imagining he was Steve Austin, The Six Million Dollar Man from his favorite TV show. At other times, a lost soldier trapped deep in enemy territory trying to safely return to the frontline. Making a game out of his hike. Avoiding anything manmade in case some adult might become suspicious or consider him a trespasser on their land and call the police. But the longer and farther he traveled, the fewer those random sightings of civilization became. It wasn't until he had stopped under a weeping willow tree earlier in the day to eat his lunch that he'd begun to contemplate how utterly alone he truly was out here.

This summer break, Rusty was staying alone with his great Aunt Madeleine. He had visited and stayed at her gigantic old house several times in the past. But this was the first time he'd stayed there without his father. The elderly widowed aunt pressed into service when Rusty's mother had suddenly departed for an overseas trip without him. (*Not that he cared*, his inner voice reminded him). A week later, his father rushed after his mom, though why was still unclear to him. All he'd been told was there had been an accident and not to worry. A day later he'd been driven across the state and dropped off at his great Aunt Madeleine's mansion on the border of Iowa and Illinois. His dad's father's sister – darkly tanned, tattooed, and deeply accented – lecturing him upon arrival how precious the area around her majestic home was.

To entertain himself, since his great aunt lived in the country and the few new friends he'd managed to make mostly lived in Almore some eight miles away, Rusty often went out exploring alone. Trailing various creeks that snaked through the thick timber surrounding his aunt's house. Looking for old arrowheads or hiking in the woods and countryside that surrounded the small lake where he'd seen the girl swimming earlier. But today he had struck out on his biggest adventure to date. The ten-year-old was determined to hike all the way to the Mississippi River and back. According to his great aunt's gardener Harold, through the woods and fields "as a crow flies," the river was less than five miles from the towering home and estate.

Still seated under the tree, Rusty lifted a dented canteen from where it hung by a fraying strap off his shoulder. The stainless-steel container was wrapped in coarse canvas and had been his grandfather's back when he had been some kind of teacher or explorer over in Egypt. Unscrewing the metal lid, he put the opening to his lips and took a swig. The water left inside the canteen was now lukewarm with a slightly metallic taste that made him grimace as he swallowed. He shook the canteen and listened to the sloshing sound inside, trying to judge how much was left. Wanting to be sure he saved some water since he was still not sure how much farther he dared go. Rusty replaced the cap and screwed it down tight before pushing himself up from the ground to stand. He reached down and retrieved the canvas bag again, pulling its strap across the shoulder opposite the canteen.

Rusty looked up at the sun, still high overhead but beginning its slow, downward retreat in the afternoon sky. One lone white cloud drifting in the near breezeless summer day. Then, looking once more across the featureless meadow in front of him, he made his decision. He had come this far after all and surely, he reasoned, he must be very close to the river by now. He would at least cross the pasture in front of him and the cluster of timber that lay beyond. Convincing himself the river must be just past those trees, Rusty began walking once more.

Once he crossed the meadow, Rusty found the tree line beyond considerably denser than the other patches of timber he waded through earlier in the day. Crowds of sticker bushes huddled together and greeted him with painful pinpricks just a few feet from the pasture. Each step forward soon became a slow, strategic dance with the wild thorns. Their prickly and wiry branches taking all of his attention to get past without ending up scratched and bloodied. Deeper inside the thistles, much to his delight, Rusty found branches full of ripe, juicy blackberries. He stopped to pick and eat these while he carefully pushed aside the clingy undergrowth. His path meandered as he moved slowly among the berry bushes. The farther he went in, the riper and juicier the fruit became, his fingers and lips stained purple before he plopped the last of the tart berries into his mouth. When Rusty emerged from the thick stand of wilderness holding the blackberry bushes, he was surprised to see the sun barely hovering above the tops of the surrounding trees.

Directly ahead of him laid a small stretch of open space full of waist-high weeds sprinkled with only a few smallish saplings and bushes. The ground itself sloped downward at a slight angle, and towering trees circled all sides like a tall, wooden fence. Finally freed from fighting his way through the thick woods, he could hear the sound of rushing water in the distance. Excited, he ran forward in the tall weeds, and they swished noisily against his legs as he sprinted down the field. Rusty felt energized by the thought of having finally reached his goal and was excited to explore the bank of the muddy water. Imagining all sorts of washed-up treasures he could lay claim to and use as proof he'd finished his quest. He bet that, besides maybe Native American Indian tribes a long time ago, he would be the only person ever to have explored this part of the Mississippi River bank.

As he ran, cutting a path through the tall weeds, clingy green grasshoppers jumped and scattered desperately in his wake. The bugs panicked by the unexpected intrusion and clamoring to avoid the rushing boy stomping past their home. Other insects chittered and buzzed noisily in the field, all complaining loudly about the kid disrupting their peace on this lazy summer day. A hundred yards into the open space, his mind distracted by the exciting culmination of his daylong hike, Rusty tripped over something sticking out of the ground. He fell face first in a huff on the thick bed of weeds. His bag flying off his shoulder and landing a few short feet in front of him.

Stunned by the unexpected fall, Rusty laid motionless for several long seconds, stretched out across the ground flat on his stomach in the itchy, weed-filled field. It was difficult to catch his breath at first, but he slowly pushed himself up to his knees. Rusty rubbed at his shoulder, which had taken the brunt of the impact when he fell, before crawling forward on his hands and knees to retrieve his upended belongings. The canvas bag had landed next to a large stone half buried in the ground and Rusty angrily snatched the strap, dragging it towards him and sliding it once again over his now aching shoulder. Barely looking at the big rock before turning to see what he'd tripped over.

Behind him, obviously what his feet had hit and sent him sprawling, was another similarly sized grey rock. Rusty stood slowly and, as he did, noticed there was another large rock of the same color beside the one that sent him flying. Turning his head, he saw another a few feet away from that one. Then another, bone white and rounded across the top. Behind it, maybe ten feet away, was also what looked like a cracked piece of rock lying on its side.

Confused at the cluster of large rocks sticking out of the otherwise flat and weedy field, Rusty walked a few steps over to the starkly white, curved stone. He used his feet to stomp down the tall weeds on both sides that mostly hid the rounded rock. When revealed, the granite proved to be flat on both sides and circular across the top; maybe six inches thick in total.

Rusty knelt in front of the stone and saw that, now with the surrounding weeds trampled to the ground, the unnaturally shaped rock resembled a large tablet sticking up from the earth several feet high. He ran his hand across the flat and weathered surface of the stone, stopping only when his fingers felt some rough carvings still hidden by the weeds near the bottom. Unsure what he felt, Rusty leaned lower until he was bowing down and practically lying on the ground in front of the strange, oblong shaped white stone. His fingers traced what he now recognized as letters carved into it. He squinted in the long shadows of the trees just beginning to block the receding sunlight. There were numbers and letters, but only two words near the bottom that the boy could make out. *Born*. Then directly below that, the second word. *Died*. With the date of 1900 clearly visible.

That was 80 years ago!

Rusty scrambled to his feet at the revelation that this queerly shaped rock was manmade, his mind working slowly to process what he found. Stepping back slightly, he looked once more across the weedy field surrounding him. He could make out the tops of some twenty stones, all about the same size as the one in front of him. Some, he now noticed, appeared thin and squared off or flat on top. While others, like the one directly in front of him, were thicker and more rounded. For the first time he saw, maybe a hundred yards away from him, two tall grey stone pillars stood as well. The rock columns had aged terribly and one had broken in two, reducing its height to half of the other. Obviously manmade and spaced apart as if they were an opening or a gate of sorts.

Rusty understood now. He had unwittingly run halfway across and was now standing in the middle of a neglected graveyard. The rock he tripped over, like the others peppered across this lonesome stretch of land, was a tombstone. This was an abandoned cemetery where long forgotten dead lay.

And the sun was setting.

CHAPTER THREE

Rusty stood completely paralyzed. His dream of reaching the Mississippi River, and the household glory that such a bold adventure would bring him, no longer on his mind. The ten-year-old thought only of leaving this place.

And now!

He tugged at the straps of both the bag and the canteen, securing both tightly around him once more before turning back to face the way he'd come. His heart thundered in his chest and he felt ripples of goosebumps spreading up his arms as he looked across the unkempt, weed-choked cemetery. Each tombstone seemed to be slyly peeking out at him from under the cover of the long wavy grass. As if waiting – now that their secretive existence was discovered – for him to pass close enough that the graves could open up and swallow him whole. Adding him to the dark tombs he imagined honeycombed the earth under his feet. Looking around him, nothing moved in the garden of the dead. Rusty suddenly felt very much alone and starkly exposed in the fading sunlight.

When he finally found the strength to move his legs again, Rusty walked quickly towards the woods he'd just exited out of mere minutes earlier. Turning his back on the river that moments ago, finding by himself, bordered on obsession. But the dark timber in front of him had somehow turned both ominous and threatening. A wall of wood that had made a pact with the jutting stones to keep them hidden. The dense forest a barrier you couldn't see into more than a few yards. On shaky legs and his head on a swivel, he headed for it anyway, back the way he'd just come.

Halfway across the decrepit graveyard, Rusty caught the faintest whiff of smoke. The smell was light in the air, but unmistakable. Smoky in a familiar and outdoorsy way, like the smoldering wood of an old camp-fire that had died down hours before. Though not daring to slow his pace, Rusty turned and lifted his head towards the smell, sniffing the air around him and trying to locate the source. Thinking it may be coming from the chimney of a nearby farmhouse before realizing that on a hot and humid day in Illinois, no one was likely lighting up their fireplace. Looking around him, Rusty idly wondered if seeing a house right now was something he hoped for or deeply dreaded. He wasn't at all sure until he saw a structure looming in the distance.

Then he was certain he wished he hadn't.

It was an oddly shaped wood building on the far side of the forgotten cemetery. Hidden among a cluster of overgrown trees crowding it tightly, seemingly ashamed of the manmade structure in their midst and trying desperately to hide it. Rusty could just make out the small wooden shape in the receding light of the sun. It was tucked away at both the edge of the forest and the graveyard, squeezed in like it didn't belong. The tiny one-room house or shed was discolored and mottled like rotted fruit under the shade of the surrounding trees. Dead branches covered its sagging roof, and a withered and colorless vine hung listlessly from one corner, as if it no longer wished to be there. The end of it swayed slightly back and forth. Rusty had the absurd idea it was waving at him and beckoning him closer for an introduction. There was no chimney or smoke, and the entire building tilted sideways off its foundation, giving it a distorted, off-kilter shape.

Like the burial plots, it too appeared long abandoned, cruelly discard-ed and left to decay by its owner. And again, like the lost cemetery, its very presence in the middle of nowhere was bizarre. Once he'd spotted the structure, Rusty never broke stride nor took his eyes from it as he moved past. Terrified if he turned his back, the loathsome building would spew malevolent spooks that would stalk him through the dark woods his entire way back.

As he hustled to leave the abandoned graveyard, and with his attention focused solely on the queer shack, Rusty barely stopped himself before walking directly into the source of the smoke he had smelled moments earlier. Despite the age-old cliché "where there's smoke, there's fire," here there was no fire. Instead, he nearly stumbled into a pile of black and white ash barely warming the surrounding air. Rusty had to quickly jump to one side in mid-stride to avoid stepping right into the smoking ashes. His sudden movement, so close to the cinders, caught the light ash in a swirl and particles of soot danced in the air at his feet. Nearly losing his balance, he had to stop himself completely to keep from tumbling to the ground a second time. Both the burn pile and Rusty stood mere feet away from the edge of the timber. Rusty was breathing hard and, though anxious to get away from the morbid graveyard and creepy wood building, he paused momentarily. Looking down into what remained of the fire pit.

The flames had consumed nearly everything, and it was only a few remnants of wood near the edges of the burn pile that still lightly smoked. But something shiny glimmered in the retreating sunlight near the middle of the ash. He looked nervously around and checked once more at how close he actually was to the tree line. Regarding it as a form of sanctuary from the deserted cemetery and odd little hut, should either of those spit out some horrible monster bent on his death or destruction. With no ghouls or ghosts baring down on him (Rusty dimly contemplated if ghosts would actually be visible or not, but quickly pushed down that terrifying thought), he picked up a long stick off of the ground. Moving closer to the burn pit, he scrutinized the ashes more closely, probing at them with the stick.

Rusty flicked the end of his stick under the shiny object and sent it flying out of the ash. The charred object resembled a buckle of sorts, but, still hot, Rusty dared not pick it up or turn it over just yet. Instead, he let it cool in the weeds where it landed and began to poke his stick back and forth into the ash again. Curious to see if anything else of interest escaped the flames and remained unburned. The long stick almost immediately sunk down and lodged itself into something soft and sticky under the ashes. Whatever it was, it made moving the stick difficult, and the wood bowed under the strain.

Rusty cautiously looked around him a second time, fighting back his fears of something meaning him harm rising from the old graves or escaping the strange, sagging building. When no creatures seemed to be lurking close by – *unless they were invisible*, the pesky voice inside his head reminded him – Rusty was satisfied he was still alone. Concentrating, he used both hands and leverage to slowly drag the sticky, heavy item out from the smoldering ash. When it finally gave, the stick he was using cracked loudly and split in two as the burned and melted thing finally tumbled out of the ash where it had lain hidden. As it rolled across the fire scorched weeds, long pieces of brown grass and twigs stuck to its sides. Still smoking slightly and oddly colored, the melted mass seemed unrecognizable.

Rusty, broken half of the stick still in hand, walked over to the blob and pushed at it with the remaining piece of wood. Turned on its side, the melted glob suddenly took form. It was a pair of shoes now stuck together from the heat of the fire. Judging by the design – what was left of it anyway – they were most likely once a pair of women's dress shoes, similar to pairs Rusty's own mom wore on occasion. Fascinated by the find, he pushed it over a few more times with the stick until he was sure of what he'd found. The shoes were either black or had burned up enough in the fire that they had turned black. With the mystery solved, Rusty now turned his attention back to the shiny brass buckle that first caught his eye. Like the blob that became a pair of shoes, this too was easily recognized once he was able to turn it over a few times in the long grass. It was definitely a belt buckle.

Confused and momentarily forgetting his earlier rush to leave, Rusty returned to the fire pit once more. Why was someone out here burning up old clothes? With the faint sounds of the tumbling river water in the background and a chorus of buzzing cicadas beginning to serenade him, he took the stick and swung it back and forth over the ashes, slowly scattering and thinning them out. Trying to see deeper into the pit until, he hoped, it gave up its next secret.

Fifteen seconds later, it did.

The unmistakable form of a badly scorched bag or purse peeked out from the ashes. Warped from the flames, the metal latch meant to keep the handbag closed had unsnapped in the fire. One bottom corner had completely burned up and it was missing a strap, but the shape was undeniable. In the middle of the handbag was a noticeable bulge where the material of the purse had melted. There was something still inside, Rusty was sure.

Using the remaining half of the stick, Rusty poked it in the soot and used it to drag the blackened purse out of the ashes. With the handbag lying among the weeds, still smoking and hot to the touch, he used the broken end of the stick to further pry apart the opening of the purse and look inside. The contents were largely unscathed by the fire the handbag had bathed in. Peering inside, Rusty could make out a lipstick and a small, round mirror now black and no longer reflecting anything. There was also a glass bottle that may have once held perfume, but was now cracked and empty. The largest item – the one causing the pronounced bulge that had first caught Rusty's eye – was a woman's leather wallet. It appeared pretty much intact, more singed than actually burned up.

Rusty's eyes opened in wide wonder at the unexpected find, and he quickly flipped the charred handbag onto its side along the ground.

Spilling the contents of the lady's purse out on top of the surrounding weeds. He squatted down next to the wallet and turned it over quickly with one finger so as not to burn himself. The top flap opened up and exposed a small assortment of credit cards tucked neatly inside. An Amoco gas station card had slipped out from its pocket. *Probably,* Rusty thought to himself, *when I'd dumped it onto the ground.* Imprinted on the front of the card was a series of numbers and at the bottom in typed, white script, was the name Laura Trace.

Rusty stayed squatted beside the purse and wallet for several long seconds, contemplating what he'd discovered. Unable to tear his eyes from the name on the credit card until a flock of crows suddenly heaved themselves into the air behind him, cawing loudly as they hastily climbed the sky. The abrupt explosion of wings and cries startling him and breaking his trance. Rusty quickly stood and watched the departing birds soaring above him before turning to see where the frightened crows had taken flight from. Looking back into the sun, he squinted and raised his hand to his eyes to block the sunlight streaming down from just above the trees.

That was the first time he saw it.

The silhouette was barely visible against the backdrop of the shadowed forest beyond. It stood stoically and unmoving on two legs. The outline suggesting a man. But the filtered sunlight able to force its way between the competing trees in the background cast long shadows that danced without rhythm. Their movements obscured and somehow blurred what Rusty could see, draping the lone figure in darkness. Its features shaded and masked. An ominous hush fell after the echoes of the departing crows faded, and the air around Rusty seemed to grow oppressive and thick. His pounding heart, and the rolling tremble creeping up his spine, all that stirred in the field of graves. He couldn't tell if the figure actually saw him or if it was even facing his way.

Instinctively, Rusty ducked down in the tall weeds to hide himself, praying he hadn't been noticed. Crouching low to the ground, he felt inexplicably guilty and ashamed. As if he was seen stealing money out of the purse or caught cheating on a school test. It was the feeling he was going to get in trouble, and, at ten years of age, "getting in trouble" was the worst fate imaginable. The very thought of having to face his disappointed father made Rusty feel queasy inside. If caught out here, how would he explain why he left his aunt's home without permission? Or taken her flashlight and his grandfather's old bag and canteen without asking? His lip began to quiver and his eyes filled with tears before he raised his forearm to wipe them away. No! He was not going to get in trouble! Rusty looked down at the two straps that crossed his chest to make sure they were still securely in place. He dared a quick look behind him to judge how close the tree line was and prepared to crawl the short distance into the woods so he could disappear. Hopefully unseen by this second visitor to the forsaken cemetery.

Rusty raised his head ever so briefly to steal a second quick glance at the looming figure in the distance. He was in luck! It had not moved, and Rusty began to feel confident he hadn't been seen after all. He crouched low once more and was about to scamper into the cover of the nearby timber when the silhouette shifted. Suddenly sinking down behind the tall weeds, just as Rusty had, the black outline completely disappeared. Somehow, no longer being able to see it, but knowing it was there, was even more terrible. Long seconds became minutes and yet it still never reappeared. Rusty's mind raced in fear and he rubbed desperately at his eyes.

Where had it gone?

But before he could begin to process any reasonable explanation for what he witnessed; the air was split by a shrill scream. It was desperate and agonized. The screech cutting him to the bone and setting his teeth on edge. It was a sound out of a nightmare. Without a conscious thought and foregoing any semblance of stealth, Rusty stood and bolted for the woods behind him. He wanted no part of this graveyard nor what haunted it.

He flung his body into the underbrush, ignoring the bristles and thorns that pierced and tore at his bare arms and clung desperately to his clothing. Sure that whatever that thing back in the cemetery was, it would do much worse than just scratch him. The uneven forest floor rose and fell under his feet as he threw himself forward. His eyes were wide and wild as he ran, darting in and out among the trees until at last he exploded out of the other side of the timber. Free of the forest's natural obstacles, Rusty sprinted across the neighboring cow pasture, barely noticing the dried cow dung he stepped into before finally reaching the cover of the second stand of woods.

Rusty ducked and turned as he navigated the next cluster of trees. The old canteen banging painfully against his bruised knee in a syncopated beat that almost matched the spasmodic rhythm of his terrified heart. Vaulting a dead, moss-covered log, he ran face-first into a spider web stretched between two tall bushes. The spider's carefully tailored home wrapping his features and hair in its sticky webbing. The dry and hard husks of the spider's last meals clung to his face, and he thought he felt something crawling along his neck.

But he dared not stop.

Rusty spit out and wiped desperately at the clingy web that covered his open mouth as he ran. Wooded vegetation of all sizes whizzed past him, and small green plants that only recently sprouted hopefully along the floor of the forest were crushed mindlessly under his frantic footfalls. His lungs soon burned for air and his gasps turned to sobs with every other breath. He was terrified the thing from the graveyard was hunting him, possibly just steps behind.

When he reached an open bean field, halfway across it without break-ing stride, Rusty finally summoned enough courage to turn his head around. Praying the thing from the graveyard hadn't kept pace or would somehow manifest behind him. Seeing nothing, he continued to cross the field at a breakneck pace until he reached the next bank of trees, forgetting about the low hanging barbwire fence he had so carefully stepped over coming the opposite way. The rusted wire seemed to reach up and grab him by his legs. Tangling and tossing him cruelly to the ground, the barbs tearing his jeans and, opening a wicked gash across one thigh.

Rusty lay on the ground, panting. Both his fear and the pain from his wound wrenched a moan out of his lips and tears from his eyes. Behind him lay the bean field. Exhausted, bleeding, and scared, he scanned every bit of it. Praying it was still empty and nothing would emerge from the trees beyond, no longer sure he even had the strength to run again. But the bean field was quiet and the line of trees remained motionless. The pesky voice inside tried to remind him again that *some ghosts were invisible*, but Rusty was too tired to listen. He pulled at the wire caught on his feet and began to painfully untangled himself from the steel barbs.

"Need some help?" Rusty screamed an unintelligible reply and tried unsuccessfully to scramble to his feet before face-planting once more in the packed dirt at the edge of the field. The startling voice had come from the darkened woods behind him, and he contorted his body and head to face the horrid wraith before it devoured him. But instead of a blood thirsty ghoul, or twisted monster with ripping talons and teeth, the girl from the lake emerged from out of the brush. She had a brightly colored beach towel thrown over one shoulder, and her blonde hair was pulled back in a ponytail. "Are you alright?" she asked timidly.

"What?" Rusty felt his face flushing. He stammered a bit before adding defensively, "What are you doing sneaking up on me like that?"

"Sneaking up on you?" The girl, Izzy she'd told him her name was, laughed. Her pinkish, slightly freckled, sunburned nose crinkled up. "I was just walking back from the lake around the edge of this field. You were the one that came chasing after me." When she smiled the second time, Rusty saw she had dimples on both her cheeks.

Rusty pushed himself up from the ground and tried to ignore the stabbing pain in his ankle where the barbed wire fence still dug into his flesh. "I wasn't chasing after you. Ew!" He tried to scowl, but found he was unsuccessful. Behind Izzy's pinkish nose and cheeks, her bright green eyes twinkled in the setting sun. When he looked into them, his stomach did a flip-flop before he could look away.

"Maybe you are right. But if you weren't running after me, what was chasing after you?" Izzy paused before adding, "You sure are lucky you can run so fast." Rusty was slowly unwinding the wire at his ankles; while at the same time trying to casually wipe his teary eyes across the cloth on his shoulder. When she'd reminded him of running, he spun his head back to the beanfield, but nothing seemed to have been following him after all.

"No one was chasing me. I just... I just like to run fast. I'm late for... I'm late for dinner, that's all." Rusty finished untangling himself from the barbwire fence and stood. Though he hurt everywhere, he pretended nothing was wrong with him. "I better get going. My aunt might be worried." He turned from the gaze of the girl. "Maybe I'll see you around sometime," he added shyly. Though the sunlight was fading fast from the sky, the remaining light was brighter out in the open field and was a comfort. Rusty felt more like himself as he hurried on. He never looked back as the girl silently watched him retreat before eventually melting back into the trees lining the field.

Rusty hurried as he moved back through the last of the wooded timber, walking quickly, but no longer running. Turning to look behind him every few steps, hiking and limping his way across the remaining landscape until at last he reached his aunt's mansion over an hour later. Barely beating the encroaching night and rising of the full moon.

Rusty crept quietly through one of the side doors of the grand house, hoping to enter through the dark and empty kitchen unseen. The kitchen staff had all gone for the day. His aunt, as usual, oblivious to his comings and goings, had already eaten and was reading in one of her favorite sitting rooms. Hearing him in the kitchen, but without looking up from the leather-bound book in her lap, she called out in her thick French accent that there were leftovers in the refrigerator. Rusty answered her cheerily, hoping he sounded normal (though feeling anything but) and not wanting to draw attention to himself or his torn and bloody clothing. He made his way carefully up the long staircase and down the carpeted hallway before entering the bathroom closest to his room. Shutting and locking the door behind him, finally feeling safe.

Drawing himself a hot bath, he slowly peeled off his ripped and stained clothes. Wincing as he tore open the barely formed scabs crisscrossing his arms, chest, and legs. He inspected himself in one of the large hanging mirrors and dabbed at the fresh blood with pieces of toilet paper until the worst of the bleeding stopped. He pulled off the rest of the spider web still clinging to the back of his head and plucked a single tick crawling near his ear off his skin, squishing it as hard as he could between his two fingers before tossing it in the toilet. Satisfied he was de-bugged with no mortal injuries, Rusty climbed into the bathtub and lowered himself into the warm water.

As he settled down into the tub, his new cuts burned, but none of them were very deep. He washed the wounds lightly with a washcloth and then just soaked in the comforting water for fifteen minutes. Puzzling over all he witnessed and wondering what to do about it. He could not get the bizarre disappearance of the silhouette at the edge of the cemetery out of his head. What had he seen? He thought again of the awful scream and the burned clothing and purse he had found. Who was Laura Trace? Was that who he had seen?

Soon, whether it was from the cooling pink-tinged water or otherwise, Rusty shivered all alone in the tub.

BATAVIA, IOWA
July 31st, 1909

The black shadow closed the window silently from outside in the yard. The path behind him, inside the house and down the hallway, splashed with gore and dripping blood. Gruesome consequences left in his wake that he'd never consider again. He leaned out from the darkened shelter the side of the home gave, silently cursing the full moon above. Though the next house over wasn't very near and still completely dark, earlier there had been quite the racket inside the one he was leaving. The man smiled grotesquely. Oh, my yes, he thought, quite the racket indeed. At least until he had finally silenced the family's dog...

Damnable mongrel!

He smiled again despite all the extra effort it had taken him. What he would give to see the look on the face of the one who finds that mutt. It had been hard work finagling the dog's entire carcass inside the splayed chest of its owner, despite the sloppy wetness. But the end result had looked absolutely glorious. Man's best friend? He chuckled lightly. The newly joined pair had reminded him of the Siamese Twins he'd once seen at a traveling circus a few years back.

And people pay to see that!

Though he was mere yards from the edge of the cornfield, he would have to cross the weedy lawn exposed under the moon's translucent beams. He padded swiftly across the tall grass, head down and collar up on the long coat he'd stolen from the home he'd just exited. The front of it glimmering and shiny in the moonlight, as if the man had hastily painted something black. No matter, he would either bury it once he got deep into the cornfield or burn it later. The man slipped between the rows of corn. His shadow trailing behind him like an unwanted little brother. In the far distance, a lone train whistle blew. He hastened across the cornfield towards the steel rails at the opposite end of the field smiling.

The train was right on time.

CHAPTER FOUR

"I meant golf. Hello?"

"You mean driving around drunk in a little clown car?" Stander shook his head dismissively. The garish image of the rocker Rob Zombie emblazoned across his chest. "No thanks, Tommy. Standing around watching guys waddle ten feet back and forth out of their goofy rechargeable carts, all the while gossiping like old women about their workplace, is not my idea of a fun time. I can go to a Wal-Mart if I want to see that. No difference between the two except the size of the battery-operated carts." When Secrist started to object, he quickly added. "Yeah, yeah, I know you dudes who golf all the time think it's different, but it's the same thing. Frustrating, sweaty and all the while you're walking around hoping no one sees how much you adjust your balls."

"Well, golf is a sport." Secrist tried again, subconsciously smoothing down the front of his striped golf shirt.

"Right," Stander let the single word roll off his tongue slowly. "Same as badminton and shuffle board. They had all three of those 'sports' (Stander made quotation marks in the air) at the nursing home where my dad lived." Stander looked expectantly across the breakfast table. When no further argument was raised, he pushed himself away from the small table and stood. "You ready to roll?"

As the two men exited the hotel's adjoining restaurant, Secrist asked, "Did you end up hearing anything from Lucas last night?"

"Yeah, he sent me an email along with a few pictures he took. I guess the little army of government archeologists are still hard at work excavating all the human remains out of the quarry. He said a separate team at the University of Caen Normandy will head up the repatriation and reburial of all the bodies they recover."

Secrist frowned, "Jesus… How are they going to do that? I thought the consensus was this was some lost burial pit from the Battle of Caen. What are they going to do with all of them? They may have been French citizens back in the 1300s, but they've all been dead for like 700 years?"

"No clue. But that was why Lucas wanted to play nice and partner with the government officials and university after we donated the land to them. Let those egghead academics wrestle with all the ethical and moral obligations around taking care of their fallen countrymen." Stander clicked his key fob and unlocked the Jeep. "This way we can still keep an eye on what they are doing while we discreetly focus on the location nearby that we kept for ourselves. Lucas still believes what we found in those deep underground scans is the key to the whole quarry." Both men climbed up into Stander's four-wheel-drive vehicle.

"So, what is next for Lucas and his little team of trusted archeologists? They've been cataloguing all the artifacts as they've been digging, right?" Secrist pulled out a pair of sunglasses and began inspecting the lenses, periodically wiping them on his shirt as he spoke. "Does he have any ideas yet about what, or who I guess, buried the anomaly shown in those underground images?"

"The artifacts unearthed so far haven't proven very helpful in identifying who. Lucas said he hopes when they get deeper, items of more value will be revealed. And he says he's not completely sure yet, but he thinks they may be closing in on a carving of a head. Or maybe even the top of a gigantic statue. One chiseled right into the granite itself." Stander started the Jeep.

"What does that mean, then? Did the English army just happen to use that deep pit in the quarry to hide their dirty deeds? Or did they know the Romans had sculpted something next door and were paying homage to it?" Secrist paused, his mind sharpened by years of detective work, trying to put the pieces together. "Like some weird tribute, maybe? Man... talk about going down a rabbit hole. This is some Alice in Wonderland shit."

"Thing is," Stander puts the Jeep in gear and slowly backs out of the hotel parking space. "Lucas is pretty confident that, whatever it is we've found down there, it predates the Roman occupation and the quarry itself." Stander turned and looked briefly at Secrist before turning out of the parking lot. "Curiouser and curiouser..."

A short time later, after filling up with gas and heading out of town, Secrist asked, "So, what's the game plan this morning? I know we are checking out your aunt's old house. But what else? That shouldn't take us very long."

"Technically, she was my great aunt, and I guess the house and property are mine now, aren't they?" He looked over at Secrist, not frowning, but not smiling anymore, either. His eyes unfocused. "Anyway, when I picked up the keys from the lawyers, I was told the grounds have been kept up. But none of them seemed to know what shape the house itself is actually in. But knowing my dad, I'm pretty sure he would have stayed on top of that as well. Guess we'll see."

"How long has the house sat empty now?"

"Well, Aunt Madeleine died sometime in the mid-eighties. Like maybe 1985 or 86, somewhere around then. The last time I visited here was a couple of years after that." Stander turned the wheel and nosed the Jeep south down a two-lane highway. The automated voice on the GPS guiding them along a route that followed the Mississippi River. "I'm not really sure what to expect after all this time."

The morning sun bathed the interior of the automobile as they drove along the twisting route. On one side of the highway, bean and cornfields spread out as far as the eye could see. A flat and featureless landscape numbing in its endless order like an autocrat's vulgar display of authority. The crops, once free to grow naturally in the wild, constrained in obscene rows of control. The chaos of nature briefly reined in by man. It was impossible to tell what might lurk behind the wavy green curtain. Like in the Land of Oz, did it conceal a greatly bloated buffoon? Or, more like a sea of green, is it full of predators barely glimpsed before they drag you deep into their world? The only breaks in the neat rows were a few side roads and the occasional farmstead. On the opposite side of the highway, the two men caught periodic glimpses of the muddy river in the distance between clusters of trees when the blacktop veered closer to the water's edge. There were several spots along the side of the river that looked like they'd recently flooded. The weeds matted down with layers of dried mud and warped tree branches left behind when the river's waters eventually receded. Long-necked and long-legged herons gracefully picked their way along the water's edge, looking for an easy snack. Their stabbing beaks poised and at the ready.

"So, we spend the day poking around the place? See what we can see?" After his decades in law enforcement, Secrist liked to have a set plan and defined goals and objectives. He'd learned over the years that Stander was very much the opposite. The tavern owner, by nature, was very laid back and comfortable going-with-the-flow, as they say. But this trip, even for Stander, the purpose seemed particularly elusive. With their destination, according to the GPS unit, only a few more miles away, the old detective pressed him. "You asked me to bring a week's worth of clothes down here with me. I can't imagine it is going to take a week to see if the house can be lived in. Or sold." He paused, but no reply came. "Or whatever you're thinking..." He let the last words hang in the air, hoping to have them picked up and filled in.

"I doubt in a week we'll even have time to explore the entire property," Stander stated cryptically. Then, responding to the command of the

Jeep's smooth-talking navigator, he made a sharp turn off the highway. Traveling down an unpainted blacktop road barely wide enough for two cars to pass each other. On either side of the winding road stood long grass and tall, shady trees. The endless fields of crops they'd driven past for the last 45 minutes all vanishing. Still driving, he faced his friend. "The thing is, it's not really just a house."

"What do you mean it's not 'just a house'?" In response, Stander simply pointed out the passenger window over Secrist's shoulder. He turned, at first seeing only dense woods. Tree branches so close to the road that he could have reached out and greedily swept up a handful of their leaves before the expanse of timber finally parted. Then, just ahead and where Stander had gestured towards, stood their destination. Over the tops of the trees and the slight hills, he caught glimpses of what appeared to be several separate roofs. The highest one likely the top of a tower. Stunned, he stupidly blurted out, "My god, why would anyone have built a home like that way out here in the boondocks? I thought you said your aunt lived alone?"

Stander, shrugging indifferently, cranked the steering wheel and pulled into the lone lane they'd passed since turning down the deserted blacktop road. A mammoth metal gate blocked off the long drive that led to a cluster of buildings on the grounds of the estate. A rusted, heavy chain was wrapped around the bars on both sides of the gate, a newer padlock holding both shut. Stander put the Jeep in park and pulled a full keyring out of the car's center console compartment.

"Why did she choose to live here? Building a mansion like this out in the middle of nowhere?" Secrist's eyes roved across the estate, trying to take the entirety of the grounds in.

"That question, my friend, opens up the door to the church of who the fuck knows." Stander, still seated in the driver's seat, smiled wryly.

"Humph," grunted the recently retired detective. "Never heard of that group of faithless parishioners. Is that a church where they want you to pray or be the prey?"

"In organized religion, has there ever been a difference?"

"Point taken."

Stander pulled himself out of the driver's seat, keys in hand, staring down at the mansion at the end of the driveway. Then, closing the door behind him, he said to no one in particular and with a hint of trepidation, "Welcome to Relict Mansion." Then, bending down and addressing his lone traveling companion through the open car window he added, "At least that's what it's known as around here."

"Relic? What? Your great aunt's home doesn't look rundown from here." Stander shook his head in a way that let Secrist know his assumption was wrong. Thinking he was correcting himself, the detective added, "Wait, you mean the locals called your aunt a relic? That's just mean. How old was she when she died?" Again, in reply, he got more head shaking.

"Not relic. ReliCT." Stander emphasized the ending of the word.

"Oh! Well, that's a pretty obscure reference for a bunch of Midwestern farmers to make. But at least not so mean-spirited, I guess. So, they call this place Widow Mansion then. Got it. So, her husband died. Big deal. How far back did he pass?"

"Which one?" A slight smile playing under Stander's thick white moustache. "She was married four times."

"Four! Really? Well, oh gee, I don't know." Secrist turned the tables. His answer dripping sarcasm, usually Stander's calling card. "Probably the one that died in the house, right?"

"They all fucking died in this house..." Stander returned his gaze evenly. Then nodded his head in response to the disbelieving stare of his friend before turning to walk over and unlock the chains across the gate. Once the driveway's entrance was open wide, he returned to the car. Only briefly glancing at the passenger, appraising him silently from the seat beside him.

The black Jeep Wrangler pulled forward; the gate behind left unlocked and ajar. The car, flanked on either side by flowering dogwood trees, made its way slowly down the long driveway. The narrow blacktop turned and dipped and the four wheels hugged its soft curves and climbed its slight hills before finally pulling around the circular drive at the end of the lane. Stander parked near the front doors and killed the engine. Both men stepped out. A look of awe plastered across the face of Tom Secrist as Stander grabbed a duffle bag off the backseat of the car.

The huge house loomed before them; three stories off the ground with several tall spires just barely visible from the front of the house. The massive home seemed to be a confusion of architectural ideas stolen from the past. Along with gothic spires, the soaring rooftop of the house was decorated in a complicated framework that bordered on art. The mansion's exterior so uniquely adorned that almost nothing was left untouched. Wrought iron lightning rods dotted the roof despite its primarily brick and stone construction and dark windows – more than could be easily counted – appraised the two men with baleful stares. Nothing stirred behind the panes. The gothic or Victorian style architecture, paired with a sprinkling of newer amenities themselves now far outdated, was startling under the bright sunshine of the near perfect Midwestern day.

Was it out of place or out of time? Secrist wasn't sure... maybe both. All that's missing, he thought to himself, are some medieval gargoyles looking down from the gables. The massive home seeming to have more in common with the grand European estates of England or France. Or maybe a few of the one-time slave plantations still standing in the deep south of America.

"Welcome to Relict Mansion." Stander repeated himself, this time addressing Secrist directly. "Let's see if one of these keys the lawyers gave me fits the front door." He started forward and Secrist fell in behind him.

CHAPTER FIVE
1982

"Oh... wowsers, Rusty!! Did that really happen?" Denny was looking across at Rusty with an awed expression. His rapt attention never wavering during the entire telling of the story. Both eyes wide behind dark framed glasses.

"You're such a spaz, Denny," said Brian. "Don't have a cow! The whole thing is baloney. He is just trying to scare us." The other twelve-year-olds around the campfire nodded in agreement as Brian continued. "If the story was true, it would have ended with Rusty crapping his pants." At this, all four boys laughed out loud together. Denny with an audible relief; Rusty, despite himself. Since he was sitting right beside Brian, he reached over and punched him hard on the bicep of his arm. "Ow! Why did you do that, dickwad?" Brian faked like he was going to retaliate but just rubbed the spot where he had been hit, frowning. Rusty never flinched.

Chris reached behind him and tossed a few more pieces of the wood they gathered earlier onto the campfire before commenting. "Why didn't you make the man or thing you saw in the graveyard a monster? A werewolf would have been cool."

"Or a vampire," added Denny. "Vampires can turn into mist, so having him materialize out of nowhere and then disappear again would have made more sense." He pushed his glasses up on his nose as he spoke authoritatively about the fabled creatures of the night. Rusty always thought that when Denny fidgeted with his glasses while he talked, it gave him the appearance of a librarian or teacher. Of course, Denny getting the best grades in school out of the four of them might have also played into that.

"I swear I am not making any of this up," Rusty began. "I don't know for sure what I saw or heard. Maybe it was just some old geezer out burning his trash and yelling at me for being on his property. I mean, I was just a little kid back then," continued the twelve-year-old defensively. He spit to the side like he sometimes saw some of the high school boys around town do, hoping it made him look older and tougher. "And whether you believe me or not, now you know the real reason we are out here."

Rusty wasn't surprised his friends didn't completely buy his story. The biggest reason he never told his dad or even his three best friends what he'd seen that day, was because he didn't think they would believe him. For the last two summers, he'd been dying to go back and find the place again just to make sure what he remembered was real. The weathered tombstones, the shadowy man/thing, and piercing scream all haunted him.

One time, last summer, he had even struck out for it once more. But he had chickened out maybe halfway there when he'd seen Izzy walking alone in one of the pastures. Not that he had needed much prodding, but she had talked him out of it. The two of them instead spending the afternoon playing together. Tag, hide and go seek, and a game they made up and named Hot Lava. Both of them jumping across water filled streams and balancing themselves on the bigger rocks and logs that crisscrossed the trickling creeks carved into the forest floor. Pretending the gullies and meandering water was hot lava and, if they fell in, they'd be scorched alive. Rusty wanted to blame Izzy for him not making the return trip. But if he was honest, deep down, the place had scared the hell out of him, and he was too afraid to go back alone.

"It was a pretty cool story, I guess," offered Brian. "Too bad we'll probably never be able to see it. I mean, if you did really find some old graveyard." Chris nodded along and both of them looked questionably at Rusty before Brian added, "Did you? I mean, is there really some long-lost cemetery in the middle of the woods out here?"

"He said so, didn't he? And we all made a pact never to lie to each other. Blood brothers and wolf brothers always tell the truth, right?" Denny, the smallest of the four, looked across the flickering flames of their campfire at the other three. As always, hungry for affirmation that he was counted as one of the gang. Their own little self-proclaimed "Wolf Pack" as they had named themselves the first summer Rusty had stayed with his great Aunt Madeleine. Now, two years later, as gangly twelve-year-old seventh graders, they rarely used that title anymore. At least ever since some of the older boys in Almore caught wind of the moniker and started teasing them about it. Sometimes even chanting "Puppy Pussies" at them when they walked past, usually embarrassing them at the worst possible times. Their old club name sounded so kiddie now that it made Rusty cringe anytime he heard it. Denny was the only one who still brought it up this summer.

"Yeah, but no one can make up stories like Rusty here. If he was Pinocchio, his nose would always be out to here." Chris held his hand a good foot away from his own nose. "He'd look like even more of a dickhead than he already does." But he was smiling as he teased him.

"Dickface," Brian corrected, laughing. He leaned away from Rusty and covered his bruised arm.

Chris snorted once before cocking his head and then continuing. "But I think you should answer the question, Rusty. We each lied to our parents so you could get us all out here, so you better be telling the truth. Spill the beans. Are we really gonna be able to find this old cemetery you said you saw back in fifth grade or not?"

Just as during the telling of Rusty Stander's hike-to-Mississippi-story, the three friends were all focused once more on him. Which was just the way Rusty liked it. Being the center of attention.

"Everything I just told you guys about that day is true. I swear it." For emphasis, he took his forefinger and made an X over his heart. "I never told you guys because I didn't want to get razzed about it." He looked down into the fire briefly, ashamed to admit he hadn't trusted them with his secret until today. "I did pack some supplies and hiked west all day to find the Mississippi River, just like I said. We all know the river is just beyond town over there," Rusty gestured in the direction behind him which was, in a general way at least, west. "I should have made it just like Harold said. But right before I hit it, I found this really old, creepy graveyard with tombstones from like a hundred years ago."

"All by yourself? Really? Weren't you scared?" Denny, who never doubted Rusty, had been the least comfortable with the plan Rusty had roped all of them into. Which originally he'd said was just to camp out all night together and then secretly hike to the river and back. Daringly, without his great aunt's or their parents' knowledge or permission. All the adults knew right now was that the four boys, all best friends since Rusty started spending his summers here two years ago, were camping out in the woods behind his great Aunt Madeleine's estate. It was this lie that had taken all three of the other boys to finally convince Denny to go along with so that none of them would get caught or in trouble with their parents.

Only now, with the moon high overhead and their tent pitched, had Rusty finally leveled with his buddies. For the first time telling them he'd tried this once before, only to stumble across the deserted cemetery and an ashy pile of smoldering belongings. He watched Denny carefully, trying to judge whether or not the smallest and youngest (by six months) would chicken out. If he did or now refused to go along, it would blow it for all of them. Rusty was ready to use that fact, if needed, to guilt Denny into sticking it out. But to his surprise, Denny did not seem reluctant or scared after hearing Rusty's story. Maybe it was his fascination with all things monster related. After all, this was his chance to go see a spooky old graveyard. Just like the ones in the movies.

"And why would you trust what Harold said? I know you say he is cool and nice to you when you visit. But around here, everyone thinks he is about as sharp as a marble." Now it was Chris casting some doubt on Rusty's ambitious plan.

Rusty quickly fired back, defending his aunt's simple-minded gardener and groundskeeper. "Oh? Well, I guess you would know since you still play with marbles."

"You mean balls." Brian chimed in, never missing a chance to tease his next-door neighbor. "Chris plays with his balls all the time, and they are the size of marbles." Rusty laughed as all four friends guffawed loudly around the fire. No one talked more crap about each other than Chris and Brian. But, since they had been best friends since first grade, neither one of them took what was said seriously.

"Oh yeah, you talk big out here. I'd like to hear you say that to my face."

As Brian started to stand, Denny quickly chimed in, "You are the one always calling him Tinkertoy Dick," snorted Denny, talking to Chris but pointing to Brian. Now all four of the boys were laughing together. Falling into the comfortable and usual routine developed since they first played together two summers ago. Any one of the four could get the other three giggling and laughing, almost telepathically at times it seemed. The four were linked and blindingly loyal to each other as only grade school summer vacation or summer camp best friends ever can be. This was the third summer Rusty was staying with his great aunt and the four of them spent almost their entire summer vacation days together. Inseparable and as close as brothers.

Or like a wolf pack.

Rusty, the tall and skinny blonde haired one who always seemed slightly ahead of the other three when it came to some of life's biggest mysteries. Like what French kissing was, how to look cool lighting a cigarette, or the best way to ride a long wheelie on your bike. Brian Naylor was nearly as tall as Rusty, but not as skinny. Dark haired, liked by all the girls around town, and always one of the first picked at dodgeball, kickball, basketball, or baseball. Chris Bond, red haired, freckled, and slightly pudgy, was most comfortable in front of a TV with an Atari joystick in his hands. He could make two dollars' worth of quarters last all day at an arcade and his initials dominated the high scores of the four video games at the local pool hall in Almore. And Dennis Reiner, or Denny, the runt of the group with dark eyes behind thick framed black glasses and with even thicker jet-black hair. A straight – A student and the one who could answer nearly any question ever raised about movie monsters. A little nerdy and needy, but his family, like Rusty's great aunt, also lived out in the country and not in the actual town of Almore. Denny and Rusty often rode bikes over to each other's house to play. All of them together, Rusty was sure, would be best friends for life. Probably buy houses next to each other when they grew up.

Of the four of them, at least in Rusty's mind anyway, he was the ringleader. That was how he was able to so easily persuade the other three their secretive adventure was going to turn out OK, even if they did have to lie to their parents. The other three always trusted him and his plans. So, under his direction, the three boys each begged their moms (because convincing dads was always harder) to let them pitch a tent in the woods close to Rusty's aunt's house. Coyly reminding them summer was nearly over and Rusty would be leaving to go back home to the Chicago area in just three days. Politely requesting bags of potato chips, cans of Shasta and Crush soda pop, and hotdogs to cook over their campfire for dinner. Promising to stay inside the big tent, each huddled in their own sleeping bags by 11:00 that night.

Then, the moms and Rusty's great aunt were told the boys would spend the next day just swimming and fishing at the nearby lake. Playing together on the water as they sometimes did during the long, glorious summer days when Rusty came to visit. Since the boys had camped out often in the past without getting into trouble (though usually in the backyard of one of their family's houses), it was not really a big deal. And the idea of them camping "for real" was not a farfetched idea. After all, Denny and Brian were true Boy Scouts now and followed their motto of "Be Prepared." Between the two of them, they'd already earned several first aid, camping, and wilderness badges. Brian even had his own pocketknife, which, unless he was at school, he always carried with him.

They were real outdoorsmen!

But, again under Rusty's direction, the boys also each secretly smuggled out peanut butter sandwiches and a bunch of bananas, apples, and oranges. Food that wouldn't spoil overnight and could serve as their breakfast and lunch the next day. Then together, the four had hiked west with their sleeping bags, the extra food, Brian's BB gun, their slingshots, and the tent. Making their camping spot in a place Rusty had scouted earlier. Close enough to his great aunt's house they could claim ignorance if they got caught, but would also give them a good jump on the long hike needed to make it to the old graveyard and back by dinnertime the next day. None of them, of course, letting their moms know they would be abandoning the tent in the woods as soon as the sun came up to hike until they rediscovered Rusty's "lost garden of the dead." Before returning to pack everything up and come home.

Rusty was pretty sure he'd thought of everything. He swatted at a blood thirsty mosquito buzzing past his ear.

"So, who is ready for a smoke? I like to have a cigarette after supper." Rusty, feeling very adult, casually pulled out a partially crushed pack of Camel cigarettes from his back pocket. He found the pack along the side of the road last week and had been saving the cigarettes for this trip. The pack looked like it might have been left out in the rain or gotten wet at some point, but the packaging had been dry when Rusty first discovered them.

"Yeah man, give me one of those, Rusty," said Chris, reaching his hand out. The other two soon followed and, using a stick from the fire to light up, all four boys were soon puffing away. Barely coughing, but barely inhaling either. A slight grimace played across Brian's and Chris's faces. While Rusty had to keep rubbing at his right eye because it wouldn't stop watering. In the past, the boys sometimes snuck Denny's mom's smokes from out of her purse when she wasn't looking, so they were used to smoking around each other. Often sharing a single cigarette, even though Denny was the only one who didn't actually seem to mind the smoke. None of them admitting to each other that they didn't really like the taste.

"Nothing like a good smoke with friends, huh guys?" Brian said this and then turned to cough. His face was red when he turned back around. "This is what life is all about," he continued philosophically. "Good times."

"Speaking of good times, gentlemen," Chris began as he stood. "I have a little surprise to help us celebrate our big adventure tomorrow." The redheaded boy reached down into his backpack and pulled out a can of beer labeled Old Milwaukee. "Let's get drunk!" Holding it up, he pulled the tab back and white foam exploded from the opening, totally surprising the boy, and covering both the can and his hand before dripping to the ground.

"Wow, Chris! Where did you get that?" Rusty was impressed. A smoke and beer shared among friends with no adults anywhere nearby? This must be what paradise is like. "Is that one of your stepdad's?"

"Yup, took it right from the back of the fridge in the garage. He had like a hundred of them in there, so he'll never even know." Chris held the can to his mouth and tipped it back. Smiling with pride, a white

Hitler-like moustache under his nose, he passed the slippery can over to Denny who didn't seem to know what to do with it. "Oh, come on, Denny. Take a drink and be a man. We are partying now, boys!" Denny tilted the still wet aluminum can, but then spit out what made it into his mouth.

"Oh god… that is awful!" Trying to recover and show he was one of the gang, he quickly added, though without conviction, "I only drink cold beer. This is warm."

Taking the can from Denny, Brian scowled at the smaller boy. "Yeah, right. Since when have you ever even tasted a beer before?" For emphasis, Brian then took a long drink, but he wasn't smiling either as he swallowed before quickly passing the Old Milwaukee can over to Rusty.

"Come on, guys! Who cares? This is practically my last night here. Let's enjoy ourselves," Rusty said before taking a sip of his own. "We are out here all alone. No parents or teachers for miles."

"And no sign of your little girlfriend, Izzy, either. I'm surprised you didn't ask her to come along with us. You might have scored." Brian was looking at Rusty with a strange expression before he added, "You're a regular Casanova this summer. Or maybe the new Fonzie!" Both Denny and Chris immediately stuck their thumbs in the air in front of them loudly mimicking the character's catch-phrase, "Ayyyy!" Trying to sound just like the Fonz did on the hit TV show Happy Days.

"I know you go swimming with her at that little lake. I've seen you." Again, Brian's face seemed to show a range of conflicting emotions that Rusty had to turn away from.

"I heard there is supposed to be some new girl with blonde hair running around here during the summertime. Did you see her? I mean, do you know her?" Denny looked across the fire at Rusty who fidgeted with the beer can in his hand before lifting it for another drink. "What's her last name? Where does she live?"

"I... I don't know who... I barely have ever even swum with her!" Rusty stammered out his answers. "Look, all I know is she lives out in the country somewhere near my great aunt's place. When you guys are busy doing family stuff and can't play, I go swimming down at the lake when I'm bored. Sometimes she is already there, and she's pretty cool..." Rusty handed the can of beer over to Denny, who took it wordlessly from him.

"Sometimes? Whatever, Fonzie. You don't have to get all defensive. I'm just saying I know you like her." Brian looked away and tossed a handful of twigs and dead leaves into the fire. "Denny! Quit being such a wimp. Hand that beer back over to me." The hurt on Denny's face was clear as he stood to hand it over. Rusty took the can from him first and quickly changed the subject.

"I don't know why we are talking about all this anyway. Tonight and tomorrow are going to be the most fun we have had all summer. Just us! We go together like spit and sweat!" Then, standing up beside Denny, defending him and knowing it would make him feel better, he howled up at the moon like a wolf. Soon the other two stood with them, all circling the campfire, joking and laughing again, passing cigarettes and the slowly disappearing can of beer, back and forth between them. All howling up at the moon and occasionally yelling, "Wolf Pack Rules!!" at the top of their lungs and listening to their voices echo around them in the forest. Throwing the spent cigarette butts, empty package, and eventually the empty beer can into the fire. Each feeling giddy at their independence, but still keen to destroy any incriminating evidence of their night of debauchery.

Just in case...

After a long debate about which of the three Charlie's Angels was the prettiest (all four able to agree that it had been Farrah Fawcett before she left the TV show), some more jokes, insults, and a farting contest won by Brian as usual, yawns began to dominate the conversations. The excitement eventually wound down and they ended their night (and the campfire) by peeing into it. Then, zipping the front door on the tent closed behind them, each boy slid wearily into their sleeping bag. Leaving the biggest flashlight on and pointed up at the ceiling for illumination. Though each would deny it if ever asked later, all four twelve-year-olds were fast asleep in mere minutes.

Early the next morning, the sun shone brightly through the tree canopy overhead they had slept under. Lighting up the inside of the tent and slowly raising the temperature of the stuffy enclosure. With four sets of shoes, sweaty socks, and four (barely) adolescent boys still not completely sold on the advantages of good hygiene, the tent quickly turned smelly and as hot as a high school locker room after a late spring PE class. The rising heat and permeating aroma soon woke the boys one by one and, still dressed in their clothes from the day before, they groggily exited the stifling tent. Greedily sucking in and basking in the cool wilderness air of the great outdoors. Hair sticking up at all angles, the four boys munched on the fruit they had packed mostly in silence and each downed a caffeine riddled soda. Then carefully packing away anything not needed for their hike back inside the tent, the twelve-year-old boys headed out on their quest. Weaving their way through the woods in search of Rusty's fabled plot of land.

Where the dead lay in wait.

CHAPTER SIX

THE FOUR BOYS HEADED west through the dewy, early morning woods. Rusty, having hiked this route in the past, led them with confidence through the trees, undergrowth, and up and down the occasional gully. But they still stopped every thirty minutes or so to consult a compass and pick out landmarks to help them navigate their return trip. Rusty was annoyed with the slow pace, but he respected Denny and Brian's caution and the safety practices learned in Boy Scouts. He also knew, though he would never admit it, he needed his friends with him if he was going to find the nerve to set foot back inside that lost cemetery. Wisely, he kept his mouth shut.

When the boys at last emerged from the patch of forest where they camped overnight, the four friends crossed several deserted meadows and cow pastures. Squinting and blinking under the late morning sunlight as their eyes adjusted from walking in the shadowy woods. Now, wide awake and enjoying the camaraderie of their brazen journey, the boys fell into their usual routine of back-and-forth banter. Joking and laughing together, each getting their fair share of good-natured teasing. At times tossing sticks and rocks at various targets and kicking at the crumbling, dried-out cow dung patties that littered some of the green pastures.

Chris kicked one old, dusty cow dung patty so hard that it flew up and hit the back of Rusty's legs before breaking into several pieces. Rusty, in turn, picked up the biggest remaining piece and playfully tossed it back at him. Then, seeing the shocked looks on the faces of his friends, he goaded each of them into doing the same. Before long, the dare evolved into a quick cow patty tossing contest among the boys to see who could throw one the farthest. The withered old cattle poop was bone dry, hard, and flat. Most pieces resembling heavy Frisbees made out of very compact grass. After a few throws (Brian was the owner of the winning toss), the four boys continued on. Discussing in great depth, as they walked, the digestive process of cattle and animals in general before the conversation turned into swapping horror stories about the worst times each boy followed behind their dads in a toilet. Each of the boys unable to explain how their mothers could ever share the same bathroom with their dads. Or what their dads ate that ended in such atrocities.

Truly baffling stuff.

The boys soon crested a small hill and were confronted by an impressive wall of green cornstalks. Being mid-August, the tops of the neatly lined rows of crops towered above them. The tall corn swayed slightly, and each of the sweating twelve-year-olds stopped briefly to bask in the gentle morning breeze. Passing around Denny's Boy Scout canteen and eyeing the next obstacle blocking their path forward.

"We must have walked five miles already," said Chris. He looked winded, sweaty, and his face was nearly as red as the hair on his head. "How much farther do you figure it is, Rusty?"

"We are not even halfway there yet, you big baby." But then, to make sure he kept the spirits of the group up, he quickly added, "But it gets lots easier from here on out. Mostly a bunch of flat fields and more cow pastures until we get really close. But, see that?" Rusty pointed at a white farmhouse with peeling paint that sat off in the distance. Bib overalls, t-shirts, skirts, and blue jeans clearly visible and hanging from a droopy clothesline stretched between the old house and a weathered red barn. "I think that house is where the farmer who owns these fields lives. We better keep our eyes peeled unless we want to get arrested for trespassing."

"Arrested!" Exclaimed Denny nervously. "You didn't say anything about getting arrested."

"Good grief, Denny. Nobody is going to call the cops on a bunch of kids out walking and hiking around." Brian took another swig from the canteen before passing it back to Denny. "So don't have a cow. Rusty has hiked out here a bunch of times before and never got caught. Right?" Brian sounded confident but, when he looked over at him, Rusty could see some doubt wavering in his eyes.

"Yeah, man. I have been this far a lot of times and never got in any trouble. I'm just saying, we should keep avoiding any houses or adults we see. After all, four kids stick out more than one." Then, not giving the other three a chance to dispute him, he added. "Last time I was here, this field was beans, not corn. No one will even see us crossing this field right now with the corn so high. You ready?"

The boys looked out across the endless sea of green cornstalks in front of them. The ground sloping slightly downhill and giving them a commanding view of the entire field. A strange mixture of anxiety, excitement, and apprehension flowing through their veins. At one time or another, all of the boys had hiked in the timber and fields now behind them. But none of them, except Rusty a couple of years ago, had ever made it this far. Or walked across the farmer's field directly ahead of them now. Rusty remembered that on the other side, just past the long rows of tall corn, was a wide creek. Once the four of them made it across that gurgling stream of water, the boys would be trekking on land that, for the other three of them anyway, they had never seen before. Virgin territory.

Rusty turned to look at his three buddies and easily read their minds. This adventure just got real for them. So, not giving them a chance to come up with an excuse to turn around, Rusty yelled, "Like spit and sweat! All together! Charge!" and stepped directly into the cornfield. Ducking under the leaves of the first row of corn, he began to cut his way straight through the cornfield rather than following one of the arcing rows. Making a direct beeline across the field towards the other side. His faith in his friends was rewarded. He could hear them sliding between the tall stalks behind him without protest.

Rusty smiled to himself.

The sandpaper-like leaves of corn scratched at their faces and arms as they trudged forward, row after row. The fragrant corn all around them, strong and sickly in their noses. Rusty started turning sideways as he met each line of cornstalks, trying his best to slide between the tall plants. Behind him, he could see the other three were mimicking his maneuvers.

Now deep inside the field, the sun streaming down on top of their heads, the temperature quickly rose. Rusty soon took to putting his arms up as he reached each line of corn as well, trying to fend off the worst of the itchy plants and keep them out of his face. Small black beetles, startled at the unwelcome intrusion into their home, clustered between his fingers and along his bare arms. Rusty reached up often to brush at his blonde hair as he walked, certain the black horseflies buzzing the tops of the corn plants were infesting his scalp just as quickly. But he didn't dare stop or show any doubt at his decision to dive directly into, instead of around, the field of corn. He stayed focused on getting himself and his friends out of this field as fast as possible. Keeping his eyes up as best he could, careful to not let them get scratched by the leafy onslaught row after row, impatiently waiting for that last line of corn to finally come. Certain they must be nearing the end and about to burst into the clearing at the other side any moment; only to encounter yet another row with each successive step. When Rusty finally saw high grass and weeds only a few rows away, he began to run, bursting out of the opposite end of the field with his arms raised like the winner of a marathon snapping the tape at the end of the race.

He dove to the ground, exaggerating his discomfort so the four of them could rest together and catch their breath. Behind him, one after another, Chris, Brian, and Denny followed suit. Sweat beading their foreheads and each huffing and puffing, feeling as if they'd just traversed the entire Sahara Desert. Finally, out in the open, the boys shed their gear and ran their hands all across their arms, face, and hair. Shaking off the bugs and corn silk the sudden plunge into the field had yielded.

Lying on their backs under a suddenly very hot sun, the boys each took turns cursing the cornfield and the farmer who had planted it. Swearing they would walk around it on the way home as they passed the water canteen back and forth once more. Rusty regained his feet first, followed shortly by the others, and Denny checked his compass to make sure which way was west. Then one row into the cornfield, over Denny's feeble protests, Rusty used his feet to kick down five or six cornstalks to mark where they had come out of the field. Then, smiling to himself (it felt good taking revenge on the damn field), he prodded the others to follow him into the weeds bordering the cornfield. Leading them down towards the creek he knew laid below.

The small stream he'd remembered from before turned out to be nearly dry and, though it made getting past it a breeze, Rusty was a little disappointed. He had daydreamed about this creek being a dangerous border of raging water. How they would have to help each other to even get across it, balancing and jumping from rock to rock, to finally conquer the water obstacle, and reach the wilderness beyond. But instead, they each barely got the soles of their tennis shoes wet before casually climbing up the other side.

Gaining the opposite bank, the four boys found themselves facing a beanfield. Also unharvested, this field was nearly identical in size to the cornfield behind them, but much easier to get across. The leafy soybean plants were not even waist high, and the tilt of the land from where they stood was also downhill. Though Rusty could sense the initial disappointment in the group (crossing another farmer's field was not exactly a grand adventure), he once again did his best to pump them up. Laughing, he took off at a jog, hurdling each row of beans like it was a track and field event, yelling out for the others to hurry and follow. Verbally painting a picture for them of the untamed land just ahead. But as he crossed the beanfield, Rusty kept his eyes up and trained on the stand of trees ahead of him.

The first pricks of fear rekindled in his belly when he reached the end of the beanfield. Rusty stopped running at the border of the field when he reached the barbwire fence. He reached out and pulled up hard on the middle strand of barbwire while at the same time putting one foot down on top of the bottom strand, pushing it down with his weight until it nearly touched the ground. Spreading the barbwire fence as wide as possible so each of them could, one at a time, safely pass between the sharp barbs to the other side. Once the other three made it out of the field, he ducked down and joined them. When he let go of the barbwire strands, they snapped back in place, just as taut as before.

Rusty led his friends through the remaining timber he knew ended at the edge of the graveyard they were seeking. Butterflies swirled in his stomach as the boys carefully maneuvered themselves past the sticker bushes. Each boy holding the sharp branches back so the one behind could have a clear path. Rusty was disappointed to see the prickly blackberry bushes were fruitless this time, but it made this part of the journey much quicker than before. Before long, the four adventurers broke into the open prairie grass that held the forgotten graves. Rusty felt a triumphant rush when he saw several of the ancient headstones poking out from behind the long, swaying weeds of the field. Though he knew he hadn't imagined what he had seen two years before, deep down he was relieved to see everything was just as he remembered it.

The four boys walked silently, almost reverently, down towards the old graveyard. Each taking in the site wide-eyed as they looked around, walking slowly forward as a group of one. Eyeballing the cracked tombstones, two broken pillars, and the oddly leaning wood structure at the edge of the cemetery. Rusty felt a brief flash of anger when he recognized part of the amazement etched on his friend's faces meant they really hadn't believed him. But then again, deep down he supposed he'd doubted himself as well.

Before reaching any of the headstones, Denny pointed out the door on the sagging wood building was ajar. It swung slowly back and forth on its old hinges. The almost casual laziness reminded Rusty of how his great Aunt Madeleine, when she would shoo troublesome flies away from her face, did so lethargically. Never swatting at them with much energy or showing any anger or annoyance. Until they landed close by and rested; going about their usual business of cleaning themselves or whatever it was that flies did to relax. Then, with a practiced hand, she would lash out with amazing speed at the unsuspecting insects. Cackling with delight as she crushed their bodies and swept aside the remnants of the bugs with disdain.

Despite the heat under the August sun, Rusty shuddered.

PITTSFIELD, ILLINOIS
AUGUST 22ND, 1908

THE PLACEMENT OF EACH corpse, especially this time, was done with meticulous care. Sated, she strode casually about the modest farm house, a flickering oil lantern in hand. With every shade drawn, and the nearest neighbors over a mile away this time, she could afford to take her time. Her ride, the twice weekly Rock Island Train Line that cut across the state, was still hours away.

Staging the scene of the bloodbath afterwards was cathartic. A creative pleasure.

Though she took great pains to remember where each family member was sleeping when she first entered the home. Occasionally, especially with small children near the same age, it could become a bit of a guessing game afterwards. Which child had been snuggled in tight between parents? What room were the boys sleeping in again? Or sometimes, if she became overzealous, the caved in heads were hard to discern. Which made putting the dripping corpses back properly more difficult. She idly wondered how often she'd mistakenly placed a child in the wrong bed. Or even the wrong room...

She giggled lightly.

But, she guessed, the appalled neighbors, or family, that would later stumble upon the houses visited were likely far too traumatized by the scene to even notice the occasional miscue here or there. Oh well, she thought, no matter really. She wandered through the house one last time. Rechecking each door and window, repositioning the occasional limb in poses that pleased her in the moment. Stepping into the parent's bedroom one last time, she stripped off the blood-soaked dress she had worn and wrapped it into a tight ball before placing it inside the cotton pillowcase she'd nabbed earlier. Crossing the room, she selected a plain drab dress from the slaughtered mother's belongings. Nearly a perfect fit, she slid it on and smoothed down the edges. Picking up the pillowcase she'd turned into a bag, she made her way back downstairs. Slipping back out the same window she'd used to enter the home hours before, she walked across the lawn and slipped between the rows of corn bordering the property.

The distant wail of a steam whistle blew in the dead of night.

CHAPTER SEVEN

"The sex appeal of a bus driver? What?"

"It's true!" Stander, laughing, was wiping the tears out of his eyes as he continued. "Your old boss on the police force back in Marquette has all the sex appeal of a school bus driver! And don't pretend you don't know what I mean, Tommy." Despite himself, Secrist started laughing along with him, nodding. "And now you're telling me that he... that... that he bought a cabin at a nudist camp?!?! God, I just can't make those two things fit together. That's all I'm saying."

"I'm just thankful his parents aren't still alive to see it. His dad was a retired Presbyterian minister!"

"My god, Tommy. *Someone's* parents *are* seeing that!" Both men burst out laughing together once more. "But like I was saying," Stander said, as their laughter subsided, pointing back again at the small outdoor balcony above their heads on the third floor. "My great Aunt Madeleine, who by the time I started coming here, had to be in her nineties, would shamelessly sunbath nude up there like three times a week. She was so dark-skinned she could pass for an Egyptian, or maybe a Native American."

"Get out of here! Right out in the open?" Secrist turned back towards where the Jeep was parked, looking out across the neatly trimmed grass of the sprawling grounds. "Although I guess as big as this estate was, no one would have seen her. But still..." He looked back at Stander, "Was she losing her marbles by then?"

"Oh no, man. She stayed sharp as a tack the whole time I knew her. My dad told me she practically worshipped the sun. Said she'd sunbathed naked as long as he could remember, too." Stander stood looking up at the mansion in front of them. He had stopped before reaching the front door, regaling Secrist with little stories and memories from the times he had spent on these grounds as a kid. He wasn't entirely sure whether he was stalling or not.

"So, *your* parents *were* seeing that." Secrist, still jovial from Stander sharing his aunt's idiosyncrasies, hadn't seen the shadow of doubt cross his friend's face. Before turning back, Stander chuckled along, hiding his uncertainty now that he was on the threshold of entering.

"My dad anyway. My mom never actually visited here or ever set foot inside the house." He turned once more and took the last three steps up to the front door. "Oh yeah, and here's another kind of weird thing I remember about her." He didn't look up as he slid the key in the lock, talking over his shoulder as he turned the key. "My great aunt was the first person, I mean except for on TV or in the movies, I ever saw with real tattoos. They weren't clear and mostly just script, but had you ever heard of an old lady back then with tats? Must have been scandalous in her day!" The old tumblers fell heavily, but easily. An audible click announcing their impending entrance. "My dad used to tease me when I first started getting inked up that it was her influence." Stander smiled, "I have to admit, she did have an undeniable presence about her." He gave the massive door a push and it soundlessly swung wide, sunlight chasing the darkness from the open foyer back into the far corners of the room.

Stepping inside, he flipped the light switch on the wall next to the doorway. Above both men's heads a massive chandelier made of brass, crystal, and glass illuminated the entryway and foyer, though not even half of the bulbs lit up. Beneath their feet, black and white squares of marble spread out ahead of them like a deserted chessboard. The floor's surface was dusty, dull, and unpolished; void of any furniture and blank like the walls of the foyer itself. Secrist stepped forward and whistled in appreciation as he gazed up at the vaulted ceiling some thirty feet above their heads. The sound partnering with the squeaking of his rubber-soled boots and echoing all around them until it was cut off by the sound of Stander shutting the front door behind them.

"If this is just the entryway, I can't even imagine what the rest of the house looks like." Secrist walked forward and looked up one of the two long flights of stairs that led from the foyer up to the second floor. He laid a hand on one wood banister before quickly pulling it back, his hand caked with years of accumulated dust. As he wiped his hand off on his pants, he said, "Guess the maid is off today, huh?"

"When I used to come here as a kid, there was a staff of at least four always working. I never saw my aunt so much as bend over to pick a piece of tissue up off the ground, much less actually clean anything. But I guess those folks must all be dead by now, too. Except maybe Harold the gardener. He was a lot younger than the rest of the people my aunt employed here."

"Is he still tending the grounds? The grass looks like it was just cut. Hell, come to think of it, I don't think I even saw any sticks or leaves on the ground." Secrist walked over to the second stairway and rubbed one finger along its banister before holding it up. "But here inside, it doesn't look like anyone has done much of anything for years."

Stander shook his head. "Doubt it. The estate probably just pays some landscaping company. I bet my dad has been the only one inside here in the last ten years or more."

"Why wouldn't he have just sold the property?"

"I think you answered that question yourself when we pulled up, right? Why would anyone want to have a house like this out in the middle of fucking nowhere? Plus, all the taxes and land to keep up with? Forget about it... Outside of a couple rich farmers that own a lot of the fields we passed, there isn't a lot money around here. So, it would be ridiculous for people who live in nearby Almore to try and manage something like this." Stander paused briefly before continuing. "And for all I know, maybe he did try to sell it and there just weren't any takers. I'm pretty sure no one locally would ever buy this…" Stander shrugged again indifferently. "Anyway, come on. Let me give you a tour of the place so you know where things are. Looks like the electricity is working right now. But I'm not sure what shape the old generator is in. Or if the water pump still works. Might take us all day to figure all that out and see what part of the house would be best to stay in."

"Ah! So that's why you brought along those tools."

"Yeah, I just didn't know what we'd run into. But I figured between the two of us we'd at least be able to jerry-rig anything we really needed working. And, if we find we need some parts for something, I know there used to be a small hardware store in Almore. Hopefully it's still there. But even if we don't need anything, I want to drive over there later today and show you how to get back and forth from town. Tomorrow, I want you to start doing some digging into the past. The little Almore Museum and Historical Society building downtown is only open two days out of each month."

"And let me guess, tomorrow is one of those days."

"As they say in church basements from coast to coast," Stander pointed a finger at him, "Bingo! Hopefully, you'll find some local volunteer just dying to have someone to talk with all day. Especially someone from out of town that they can share a few of the town's secrets and gossip with."

Secrist nodded, "Well, that sounds slightly more fun than hanging out here with you and cleaning all this up. You want me to look into the history of this place? Get some backstory on the land. Real estate transactions and such?"

Stander shook his head. "Nope. The history of this place started with my family. I'm not concerned about any of that right now."

"What then?"

"For starters, I want you to look up someone who I think lived around here back in the 80's. Her name was Laura Trace." Stander's face grew serious, the smile running away from his lips.

"Jesus, Stander. Are you really going to waste my time looking for some old girlfriend of yours? Just go creeping on Facebook like everyone else does..."

"Trust me, it's not like that. I never even met her and I'm pretty sure she was way older than I was back then. Just see what you can find out about her, OK?"

"Fine, fine. You said for starters. What other lost adolescent fantasies do you want me to help you reclaim? Was there a town librarian you used to think about while jacking off?"

Stander rolled his eyes and gave the retired detective a different finger to look at before starting again. "I also want you to find out everything you can about an old cemetery about five miles from here. When I was a kid, I stumbled upon a graveyard that hadn't been used in almost one hundred years. Supposedly, no one around here had ever heard of it. But I have always had my doubts about that."

"And...?" Secrist prodded, "You think this old cemetery ties in with what we saw up at Mount Arvon in Michigan?"

"Maybe not the cemetery itself. But what my buddies and I found underneath it..."

CHAPTER EIGHT
1982

"Where was the fire pit you found that purse and stuff at?" asked Chris. The four boys had spent the better part of an hour moving back and forth among the tall weeds of the open space. Meticulously inspecting, counting, and looking at each individual headstone. From what was still legible on the badly deteriorated grave markers, it appeared all the cemetery's inhabitants were buried over roughly a thirty-year span. The oldest tombstone they could find was 1870, and the newest ones were dated 1900. But as Denny pointed out, more than half of the burial markers, the ones that were still legible anyway, were all dated 1900.

The boys counted a total of twenty-nine tombstones, but in places it appeared there may have been more at one time. There were several blank patches of weeds, oddly without any marker at all. Yet considering the grid-like placement of some of the largely intact markers, it was hard to imagine those plots would not at one time had interred some unfortunate soul. To be fair, though, many of the severely weathered headstones had broken and eroded over time or had tipped completely over. Making it hard to judge where some of the graves began or ended. Plus, there were several other large rocks within the natural boundary of the cemetery that could have been crudely placed grave markers as well. It was just hard to know for sure.

"It was back up the hill. Kind of where we came out of the woods." Rusty hitched a thumb behind him, but his gaze remained locked on what clearly was once the cemetery of a small community. Neither he nor Chris moved to explore the area where Rusty found the burned-up clothing two years before, and all four boys stayed rooted together near the middle of the abandoned graveyard. In the bright sunlight and surrounded by friends, the small group of old grave plots was much less intimidating than the last time Rusty had stood here alone. But it still gave him the creeps. He said aloud what they all were thinking. "Why would there be a graveyard out here in the middle of nowhere?"

"Maybe this was a Civil War battleground. Or they were all killed by river bandits," offered Brian. "Attacked or drowned out in the river so they buried them right here." Denny, who had spent the most time looking at each specific marker, however immediately shot down that theory.

"The dates you can still read are spread out over decades, dummy."

"Well, maybe some of them were killed and others were wounded and just died later... Duh! Most of them died around the same time at the turn of the century," replied Brian defensively. Chris, literally the redheaded stepchild of his family and ever the diplomat of their group, jumped in to offer his take and subtly defend Denny.

"No way bandits or river pirates were raiding and killing settlers into the 20th century." Then, less sure of himself, he added, "At least not in Illinois or Iowa anyway. Right, Rusty?"

Rusty shrugged without conviction, more puzzled by the location of these burials rather than how or when the dead under their feet left the earth. "But why here? And how come no one knows anything about this place?" He looked up and searched his friends' faces for answers. "You all grew up around here and so did most of your parents. Have you ever heard anyone talk about this place before? I mean really, like ever?" He held his hands out with his palms upturned.

"Maybe we can find the answer in there?" Denny offered this idea while pointing at the rotting wood shack in the far corner of the open space. Its door still hanging open as if inviting their scrutiny. "It's made of wood, so it has to be newer than these graves." Each of the boys looked across the cemetery at the queer little structure, nodding, but not moving.

"You guys are a bunch of pansies," Brian finally declared as he took the group's first steps towards the little building. "Come on," he added, marching towards the sagging structure. Without a word and with less desire, the other three followed behind him. All reaching the swinging door at the same time. Brian turned to Denny, "Hand me a flashlight, will ya?" Denny pulled the battery-operated torch out of the bag of food and supplies the boys brought along with them. Brian, switching on the bright beam, shone the light inside the open doorway and peeked inside. The crude door, standing a couple feet open, was warped and dramatically curved along the bottom. A terrible smell of musky rot emanated from inside, and Brian pulled his Chicago Cubs t-shirt over his nose and mouth as he peered inside. "Whew! I think something must have died in here..."

Rusty approached the small building slowly – the last in line – and hung slightly back from the others. Wordlessly, he inspected the outside of the drab, colorless structure. Looking for clues that might give away its age or who or why it had been built to begin with. The wood the old shack was built from looked impossibly old. The drooping roof was covered in rotted and splintered branches, and the entire building leaned to one side. With multiple trees pressed tightly around it on all four sides, there was no way to tell if the structure could have actually stood on its own without their support. It was also obvious that the trees pressed so closely to the sides of the rotting building had all sprung up and grown tall long after it was built. No one would have bothered to build anything so close to so many existing trees, even if they were mere saplings at the time. Yet the tree branches all stretched high in the air, and the trees themselves were scarred with age as they had grown around it. But, Rusty realized, he really had no idea how long it took trees to grow that big. Or how to date them.

"Empty," announced Brian, after barely stepping one foot inside. "There is nothing in here at all," he added as he walked back out, grimacing and gagging after being inside for less than a minute. Chris, who had been standing just behind Brian, grabbed the flashlight from him and stepped forward next to Denny crowding in beside him. Rusty walked up to the doorway and peered over Denny's shoulders while also trying to look around the much bulkier Chris. When curiosity finally got the best of his fears, he slid in behind the other two. All three of them elbow to elbow inside.

"What is that smell?" Denny's voice sounded hollow in the constrained space. The inside was as colorless as the outside of the single room building. The entire shack was maybe ten feet by fifteen feet, if you were being generous. In some places, the walls were warped and had split open; moss grew down one side from a soggy hole in the roof. But otherwise, it was bland without furniture, adornment, or unique features. Rusty expected to find some woodland creature's nest inside or, based on the odor, some animal's carcass that had crawled in and died. Yet there was no evidence even a single wild animal had ever ventured inside, much less made a home out of it.

Which struck Rusty as strange...

The little building had a distinctively stark and grim personality. Much of that, no doubt, stemming from its placement in the middle of nowhere beside the old abandoned graveyard. That, and the truly horrible odor that seemed to permeate the entire structure despite the open doorway and rotted exposure to the outside. But otherwise, it was just a small deserted old wood building. Nothing inside or outside gave any hint of its prior use.

"Where is the smell even coming from?" Rusty craned his neck and leaned against the backs of both Denny and Chris, trying to pinpoint the horrible odor. Crowding in and pushing both Chris and Denny two steps deeper into the empty wood shack. Behind Rusty, Brian stepped back inside as well. The boys covered their noses and watched as Chris pointed the flashlight in various directions. The light exposing nothing and soon both boredom and the overpowering smell drove all four of the boys back outside once more.

"This is lame. Let's go the rest of the way until we hit the riverbank. I bet we'll find something cool along the shore." Brian looked across at the other three as he spoke. Rusty was the only one still looking back at the wood shack. He felt let down by what little they'd found here so far. This was supposed to be his big secret and an amazing mystery. A "lost" cemetery, old shack, and a strange burnt pile of clothing. All guarded by some weirdo that had scared him to death when he was ten. But now that they found the place, the four of them together on a bright summer day, there was nothing really here to see after all.

"Or we can check out the place where I found the ashes and…" Rusty started to say before he saw the other three already turning and walking away. Picking their way along the weeds and woods, heading west again towards where the Mississippi River ran. After a minute, he followed behind them, sulking slightly at his friends' indifference to his grand discovery.

The river proved to be only a ten-minute walk from the cemetery. The boys combed up and down the riverbank, shouting out when they uncovered a single car tire, a broken oar, and a cracked red cooler with a missing lid. But after thirty minutes of scouring the shoreline, they ended up finding nothing much of interest among the trash the winding river water at one time or another deposited on land.

They took turns using Brian's BB gun to shoot holes in the old beer cans and soda bottles lining the side of the river. Tossing a few cans that looked like they might still float back into the water before launching rocks at them with their slingshots until they sunk. But soon the novelty of having conquered the stretch of land between their houses and the massive river wore off. The anticipated celebration of finally making it all the way decidedly muted by the lack of discoveries. And with nothing to show for their efforts, the long hike back home under the hot August sun was soon staring them in the face, and none of them were looking forward to that.

Eventually, the boys sat together on a couple of downed trees near the lapping water's edge. Pulling out their sandwiches to eat and drinking the last of the soda pop they brought along. While they ate, a lone barge without cargo chugged wearily upstream but otherwise they saw no one else. In the far distance, stretching from one side of the Mississippi to the other and connecting two states, was an old railroad bridge sitting empty and silent as well. With the summer sun high overhead, the boys soon agreed it was time to start making their way back home.

When they reached the cemetery for the second time that day, nothing had changed. Still disappointed at how the day was turning out, Rusty began picking random rocks off the forest floor. Using his slingshot, he started launching stones at the leaning wood structure as they hiked towards it. After a few misses and getting a few steps closer, he began to nail the rotted door repeatedly and dents began to appear along the soft wood sides of the decrepit building. Soon the others joined in and, between the slingshots and the BB gun, the outside of the old shack was soon peppered with holes and jagged cracks of various sizes.

In a pause between shots, Denny said, "Should we be doing this? I mean, someone must own this, right?" But then, pulling back hard on his slingshot, he let fly a perfect shot that punched a ragged hole in the warped door. Forgetting his concerns, he yelled, "You see that? Bet you couldn't make a hole that big from back here," he challenged. The others redoubled their efforts and a barrage of gradually larger rocks were launched until the door came completely off its hinges and everyone stopped.

The four boys exchanged nervous glances before Brian said, "Oh, fuck it. Let's tear it down!" Dropping his BB gun to the ground, the brown-haired boy took off running and jumped up at the corner of the shack. Grabbing hold of the outside corner of the roof with both hands and hanging down from it. When it didn't budge, he swung himself back and forth, trying to knock the tiny building off its foundation. He yelled for the others to help him, and the three others soon joined in. Pushing on the outside walls and taking turns jumping up to hang down from the roof with all their bodyweight.

Within minutes, a loud screech was followed by a sizeable split that spread quickly down to the opening of the door. The boys all stepped away and jumped down in time to see one side of the structure cave in just before the other three walls followed. Like a house of cards, the entire structure folded in on itself. The boys stood panting beside the collapsed shack, first exchanging worried glances before breaking into grins. Then whooping, they danced around the ruined shack, laughing and slapping each other on the back and high fiving in midair.

Still pumped full of adrenaline, Brian leapt on top of the collapsed wood structure and raised his arms in victory. "Take that, you smelly old shack!" Pausing, he came back with, "You smelled worse than Rusty's old aunt's butt crack!" The witty (in a 12-year-old kind of way) rhyme and insult soliciting howls of laughter from the other three as he jumped proudly down from the top of the wood pile where a building stood minutes before.

Rusty, not to be outdone, scrambled next to the wood pile and climbed it like a stage. Turning to face his three friends, he also raised his arms above his head and yelled out to the collapsed building, "As a house you were such a big wussy, and you stunk like Brian's mom's hairy pussy!" When he was done, for good measure, he jumped up and down several times on top of the pliable wood. Bouncing around like he was on the world's lamest trampoline. The whole time laughing loudly along with his friends, none of them harder than Brian, who collapsed to the ground holding his stomach. Rusty scooted off and held a hand down to Brian to help him up. As he did, he added, "Remember when we found that Summer's Eve douche in your parent's bathroom last summer?" Both boys stood leaning on each other laughing so hard there were tears in their eyes. "And you... you thought... you said you thought it was mouthwash!" Rusty was howling now, bent over at the waist.

"I know, I know..." Brian wiped the tears from his eyes, still smiling and laughing. "Then we, oh god, then we opened it and smelled it..." The two boys still laughing together at the memory. "God that was terrible!"

"You were saggy, smelly, and went down with a kick," started Denny, now perched on top of the remains of the wood shack. "Just like when Mr. Goben got hit by that ball in his dick!" Once again, the boys erupted in howls of laughter. The three local boys gleefully recalling how, in fifth grade, during a kickball game in PE class, an errant strike sent the ball awkwardly off of one classmate's foot and straight into the distracted PE teacher's crotch. At Almore Grade School, that event had become legendary. Nearly every single person, young and old, in Almore had chuckled about it at one time or another. Well, except maybe Mr. Goben. As he was struck, he had collapsed to his knees, eyes bulging and mouth open in a perfect "O" as he moaned loudly. In grade school, a scene like that became an instant classic and one that may never be forgotten. Embellished perhaps, but never forgotten. Rusty, who had heard the story many times before, only wished he had been there to see it as well.

Denny, proud of himself, also jumped up and down on the pile of collapsed wood before Chris rushed up to take his spot. Denny jumped down just as Chris jumped on. Chris spun around to face the audience of three and began his turn. "There once were four guys that had the balls, to knock down this crappy house's walls. When they were done with the house that smelled like poo, they all laughed out loud and screamed, 'FUCK YOU!!!'" With Chris still standing on top of the wood pile, the other three joined in for several more choruses of "fuck you" as they raised their middle fingers skyward in defiance of the vandalism they had perpetrated.

Then Rusty, feeling redeemed by the fun twist the hike had now taken, started chanting, "Chris! Chris! Chris!" Saluting his two rhymes as well as the boy who had come up with them so quickly. Soon, all three boys made a semicircle around the ruined shack where Chris stood tall and basked in his friends' adulation. "Chris! Chris! Chris!" rang out and echoed among the surrounding trees before it was replaced by a singular crash. In a moment, Chris was gone. Swallowed whole by the collapse of the rotted pile of wood under him. In a flash, he disappeared below ground. Above, the remaining three boys stood frozen and mute around the gaping hole he had fallen into.

Just like Chris, as he tumbled down into the new hole, they fell silent.

CHAPTER NINE

I⏢ was Rusty who broke his paralysis first. Audibly groaning as he ran to where the collapsed walls and roof of the wood shack were stacked before vanishing, along with Chris, below ground. Nearly losing his balance when the bottoms of his tennis shoes slipped on a couple of the broken planks still scattered around the edge of the newly formed pit. The remaining pieces of splintered wood were moist and weather smoothed, slick with decay. Nearly upending the twelve-year-old and sending him gracelessly skidding towards the cave-in. Behind him, Rusty felt someone grab a handful of his t-shirt, stopping him in his tracks before he toppled over. "Hold on! Don't go flying in after him!" The steady grip was Brian's. Moments later, both boys stood peering over the ledge with a hand on each other for balance. Denny let out a single sob in the background.

"Denny! Gimme me that flashlight!" Rusty held out his hand behind him as he hollered at his friend. Stretching for the lone light they'd brought along, anxious to see where Chris had dropped down into and get him back out.

The new rift in the earth was dark and shadowy. The dank scent of rot rose in the still air to greet him as he peered over the ledge. The sickly smell mixed with the deafening sound of silence, adding to the surreal feeling that hung heavily around the three boys. The surrounding trees blocked much of the natural sunlight from reaching very far down inside the new crater, adding to the confusion as well. While Denny scrambled back to their bag of supplies for the flashlight, Rusty began calling down into the chasm. "Chris! Are you OK? Chris!"

"Can you hear us? Where are you?" Brian was calling out as well, but no reply came back to them from below ground. Brian turned to yell at Denny to hurry up just as the smaller boy placed the flashlight in Rusty's outstretched hand. Denny's eyes were wet, and he pulled off his dark-rimmed glasses to wipe at them with his skinny forearm.

"Is he... is he hurt?" Denny hung back from the edge of the new pit. Asking Brian or Rusty to report rather than looking down himself. Rusty switched on the battery-operated light and aimed the yellow beam down into the new hole. "What are we going to do? What if..."

"Chris!" Rusty ignored Denny's questions and continued to call out as he swept the light back and forth across the bottom of the pit. Dust and dirt from both the fallen shack and the earthen walls of the chamber it collapsed down into danced and hovered in the air. This mass of slowly settling particles, still momentarily suspended in the air, reflected the flashlight's meager effort and created a dizzying, snow globe like effect further obscuring their vision.

But even within this unnatural blizzard, the top of Chris's red hair stuck out starkly. Chris was only down about ten feet below the surface and was sitting on top of all the collapsed wood beneath him. Both of his legs were stretched out in front of him, although the bottom of his right leg was hidden under a portion of one of the buckled walls. He looked dazed and one of his elbows was bleeding, but he was both alive and conscious. "Chris! Jesus H. Christ! Are you OK? What happened?"

"The floor just gave in, I guess." Chris looked up out of the hole at his two friends almost quizzically, as if they could educate him about what just happened. He sounded so matter of fact that Brian instantly barked at him.

"Not cool, man. We thought you just died!" Brian was breathing hard and the troubled look on his face seemed to delight Chris. He started to smile as he held his hand up to block the beam of the flashlight shining directly into his face. Now that Chris was obviously still among the living, Brian added, "Dickwad" before beginning to smile himself. Denny finally crept to the edge of the new pit and, still wiping at his eyes, grinned in relief as well.

Rusty was the only one still upset.

"You are such a dipstick! You could have been killed." Rusty switched back off the flashlight and set it angrily on the ground. "Now get out of there before someone sees us." He looked nervously around once before dropping to his belly and stretching out one arm. Reaching down into the hole, intending for his friend to stand so he could help pull him out. But Chris remained seated where he was. The pudgy boy leaned forward on the remnants of the shack's roof, walls, and floor underneath him. Wiggling his right leg back and forth and trying to work it free from under the section of wall that covered it, while simultaneously struggling with his hands to push the piece of collapsed wood off his hidden leg. After a minute, he gave up and looked back up at his three friends.

"One of you is going to have to help me. I can't get my leg out by myself. Someone come down here and lift this thing off of me." Chris gestured at where his leg disappeared from view. Without any hesitation, Brian sat down at the edge of the hole and reached over to grab Rusty's still outstretched hand. Using it, and Rusty's help, to slowly lower himself down the side. Pieces of the dirt wall cascading down as his feet scrambled under him until he reached the bottom.

Denny warned shakily from above, "Be careful where you walk. The wood could still split some more or break apart under you." Brian nodded and began to gingerly step over to where Chris still sat waiting. Once he reached the downed wall trapping Chris's leg, he was able to lift it enough for Chris to slide his leg out. With Chris's leg now freed, Brian let the wood fall back in place. As it settled, everything under the two boys shuddered once and creaked loudly. Again, Denny warned them from above, "Don't walk together. Stay spread out." Without looking back up, Brian gave Denny the finger dismissively with one hand while reaching down to help Chris up with his other.

With Brian's help, Chris made it to the side of the pit and reached up for Rusty's outstretched hand. With both Rusty and Denny pulling from above, Brian pushed Chris from below while complaining about his best friend. "Man, you have a fat ass..."

"Well quit looking at it then," Chris fired back, sensitive about being known in school as the fat kid. "And watch what you are grabbing down there!" Brian grunted while shoving as hard as he could with both hands at Chris's backside. Once Chris made it safely back above ground, Denny made him pull the bottom of his right pant leg up. His injured leg was beginning to swell and already there was colored bruising around his ankle, but it wasn't bleeding anywhere and it didn't appear broken. As he put weight on it, he grimaced. "Shit, that hurts. Walking back is going to suck a big one."

"I thought you were a goner, Chris. You just disappeared in like a second. It was like the earth was swallowing you up!" Denny had regained his composure and was babbling as he sometimes did when he got excited. "That was amazing! It was just like Raiders of the Lost Ark when Hans Solo, I mean Indiana Jones, runs while the whole place is collapsing all around him." Denny paused a beat before going on. "Were you scared?"

"Not really. It was all like in slow motion for me. I heard something crack and then I sunk down. But it was more like I was in quicksand or something. My feet never left the top of the roof I was standing on. It just sunk down under me, kind of like being in an elevator." Chris was shaking his head as he spoke. "I never even lost my balance going down until that piece of the wall fell on my leg."

"You are so lucky, man." Rusty passed Chris the water and then added, "What was that under there? A basement?"

Denny chimed in, "No one would put a basement under a little shed like that. There was no doorway to get down there, and it was just dirt walls, right?"

"There could have been a trap door in the floor," offered Chris.

"Or maybe the old shack was hiding something. You know, built over the hole to hide it... what?" The look on the other two faces caused Denny to stop talking. "What?" he asked a second time.

"Maybe it's hiding a pirate treasure!" Chris exclaimed.

"On a river? Have a clue..." Denny pushed his glasses up on his nose.

"Well, maybe it's an opening to a mine shaft." Chris countered, more than a little defensively. "A goldmine." He added, warming to his own idea.

"You guys ever hear of a place called Oak Island?" Now it was Rusty adding his voice to the mystery of the old shack and the pit it had been hiding. "My dad has this book called Pit of Money or Money Pit, something like that. Anyway, somewhere up in Alaska or Canada, some boys one time found a pit like this hidden under an oak tree." Rusty paused, trying to remember what he'd read. "Under it was a hidden treasure. Maybe someone is digging for treasure here."

Denny wrinkled up his nose and then pulled off his glasses and began wiping one of the lenses on his t-shirt. "I don't think anyone ever found a treasure in Illinois. And there aren't any goldmines around here either."

Chris jumped back in. "Well, what about that guy Rusty saw before? Maybe he was hiding something and tried to scare Rusty away so he wouldn't find it." He looked over at Rusty, "You said he was burning up clothes, right? What was the name on the ID again?"

"It was just some gas company credit card, not an ID. But the name was Laura Trace. I'll never forget that name."

"Right. So maybe this Laura Trace found out what he was doing."

"And what? He killed her? No way, Jose." But Rusty knew the reason her name had stuck with him was because he had wondered the exact same thing. Rusty's older half-sister Sherry had disappeared back when he was eight years old. And, still to this day, no one had ever figured out what happened to her. The vanishing had crushed Rusty. The sixteen-year-old girl had gone missing one night after her shift at K-Mart ended. Her car later found abandoned, no trace of her was ever found. Had this Laura Trace also been in some kind of trouble that day? And if so, maybe if he hadn't been such a scared little wussy back then, he could have helped her. Like he wished someone had helped his big sister...

Rusty didn't want to think about that now, so he blurted out what he'd told himself for the last two years. "What I saw was just a burn pile for trash." But as he spoke, he looked down, not meeting either of his friends' eyes. "Come on. Let's get out of here before we get caught." He pointed over to where the shack had recently stood. "We just destroyed that and I don't want to have to pay for some farmer's new shed."

The other two boys nodded before breaking into smiles. "Yeah, but man, that was so cool. Did you see how we took that whole thing down?" Chris was beaming. "I'll never forget this day as long as I live. We go together like spit and sweat." Then raising his voice, he added, "Wolf pack rules!"

The three boys, in unison, echoed "Wolf pack rules!" Then the boys realized Brian wasn't beside them. He hadn't climbed back out of the hole the shack collapsed down into. Together, they leaned over the dirt ledge to see what Brian was doing. Below them, he was pulling hard on a couple pieces of loose wood boards covering something along the wall on one side of the pit. As they watched, he successfully yanked off a piece of planking that seemed to be part of a crude door covering an underground opening. With the piece of wood still in his hand, Brian grimaced and turned quickly away from the black, yawning hole.

"Ewww! This is where that smell is coming from..." Brian tossed aside the old piece of wood and pulled the collar of his shirt up over his nose. He looked out of the hole at his three friends. "God! That is awful!"

Ever cautious, Denny yelled out another warning. "Does it smell like rotten eggs? It might be sulfur or poisonous underground gas. Don't breathe it!"

"Too late. I got a mouthful." His eyes were watering, and he coughed twice. After a couple deep breaths of relatively fresh air, Brian turned back around and once again faced the opening. "It doesn't really smell like rotten eggs, though. It's the same thing we smelled when we were inside the crappy shack. Just stronger." Brian took a tentative step towards the new find.

"What are you doing? Let's get out of here. Chris is hurt, and it is going to take us forever to get back home." Rusty tried to sound annoyed, but at least to him, he could still hear the fear he felt come through in his voice. "Let's get out of here before someone finds us here." Now his voice sounded desperate.

"Would you be cool, man? No one is way out here. Besides, I'll just take a quick look. Throw me the flashlight." Brian looked back up at the other three. The lower part of his face was still hidden under the neck of his shirt. Rusty thought he looked like a bandit about to rob a train.

Mutely, Denny bent down and started to hand Brian the flashlight as the boy reached up for it. But Rusty snatched it away first and shot Denny his meanest look. Then, switching the light on, he lowered himself down into the earthen cavity with Brian's help. Mumbling and complaining the entire time they all were going to get caught if they didn't leave soon. Once he was standing beside Brian, Rusty pulled his shirt up over his nose as well. The thick, rancid smell was strong. Together, the two boys made their way to the black opening, and Rusty pointed the beam of the flashlight inside.

The wood board Brian pulled off the side of the dirt wall had not been very wide. To see inside at the same time, the two boys huddled together around the new opening. The flashlight's dull yellow beam only penetrated a few feet into the shaft, and it took several long moments for their eyes to adjust enough to make out much of anything. Even then it remained difficult to see clearly what or why this gash in the earth was ever dug out. Or why it had later been crudely boarded up and hidden for who knows how long underneath the queer old shack the four boys had just destroyed. The underground hole-in-the-wall looked like it might be the beginning of a cavern of sorts. The tunnel, if it was one, seemed to snake away from the opening. The two boys now stood nearly cheek to cheek peering inside. The passageway appeared to lead deeper underground and in the general direction of the old cemetery. But whether it ran all the way to the graveyard, or ended a mere few feet in, was impossible to tell.

Just inside the small opening, lying on the ground of the newly dis-covered underground shaft, was a small collection of shiny and weirdly reflective rocks. The biggest of the smallish rocks or beads were golf ball size; the smallest marble size. They each looked like they had possibly been worked or carved like jewels sometime in the past. Instinctively, Brian bent down lower and, before Rusty could say anything, he reached his hand inside the opening to grab several of them. As Brian pulled his arm back outside, his eyes were glued to his new discovery. He stepped away and held them aloft in the shadowy sunlight streaming down from the forest canopy overhead, inspecting them and exclaiming out loud to Denny and Chris what they found.

Rusty barely noticed.

While Brian had quickly focused on the strange shiny beads, some-thing different captured his attention. Rusty remained rigid with his face pressed tightly against the wood opening, his eyes darting and searching for an explanation to what he saw. His heart lurched in his chest and, if his legs hadn't turned to spaghetti, he would have bolted right then and there. A chill creeping slowly into his bones.

Deeper inside the tunnel, where the light barely reached, stood a single twisted figure. Terrified, Rusty caught his breath and refused to let it go, fearing it would be his last. Certain this being would see him and spring to life any second. Knowing if it did, the scream bubbling up inside him, the one he was barely holding in check at the moment, would most likely wake the dead of the nearby graveyard. Yet despite wanting desperately to be anywhere but where he was, Rusty found he could not tear his gaze away from the form. Or breathe. Though, with the foul stench permeating the air around him, that was hardly a loss.

The figure was far enough away that the meager beam of the flashlight could barely punch all the way through the darkness and touch it. (Somewhere a voice inside his head asked Rusty if ghosts could control electronic devices to keep hidden, but he ignored himself.) For several long moments, the form remained motionless and completely still. Rusty slowly began to relax as his eyes, gradually adjusting to the darkness, revealed the figure to be lifeless.

The stationary, bizarrely shaped form appeared black, but in the limited illumination of his light it was hard to assign any color to what he was seeing. Rusty strained his eyes in the gloom of the hollow cavity and continuously moved the beam of the flashlight to try to shed more light on it and peer deeper inside. Behind him he could hear his friends talking excitedly and, now that he was breathing again, each breath he drew was a struggle as the stale, pungent air flooded out from inside the chamber. Despite these distractions, Rusty remained transfixed at the scene in front of him.

The statue or being – Rusty couldn't tell what material the image was made of – appeared to be about the same height as the twelve-year-old. But it was impossible to tell from his angle if the thing was kneeling or standing. The head resembled a skull with two hollowed out eye sockets and a row of teeth jutting out from an elongated, tapered, black lipped mouth. The odd shape of the jawline somehow gave the entire figure's head an insect-like appearance. Or maybe a bird with a long, sharp beak.

Rusty imagined the mouth opening and shutting with a clack. The skull itself was bowed forward, as if acknowledging it had finally been found.

The back of the thing was pressed tightly against the far wall of the underground cavern it occupied. Rusty thought it may be leaning back against it, like a statue with a rounded base that might topple over if it wasn't tilted against something. Or perhaps, the boy further pondered, the entire figure was somehow nailed to the wall to keep it from collapsing forward.

Or maybe mounted like a ghastly keepsake.

He squinted in the darkness and kept trying to change the angle of his view into the narrow opening. Desperately wanting the thing to reveal itself fully to him, hoping for some sort of familiarity that would be a comfort. But the dismal light and long shadows cast by the flashlight only made it appear even more disturbing. Studying it as closely as he could, Rusty made out the thing's two hands clasped together in front of it in a mock prayer. Each hand held an impossible number of digits of various sizes and they all were folded over each other.

Strangest of all, however, were the vestiges of what looked like two wings sprouting absurdly out of its back. Both of them, like the entire effigy, seemed fleshless. Or so dried out the bones of each were all that remained of them. Rusty couldn't help but think of pictures he'd seen in his father's National Geographic magazines, or on PBS shows when they featured real Egyptian mummies who were dried out and mummified in ancient times. Parched husks of what once held life, left withered and misshapen by time and the desert climate. But that was as close to a human appearance as this thing in front of him became. From so far away, the boy couldn't even be sure what he was looking at was real. Was it a statue? Perhaps a sculpture of a gargoyle, or maybe a bizarre parody of a beaked angel?

Rusty, his fear of getting caught forgotten, desperately wanted to inspect it further. Still holding the flashlight in one hand, he tried to grab and pull at the warped plank next to the opening Brian created. But as he went to pull the next wood board off, his light dipped lower and lit up the dirt at the effigy's feet. There lay a riot of large, hollow rocks broken apart and scattered along the ground. The strange image of the angel, demon, or gargoyle seemed to be positioned among them as if in a nest. Or perhaps they'd been, along with the shiny stones now in Brian's hand, laid at the thing's feet like an offering. Rusty stopped pulling on the wood plank and aimed his flashlight at one of the hollow shells slightly separated from the rest of the pile and closest to him. He had the absurd thought he was looking at giant egg shells. But from what? An ostrich? As he peered closer, a more sinister thought occurred to him. The hollowed, broken, and scattered pieces were also about the same size as human skulls...

"Rusty! We better get out of here, someone is coming!" Brian grabbed Rusty's shoulder and spun him around. "You hear that?" In the distance, barely audible, came the unmistakable throb of a large motor. But from down inside the pit where the two boys stood, it was impossible to tell where it was coming from or how close it might be. Rusty looked from Brian up to the top of the dirt ledge where Denny and Chris were looking down at them. Anxiety clearly showing in both their eyes.

"What is that?" Rusty asked looking at each one of his friends in turn. Not caring who answered and hoping at least one of them knew. "A truck maybe? Or a tractor?"

"I don't know, but it sounds like it is getting closer," Denny finally admitted. "Come on! We need to split unless we want to get caught." Then, with Chris leaning on the smaller boy, they both turned and disappeared, moving in the opposite direction from both the approaching rumble and the pit where Rusty and Brian stood down inside of. Brian turned to follow and began to scramble up the side to join them on the surface. He pulled himself up by grabbing several long roots from neighboring trees dangling down from near the top. Pieces came off in his hands as he climbed out, but he found sure footing on some of the broken pieces of wood from the shack lining the sides of the dirt wall pit. When he reached the top, he turned to help Rusty. But the blonde boy hadn't moved. He was looking once more at the opening where the bizarre figure was hidden.

"What are you doing? You were the one so worried about getting caught!" Brian was holding his outstretched hand out as he yelled at Rusty. Seeing his friend's indecision, he added, "We can come back sometime later. But right now, we need to move."

Rusty finally relented and ran to the side, jumping up to grab a hold of Brian's hand and quickly reaching the surface with his help. In the distance, he saw Denny helping Chris make his way slowly across the cemetery. Chris was limping badly and leaning heavily on Denny who was struggling under the larger boy's weight. Both Brian and Rusty sprinted after them with Brian taking Denny's place and helping Chris move more quickly.

Halfway across the graveyard, with the dull rumble of what Rusty now felt pretty sure was just a tractor, Chris looked over at him. "Show us where this burn pile was before we get out of here." Rusty turned, and was about to argue with him, when he saw all three of his friends were looking expectantly at him. Sighing, he started walking at an angle that would bring the four of them to the spot where two years before he'd found the burned items of clothing and purse. It was right where he knew it would be. Like before, nothing grew and white ashes mixed with black soot dominated the spot. Clearly, it was used multiple times since he'd last seen it. Though probably not recently, at least sometime in the last couple months.

"This is it. Same spot." Rusty couldn't help but look back across the open field towards where, as a ten-year-old, he'd seen the outline of the creepy silhouette. But nothing was there. He thought again of the bizarre statue or effigy standing solitarily underground, and how the silhouette from two years ago seemed to suddenly have shrunk down and disappeared. He wasn't sure if he was still shaken from these twin experiences or if it was because they'd destroyed that creepy old shack. But now he was once again the one pushing to leave. "See? Just some farmer's burn pit for garbage. Let's go..." But Denny began kicking at the ash with the toe of his tennis shoe and Chris squatted down beside the burn pit, massaging his swollen ankle. Brian, just as Rusty did two years before, was already poking a dead tree branch into the burn pile.

"Let's see if we can find anything." Brian was using the tree branch to spread all the ash out across the grassy field. At first, only ash and small black embers from long ago fires were visible. But a few minutes later, Denny spied something odd and reached out to stop Brian's raking.

"Is that just gravel or little rocks? Maybe pieces of wood?" Denny walked over to the spot that caught his eye. Reaching down, he picked up what appeared to be three small white pebbles from out of the cold ash. Holding them in his hand, he stood, and the other three boys gathered close when he reopened his hand. "Sure are weird looking rocks..." Denny began to say but stopped himself. Using his opposite hand, he picked at one of the small objects and turned it over. It might have been a rock, but as Denny brushed it off a small black spot directly in the middle would not come off. He rubbed at it hard with his fingers. Troubled, Denny brought it close to his face and squinted behind his dark-framed glasses. "That looks just like my cavity." Then Denny looked back at his other hand where he still held the other two sister items. He stated flatly, "These are teeth."

"No way! Let me see those." Brian stuck his hand out and Denny quickly dumped the three teeth into his outstretched palm before wiping his hand on his jeans. Brian turned them over in his hand while the others looked on. It didn't take long before Denny's initial observation was agreed upon.

They found three teeth.

With one of them cavity-filled, a dawning realization slowly filled the boys with a flood of mixed emotions as they stood shoulder to shoulder beside the burn pit. "These are human teeth," stated Brian, as he looked down in astonishment at what he held in his hand. Then, as if he wasn't sure if he'd said it out loud, he repeated himself. "These are human teeth."

In the distance, the rumbling of the unseen motor or tractor grew louder once more. Brian stuffed the teeth in the front pocket of his blue jeans next to the weird colored beads found earlier. All four boys traded worried glances as the grumbling engine continued to drone out its one lone note in the background.

Rusty hoped, if it was a farmer, he hadn't seen them earlier crossing all those corn and bean fields. Or that he wouldn't stumble upon their vandalism before they got far enough away from here. Once again, the fear of "getting caught" drove Rusty to grab Chris's opposite arm, so both he and Brian were practically carrying Chris by the time the four boys exited the woods bordering the lost cemetery.

SPICKARD, MISSOURI
JULY 28TH, 1907

HIS CHEST HEAVED, AND his mouth worked in the dim light of the kerosene lantern. Despite himself, soft moans of pleasure escaped his dripping lips. Each tender pink scrap he partook of seeming to taste better than the last. "Mmmm…" he hummed and cooed as he feasted, "Mmmm…" His lips smacked and he greedily licked a small pink morsel from the side of his mouth. "Mmmm…"

When he looked back down inside the perfectly symmetrical red seeping hole, he could see the delicacy was now gone. The bone bowl he ate out of now hollowed out. He pushed the empty-headed corpse off himself and turned his attention to the woman lying next to him. Her eyes stared unseeing, pieces of white bone where he'd opened her skull stuck to her cheek. The man callously flicked the particles of bone away with his middle finger before pulling her head into his lap next. Though he was nearly full now, the thought of not finishing never entered his mind. He bent over her as he had her husband, quivering with excitement.

"Mmmmm…"

Once every piece had been devoured, he pushed the woman's head off his lap. The hollow head lolling awkwardly on one side; a slow trickle of curdling blood running down her forehead. As he rose from the married couple's bed, the husband slipped silently off the mattress, landing face first on the floor beside the small bedside table where the lantern sat. The man bent down and retrieved the husband, placing him once more next to his spouse before pulling the covers of the bed up to both of their chins. The man looked down at the couple with satisfaction. If you looked past the bloodstains, they seemed to be sleeping peacefully. Just as they had been when he first entered the bedroom.

"Nice," he muttered to himself before walking back into the little girl's room across the hallway. There he retrieved the family's wood axe he'd used to bludgeon their daughter earlier, barely glancing at the ruin he'd so painstakingly arranged when he'd finished with her. Returning to her parents' room, he raised the axe above his head twice. Caving in the empty skulls of both before dropping the axe onto the floor of the bedroom. He looked down at the ticking alarm clock on the bed stand.

"I must take my leave of you now," he spoke to the unhearing farming couple. "I have a train to catch."

CHAPTER TEN

"That guy couldn't organize a panic in a flooding submarine." Stander shook his head, smiling. "But I guess even if his place of business was a catastrophe, at least eventually we were able to find the old-timey screw-in fuses we needed. Hopefully, the historical records in town will be more organized than the Almore True Value Hardware store was."

Secrist leaned out the driver's side window of Stander's black Jeep. "Yeah, no kidding. That place was a dump. I bet the live bait and little tubs of night crawlers are about all he actually sells in there. Anyway, wish me luck, Russ. Unless I completely strike out, I'll plan on eating lunch in town. You want me to bring you anything back?"

"Nah... we brought plenty of food back yesterday. I'm set." With that, Stander took his hand off the side mirror where it was resting. "See ya' when you get back, Tommy."

Secrist pulled around the circle drive and headed down the long driveway of Relict Mansion. Turning at the "T" at the end of the drive and pulling onto the blacktop road that led back into town. Twenty minutes later, he pulled into an angled parking spot in front of an unremarkable house with black shingles and peeling white paint. The modest two-story building was one block over from the tiny downtown area of Almore. The entire small village's commerce comprised of a café, post office, bank, chiropractor, and a real estate office that shared a roof with the neglected hardware store both he and Stander had stopped in yesterday for the fuses. On the far side of town, closer to the highway, stood a sad looking bar and a lone gas station with two pumps and a decrepit single stall car wash. As he killed the engine, he looked up at the equally unremarkable sign stuck in the ground out front of the building. The sign read "Almore Historical Society," clearly hand painted in plain black lettering.

He smoothed down his windblown salt and pepper hair and ran his fingers over his moustache before stepping out of the car. The sidewalk in front of him was empty, and on the entry door hung a slightly askew "Open" sign. Secrist stepped up the three cement stairs that led to the creaking wood porch and pushed the front door open. Above his head, a small discolored bell tinkled twice as he swung the door open and then closed it behind him.

Inside he was greeted by brown paneled walls full of glass frames containing mostly black and white photos. Many of the bigger ones, as he glanced over them quickly, were clearly pictures of the downtown area he'd just driven through. Some shots were posed groups of sober looking men and plain faced women looking as if they wanted to be anywhere but in front of a camera. Other photos were of small crowds gathered for parades and various events from the preceding decades. There were also spectators alongside uniformed baseball players and brass bands of geeky looking kids. Some of the other pictures were of high school graduating classes which, in the 1930s and 40s, seemed to routinely only be 7 or 8 students. Most of them female.

Filling out the rest of the room were several wood and glass display cases, themselves nearly antiques. Underneath the glass partitions were countless old farm tools, medals, and various sew-on patches. Behind these stood badly scarred mannequins decked out in officer and combat uniforms, and in the far corner sat a massive black antique typewriter and part of an iron printing press. Hanging above both of these were two crank-handled wood telephones and draped down from the ceiling were three weathered American flags.

Secrist stepped towards the middle of the room about to callout and see if someone was in one of the unseen backrooms when the slatted wood floor under his step creaked loudly. As he stepped back, the floor creaked a second time, just as loudly. Like magic, out from behind a drab, olive colored curtain stretched across a hidden doorway, an elderly man stepped lightly behind a rolling walker.

"Oh! Well, you aren't my granddaughter now, are you?" The man wore beige hearing aids with yellowing tubes above each ear, and the light from the ceiling fan above glared off his shiny head. His red walker was adorned with various war veteran decals and bumper stickers of assorted sayings. He wore a badly faded Rock-the-Vote t-shirt with the iconic winged MTV emblem blazoned across the back. He shoved his walker to one side and stretched out his hand to shake Secrist's in greeting. "Name's John Gilmore." As the two men shook, he leaned in close and whispered conspiratorially. "Now if my granddaughter shows up, don't tell her I was walking around without that contraption. I can do without her scolding." When he pulled back, he grinned warmly.

"Your secret is safe with me, sir." Secrist nodded once, smiling sincerely.

"Fine! Thank you, indeed. Now forgive me, but there are very few folks around these here parts that I don't know. So, since I don't recognize you, I am guessing you are a visitor to our little neck of the woods. How can I help you?" The gracious old man bowed slightly.

Stander had already cautioned Secrist about referencing Relict Mansion, saying it might skew the responses of the locals if they knew he was involved with the place. Or the family that owned it. So Secrist recited the story he'd concocted the previous night. One he hoped would help him get the most information with the least amount of dishonesty. "Well thank you, John. My name is Tom Secrist and I have recently retired to start a second career in writing," he began. "I am hoping to pen some of the interesting stories, myths, and legends of the smaller communities along the Mississippi."

"Forget it!" The man said abruptly before turning to reclaim his red walker. "That old house stroked the imaginations of a few impressionable village idiots. But none of it is true. You are wasting your time." The old man moved away before adding over his shoulder, "And mine!"

Shocked, Secrist stammered. The local historian's curt response conveying a finality. "Excuse me... sir, please excuse me. But I am not sure what you are referring to." Lying again to the old man, certain he was, as Stander warned, unwilling to speak with him about Relict Mansion. What the hell have you got me into, Russ? "I was told there once was a small burial plot down by the river. My interest is in the history of those early residents of Almore, not some house."

The old man stopped walking, but didn't turn around. Instead, tossing his words over one hunched shoulder. "Well, you're wrong. Those people were *never* considered Almore citizens." After a moment of silence, the old man turned back slightly, still not meeting Secrist's eyes. "But what would you know?" Finally, he looked up, his eyes narrowed in suspicion. "That place, those people are all long gone now. How did you hear about what you think you know something about anyway?" The last sentence laced with more than a bit of sassy sarcasm.

Initially flummoxed, the detective quickly spun out more of his tale. Hoping something out of the little bit of information Stander shared about the forgotten cemetery might stick. "You are right, sir. I am not from around here. I actually live in Michigan. But my granddad used to tell me stories about his adventures as a youth going up and down the Mississippi. He would, if he was still alive, tell you he was kind of a rolling stone when he was a young man. Hitched rides with early barge operators, ran a little 'shine' as he called it, and rode motorcycles back when they were pretty much death traps."

"Motorcycles, you say?" Clearly this was a topic of interest to the local historian, and he noticeably perked up. "I had my share of motor driven bikes back in the day. Loads of fun, but not very reliable as I recall."

Secrist lurched for the opening the man had given him. Grasping for anything to get back in his good graces and keep him talking. Knowing from his past experience interviewing witnesses, suspects, victims, and everything in between, that finding a neutral subject to discuss often successfully led back to the original line of questioning. The tactic, hardly unique, usually proved very effective.

"Yes, sir! My grandad loved his bikes." Though he didn't ride himself, nor did his grandad as far as he was aware – Secrist had been adopted and never knew his real parents, much less any grandparents – but he knew enough guys with motorcycles that he could keep the conversation flowing. He hoped. "Were you a Harley man? I love those old Harley Davidson motorcycles."

The man took a few steps back to where Secrist stood, his face softening slightly. "Oh, now I rode just about anything back in the day. Excelsior was really my favorite. But I also owned Triumphs, Indians, and all... loved those old bikes."

"How about Harley Davidson? That was my grandad's favorite. Bet you had a few of those back in the day, huh?" Secrist kept his poker face, still smiling amiably.

"Yes, I did. Last bikes I owned back in the seventies were Harley's."

The conversation was warming again. Relieved, Secrist was keen to keep him talking. "Those must have been amazing machines."

"Nope. Pieces of shit, if you'll pardon my French. Part of why I quit riding was because of those. Like I said, fun but not very reliable. Kept breaking down, parts would fall right off them sometimes, and heaven forbid you ever try to ride one in the rain. I'd take back my old Indian Chief from the 50s' over any of the 'Hardly Ableson' bikes I had later on in the 70s." He pushed himself back towards the front of the building frowning.

Secrist's heart sank, thinking he may have just blown it. "Hardly Ableson? I thought, er... I mean, I know my grandad thought they were the best. You sure see a lot of them on the roads these days."

The historian stopped near a counter by the front door and sat on a high-backed stool directly behind it. Thankfully continuing the conversation with the lone patron. "Lot of McDonald's around nowadays too, ain't there? That don't mean you get the best cheeseburger there though, does it?" But the man's friendly demeanor seemed to have returned and inside Secrist breathed a sigh of relief. "People are sheep and can't think for themselves anymore." Secrist nodded, trying to decide how to steer the topic back without offending the old man when he suddenly spoke again, bailing him out. "That was the problem with those poor souls that settled down by the river. Back at the turn of the twentieth century. They were just pathetic sheep following a bad shepherd."

"Bad shepherd? How do you mean, sir?" Secrist couldn't believe his luck. But then again, patting himself on the back inside, this was what he was aiming for. Getting the local historian comfortable and talking.

"Nothing sadder... few know the story, less ever wanted it talked about. But after all this time, how can it hurt? Nothing left there to see anyway." The man looked up, sighing, seeming to make up his mind. "You gonna write this down?"

"Better than that, sir. With your permission, I'd like to record our conversation, so I don't get anything wrong later if I decide to use this in my book." Secrist pulled out his iPhone and showed it to the historian before laying it on top of the glass counter, setting it to record.

"So, what did you mean by a bad shepherd?"

"Oh... now, that was just what my grandfather called the fella. Said those folks who tried to make a go of it riverside had lots of bad luck. Most of it on account, as he told it anyway, of their leader." As the historian spoke, he pointed to a second high backed stool behind the glass topped display next to Secrist. Silently inviting the supposed author to pull it over and have a seat.

"Why? Was their leader not up to the task? Made stupid mistakes or...?" Secrist, after scooting the offered seat closer, sat down, intrigued. "Or corrupt, maybe?"

"Corrupt, you say? HA!" The historian snorted derisively once before continuing. "Corrupted soul more than likely, as I heard tell." But then, stopping, he glanced out the large picture window behind him. Walking up the street was a casually dressed woman of perhaps 40 or so. Pleasantly plump and pretty under a pair of wide rimmed glasses. She had a lit cigarette in her mouth and her brown hair was tied back in a ponytail. In one hand, she carried a small white paper bag. "Ah! Now here is my granddaughter, Jenny." Perhaps subconsciously, the historian laid his hand on one of the handles of his walker. His eyes darting across at Secrist with uncertainty.

"Your secret is safe with me," Secrist managed to get out right before the dull brass bell tinkled above the doorway. The old man smiled and winked back at him as the bell sounded a second time. Secrist stood.

"Here you go, Paps." The woman cheerily tossed the white bag she was carrying, clearly a newly filled prescription, on the countertop in between both men before she noticed Secrist's presence. "Oh! Excuse me. I didn't realize we had a visitor. Sorry!" Though smiling and friendly, she walked past both men without introducing herself. Saying, before disappearing behind the same curtain the historian had emerged from behind earlier, "Go on ahead and keep talking. Just ignore me. I'll be out of here in a bit, Paps."

Distracted, the local historian picked up the bag Jenny had dropped off and began reading the paperwork stapled to the outside. After sitting back down, Secrist waited another minute before trying to engage the old man once again. "So...," he started slowly, "I guess the shepherd wasn't thought of too highly around here then, huh?"

"That foreigner wasn't thought of much at all." Though speaking once more, he continued to look down at the prescription, reading and still distracted.

"Foreigner? So, he wasn't an American, then? Where did he come from?" The elderly man looked back up, apparently satisfied the newly filled prescription was correct.

"I asked my grandfather the same thing. He said maybe he didn't look it, but he thought he was Spanish on account of his accent."

"Really?" This surprised the detective turned alleged new author. "So, the whole group was a bunch of Mexican immigrants? Do you know why they stopped here?"

"Now, I never said they was all Mexicans. My grandfather said most of the group of settlers who lived down at the river's edge were God fearing white people led astray. Said for some reason, they all were smitten with the Spaniard or Mexican. Or whatever he was. Treated him like a god and..." The man paused, lost in thought. "Now what was that there fellow's name again? God bless it! It was, no... it was..."

"Norte, you told me his name was Norte." Jenny, a mug of something steaming held between her two hands, walked out from behind the curtain. "I remember because, when you first told me about him, I thought you said 'naughty' like his name was naughty." She walked over and placed what looked like a mug of hot milk down in front of the local historian, smiling. She turned and introduced herself to Secrist. "My name is Jenny, by the way. The town crier here," she tossed a thumb up over her shoulder towards where she put the mug down, "is my grandfather." Secrist stood once more and introduced himself, giving the agreeable woman the same story he'd shared with the historian about hopefully writing a book. She seemed intrigued and, without asking, pulled up a third chair next to her grandfather and sat beside him. She didn't question the premise of Secrist's arrival at the Historical Society.

"So, this Norte," quizzed Secrist, "was leading a group of white men, women, and families that revered him? Leaving their own homes and family to start a new life with him right around here? Down near the shoreline of the Mississippi River? Why there?"

"They were traveling up the Mississippi River. I don't know why they picked the spot they did, but I'm sure they all regretted it." The old man sipped his hot milk gingerly as he spoke. Jenny was mostly silent beside him.

"Well, what happened? I know about the graves down near the shoreline. I understand the dates still legible are from before the turn of the twentieth century, and a lot of them seemed to have died right around 1900."

"Graves?" Jenny looked across at her grandfather, clearly unaware of any remnants left from the settlement. "There are graves leftover from the Norte cult?"

"Cult!" Secrist looked down at his phone, amazed at what he was hearing and thankful it was being recorded. "So, was this some Jonestown massacre-like situation that happened? Right here! How many people died? I can't believe this story has never come out and been..."

THWACK!!

Rising to his feet, the historian slammed both hands on the top of the wood and glass counter where he and Jenny sat. He pointed a bony, gnarled finger at Secrist and spoke loudly, not yelling but clearly taking exception to the assumptions made by both his granddaughter and the newcomer.

"See? This is why I should have kept my mouth shut." He looked down at the iPhone still recording. Secrist suspected if he knew how, the old man would have turned it off. "There was no massacre. Or a crazy cult running around Almore like a pioneer version of the Manson Family.

A lot of those poor souls died the same way everyone back then died. Disease, unsanitary conditions, exposure, you name it. And I'll remind you, sir, that I am speaking with you out of kindness. This community does not have any need for the fictional drama you are dreaming up. God knows this town has had enough tragedy without talking about..." The old man seemed to waver. His voice lowering before he sat once more. Jenny looked concerned at the outburst and shot Secrist a look that told him he needed to tread lightly. He nodded back discreetly to let her know he understood.

After a moment, Secrist spoke, his voice low and calm. "You are right. Please let me apologize. Sometimes I get carried away when I find what I think is a good story. But I promise you I will not write a word that isn't true." Secrist, promising to not write a word, was being honest. The old man did not need to worry about some sensationalized version of his tale bringing shame to the town of Almore. "Please correct me. What did really happen?"

"Nothing! Nothing happened here that didn't happen a hundred times over up and down the Mississippi. God bless it! Still happens from time to time." Jenny looked across at Secrist and their eyes met briefly. Both seemed anxious to hear the story, and both seemed surprised by the historian's behavior. Jenny reached across and squeezed her grandfather's hands.

"What happens from time to time, Paps?"

"Floods! A big flood came and washed everything away. The whole settlement. Killed just about all of them. Including their leader, Norte. Or if it didn't, he took off just the same. Might have found some other kind hearted Christians to bamboozle. Who knows?" The historian looked up. His eyes daring Secrist to challenge his story. The longtime detective recognized the look from a thousand previous conversations.

The look of someone telling a lie.

"That makes complete sense," said Secrist, the far more seasoned liar. "Washed everyone and everything down river. What a tragedy. I suppose locals here in Almore had to clean it all up. Bury the dead. What a horrible ordeal for the town. No wonder folks were hesitant to talk about it." The historian nodded numbly, not meeting either of the two listeners' eyes.

"This was in 1900, right?" Jenny asked softly. "They all drowned?"

Still not raising his eyes and to meet hers, he replied. "They all died. That's what I said wasn't it?" Secrist reached over and stopped the recording. The three sat in silence until finally the local historian excused himself, mumbling he needed to use the bathroom. He pushed his walker in front of him and disappeared once more behind the faded curtain at the end of the room.

"I am sorry if I upset your grandfather," started Secrist. "I never intended that. I just was curious to hear what happened."

"Please, it's fine," Jenny replied. "But I will tell you that one part of the story, well two, I guess, since he'd never shared there are still marked graves." Her brow furrowed in thought before continuing. "Anyway, the part about them all drowning? That isn't what he'd told me in the past. I remember one time, when I was a little kid, there was a fire down by the river. Some teenagers were messing around and caught an old wood train bridge on fire. One of the local kids even fell to their death trying to escape the blaze. It was so sad. But that's not the important part. It's what he told me back then, afterwards. When he refused to take me down to see where it all happened. See, all of us little kids were so curious. It was the biggest news event around here for years! But he wouldn't even tell me exactly where it even had happened. I had to find out later on my own, when I was older."

"Why was that? Was he still trying to keep the graveyard a secret?"

"I don't know for sure. Until just now, I've never heard the Norte settlement had their own cemetery. But what I do remember is him saying the teenager, the one that died, their head was caved in." In Jenny's eyes, Secrist could see the story still resonated with her.

"Well, if they fell from somewhere up high, like a train trestle, that wouldn't be that unusual." With the historian not seeming to be in a hurry to return, Secrist pocketed his phone and stood. "I was in law enforcement before I retired. I saw plenty of tragedies like that over the years. Teens think they are invincible. A lot of them don't figure out they aren't until it's too late."

"Yes, of course. But at the time I distinctly recall him saying the teen's pulverized skull looked just like the old skulls from the Norte settlement. Caved in and empty. If they all had drowned like he just said, why would their skulls have been caved in?"

Secrist nodded. Everything he'd heard, from the old historian, and now from his granddaughter Jenny, was hearsay. Likely embellishments at best, stories or lies at worst. All fascinating for sure, but not of real interest to him. He'd gotten what he'd hoped for. Acknowledgement of the lost graveyard from Stander's youth, how it came to be, and an explanation as to the clustered dates of their deaths. Whether it was from drowning or not. He would mention to Stander the version Jenny was sharing from her childhood. But since she was so young at the time, she was likely not the most reliable narrator.

"That is odd." He looked over at the entrance of the Historical Society building. It was now near lunchtime already. Perhaps he'd walk down to the little café on the opposite corner. He paused, debating if he should ask Jenny or her grandfather to join him before deciding against it. Stander advised him to keep a low profile, probably better to eat alone.

"So, you are a struggling writer, but you used to be a cop?" Jenny suddenly asked him, interrupting his thoughts. "Would you be interested in hearing about another puzzling local mystery from this part of the Mississippi River? Maybe it could make it in your book as well?"

Feigning interest, Secrist nodded, "Well sure, I'm all ears, Jenny. I'd invite you to lunch to hear about it, but I don't want to cause any trouble for you." He pointedly looked down at the shiny gold wedding band around her finger before adding, "I know how small-town gossip can be."

"Oh! Don't worry about any of that. The café is likely pretty empty and my best friend is the waitress, so there won't be any trouble. But that was gentlemanly of you to ask." She stood and moved her chair back over to where it had been previously while Secrist made his way slowly back to the building's entrance.

Smiling, he opened the front door for her and they both walked outside. "So, what is this other local mystery you want to share?"

"Well, it started with a missing relative back when I was still in grade school. But since then, I've uncovered some other interesting facts that are, well, mystifying to say the least."

"Really?" Inside he cringed. He couldn't count how many times during investigations he'd heard something similar. Usually wasting his time and sending him on a wild goose chase. But to be polite and make conversation as they strolled towards the café, he started to ask questions. "So, who was this missing relative?"

"Her name was Laura. Laura Trace."

CHAPTER ELEVEN

"Shania. Shania Twain."

"Really?"

"Yeah, you both are huge fans of Shania Twain. So, see? You and Secrist do have something in common, Lucas. You both love Shania Twain. Just maybe in different ways." Stander tried his best to keep a straight face. But as glitchy as the wireless video call was turning out to be, he doubted Lucas could have read his expression anyway. "So quit worrying about it. When you two do finally meet in person, you'll have something to talk about. You know, an icebreaker."

"Um... well, OK. But, um... question? Why would I casually bring up I sometimes masturbated in college while watching her music videos? You only goaded me into admitting that when I clearly had way too much to drink the night before you left France." Lucas was smiling good-naturedly, his calls with Stander were always unpredictably entertaining.

Dr. Lucas Chanet, French born but educated across the pond in the States and now employed by Stander, was the lead archeologist working the dig next to the ancient Roman quarry he'd helped Stander locate back in France. Both the quarry, and all the surrounding land, as they found out later, owned by Stander. The acreage part of a real estate conglomerate he had unknowingly inherited by way of a French trust named Noviodunum Suessiones. A trust dating back farther than any legal paperwork could be traced. Versions of the trust itself had been handed down over countless generations of family before Stander until it had ultimately landed in his lap as his dad's lone living heir. Now, using monetary assets from his inheritance, Stander was funding an excavation on a site adjacent to the ancient quarry where a series of deep underground scans showed an object of exceptional density and size was buried.

"Maybe I can casually pull up a few of her songs at some point? Then you can just share how much you 'loved' her while you lived in America. The fact you both show your affections differently shouldn't deter from your common appreciation of her many, uh... talents and assets." Stander was grinning widely now, no longer hiding it. "And you don't need to be embarrassed. You know what Tommy does when he hears her music come on?" Lucas, thinly bearded, wearing his usual wire rimmed glasses and with his long black hair tied back in a ponytail, shook his head no on the screen of Stander's tablet. "He dances. And the way he dances in public should be way more embarrassing to him than anything you might do in private."

After a few more minutes of banter and casual catching up, the two men turned their attention to the topic of the hastily arranged video call. A call Lucas had initiated after clearing away a substantial amount of earth and material from the spot he had chosen to focus on. After showing Stander a detailed listing of the small, and likely inconsequential finds uncovered over the last couple of days, Lucas also began to share some of the most recent pictures taken. The listing and digital photos showed just a small part of the painstaking documentation being compiled during the clandestine dig.

Lucas briefly narrated the images as he quickly clicked through them, anxious to get to the ones he'd personally taken mere hours earlier. "OK, this one is from right before we started excavating around what I believed was the crown of a head. See how the cuts are so perfectly angled? This level of detail would have taken an artisan of considerable skill to make these."

"Amazing, Lucas. I can see why you got so excited. The age of this and the craftsmanship shown is startling. Such precision! It looks like it was carved by modern tools, almost laser cut." Stander leaned forward, silently cursing the poor connection as the image bounced back and forth from crystal clear to fuzzy and dull. "God, I wish these satellite relays were better..."

"Here is the thing. Check out this next picture. Talk about going down the proverbial rabbit hole. Took us all day to get down another two feet all around it. And I want to be clear on this point: the surrounding dirt, rock, and debris was all completely undisturbed. There is nothing in this dig that would make me believe – and I would stake my professional reputation on this, by the way – that anyone has seen this thing for thousands of years." He paused, waiting for the gravity of his words to sink in. "Yet, look what we found!" Lucas suddenly felt giddy, unable to hide his enthusiasm, sure Stander would be floored. "Can you make that out?"

"What the fuck? Is that the top of a face?" Stander, squinting, used his fingers to expand the image on his tablet. "How wide is that?"

"A quick measurement before we started digging showed it was roughly eight feet across. But with barely the top of it showing I am still holding back any final judgements just yet." He paused until he was sure Stander could still see and hear him. The connection between the two devices was tenuous at best. "And yes, now I am sure that once we dig a little lower, the bottom half of the face will be revealed. But look here," he advanced to the next photo. "These two places, it's pretty clear, are meant to be the eyes. I think this raised portion here in the middle is likely the bridge of the statue's nose. It's just still buried."

Flipping to the next image, Lucas stopped talking so Stander could take everything in. After 20 seconds of silence, he could no longer contain himself. "See anything that looks familiar?"

Stander's face was a mask, sculpted and so unemotional Lucas first thought the satellite image froze again. But then, abruptly, Stander rose and stepped out of the picture briefly before returning to sit once more in front of the camera on his tablet. He looked down at something off camera, then looked back up once more. Doing this twice more while alternately squinting and altering the image several times on his end to see it more clearly.

The image was unmistakably the top of a face. Of that, Stander had no doubt. The bottom of the face, and anything else below it, still buried under tons of rock. Only the top showed, as if the owner of the face were standing underwater, rising slowly up from the depths, eyeballing its disturbers before either sinking back down into the depths or rising completely up to free itself. The middle of one eye, where the pupil would be, was hallowed out, concave, and empty. No different than many other unadorned statues or carved faces.

But the pupil on the other eye was filled.

Smooth and shiny, clearly worked and somehow carved. It was the black pupil of a watching, unblinking eye. Yet despite the enormity of the find — something discovered buried after an incalculable amount of time, if Lucas's hypothesis was to be believed — the casual onlooker's hands might not shake as Stander's were. For in his lap sat the black pupil's twin. The shape and odd lines, details that before now made little sense, aligned perfectly with the image on the screen. With Lucas having previously analyzed the odd rock now in Stander's lap and being onsite to compare with what he'd just unearthed, there was little doubt. But Stander asked anyway.

"Measurements?"

"It matches perfectly. The two are a matching pair." Lucas had anticipated the question from Stander. It had been one of the first things he'd wondered and checked as well. "But, although it may seem implausible, what you found in Michigan I suppose could be from this stone head's twin rather than having actually come from this site."

"Not likely."

"Agreed, but I am just saying we can't rule anything out just yet. Remember what I said earlier? The undisturbed layers of soil means whatever is buried next to the quarry hasn't been touched for a millennia. So, I can't square how the eyeball or pupil off *this* stone face could have ended up in a cave in North America." He paused. "Hopefully, more answers lie deeper down. Plus, we need to do carbon dating and..." But Stander was no longer listening. His mind trying to sort everything out. Was what they were doing dangerous? Should they stop? He thought again of Liz, the university professor who'd helped authenticate and document the discovery he now held in his lap. She'd somehow disappeared from inside the cave atop Mt. Arvon where it was discovered. Using the odd rock now in Stander's possession, the twin eye from Lucas's discovery in France, to somehow accomplish that feat. The idea of teleportation seemed absurd, yet both he and Secrist had seen the same thing. The stone had glowed brightly, blinked once, and she'd vanished. He pulled back up the last image and scrutinized it again. There was something else that had caught his eye.

"Can you still hear me? Or did we lose our connection again?" Lucas was gesturing as he spoke, trying to get a response. "Earth to Stander. Hello."

"I'm here. Sorry about that. This is just a lot to consider. I'm not sure how, or even if, we should proceed. What are your thoughts?"

"Are you kidding? This is potentially the find of the century. Hell! Could be the find of all mankind! I don't want to stop now." Lucas was animated, his passion for the dig clear.

There! That was it! That was what had caught his eye. Stander leaned forward and asked Lucas if there was another image of the top of the half-buried face, one that showed a closeup of the odd rounded etching in the middle of the stone face's forehead. After a minute of cycling past numerous photos, Lucas confirmed the one he was showing now was the best image he had of that spot. Stander enlarged the image and peered closely at it once more.

"Are you just looking at the circular, almost teardrop shaped carving on the forehead?" Stander nodded, still deep in his examination of the photo. "We noticed that as well. It could just be some anomalous scratching. Damage that might have even happened when this was first buried. Or, I suppose, it could be a carved symbol of sorts – the outline and shape does kind of resemble an Egyptian Ankh – but I'd need to get it cleaned up and digitized to be sure. I have to admit, now that you are pointing it out, it does seem to look intentionally carved. Might even be similar to a few of the celestial carvings we saw on some of the finds from inside the quarry itself. Or at least shares a few characteristics with them anyway. But if it is, it's nothing myself or anyone on my team recognizes. Why so curious?"

"It's a symbol."

"Really? OK, how can you be sure?"

In response, Stander grabbed his tablet and began walking away from the wood table he'd been sitting at during the call. Random images from inside Relict Mansion streaked past as Lucas looked on patiently. Stopping, Stander tilted the tablet, pointing its camera at a spot above an enormous fireplace mantle. There, carved deeply into the stone workings that made up the hearth, was the same unknown symbol. "I can be sure because that same symbol is carved above the stone fireplace of my deceased great aunt's home."

"What?!?! No way..." Lucas's face visibly blanched and, though only he felt it, his stomach lurched. "That looks like a distorted version of the Tree of Life. What in god's name is going on?"

"I'm starting to think the question might be what god's name," Stander replied grimly.

CHAPTER TWELVE
1982

THE RETURN HIKE TO where they pitched their tent the night before was slow and somber. The boys took turns helping Chris at the beginning but, by the time they reached the cornfield they'd plowed through earlier, the redhead was once again walking, or rather limping, on his own. Though the pace picked up with his independence, conversation remained muted. Each boy trudging slowly onward, feeling drained and exhausted by their lack of sleep the night before.

"Here's the spot we came out of." The precise rows disturbed and surrounding weeds chaotically trampled. "Do we still want to walk all the way around the field?" Rusty was looking at Chris, but the question was meant for the group. "It will save us time if we cut across the cornfield again. Be less walking for Chris, too." Rusty shrugged indifferently.

"Cut across," announced Chris. The other two nodded silently and all four boys stepped back into the cornfield. Instantly vanishing within the tall stalks, the sword-like leaves sharp and biting as before. With Rusty taking the lead once again, they began to retrace their earlier path. As they plodded forward, the wind softly rustled the tops of the corn, blowing first in one direction and then the opposite way. The summer breeze abruptly swirling back and forth like a deep inhale and exhale. The wind through the tops of the corn making oddly soothing sounds.

Five minutes in, Denny spoke up. "Do you guys hear that?" He stopped walking and cocked his head to one side. "Is that voices?"

"I don't hear anything," Rusty paused only briefly before pressing on. He slipped into the next row and the corn closed behind him like a surging green wave in an ocean, pulling him into deeper depths. The three boys behind him stayed motionless, silently questioning each other with their eyes.

"I thought I heard something, too." Chris said as he squatted, pulling up the pant leg on his sore ankle. "But I thought it was just..."

"The wind. Are you freaking out over the wind? What a wussy!" Brian interrupted, rolling his eyes and looking very annoyed. He turned to march after Rusty when the sound came again. This time, all three boys froze. The wind across the leaves swaying them. "Shhhh! That was a voice I'm sure of it." Denny, staring right at him nodded vigorously in agreement, silently mouthing "duh."

Chris, low to the ground, could see more clearly through the rows of single cornstalks. His view uncluttered by the leaves waving high above him. He stopped. Suddenly afraid. He whispered quietly up at his friends, "Wait. I think there is someone in here with us. I can see something moving over there." He rose slowly, pointing in the direction the boys entered the field from. He leaned in close to the other two, lowering his voice even more. "Whoa... it stopped moving as soon as I said that."

"What do you mean, *it*?" All three speaking in hushed whispers.

"It? Him? Mr. Green Jeans? Whatever? I'm just saying there is something out there in the field coming up behind us. Let's split, guys."

"Yeah, let's get out of here!"

"What about Rusty? Where did he go? We can't leave him..." Denny looked from Chris to Brian, then back at Chris again. "He wouldn't leave one of us."

"Yeah, how do you know that, huh? We play with him each summer for a few weeks when he visits his great aunt down here. But that's it. It's not like he's from here. He's just some rich doctor's kid from Chicago.

You think he really gives a piss about us?" Brian hissed the words out. The sound still low, but severe and cutting.

Chris chimed in, "And he stays all summer at Widow Mansion with that weird old lady. Everyone knows that place is haunted. You'll never catch me in that old house. Ritchie Shockey says she killed all her husbands, you know."

"And guess whose mom supposedly just up and disappeared a couple of years ago?" Brian smirked. "Oh yeah, and his big sister. What was her name again? Shelley? Sherry? Whatever... she vanishes in Michigan at their lake house? Lake house! Give me a break. I bet his whole family is a bunch of weirdos." His face had turned red now, hands clenched in a fisted rage.

"Guys..." Denny pleaded with his eyes. "What are you saying, Brian? We are brothers, right? Aren't we a wolf pack? You always say you can't wait for Rusty to come back so we can all hang out over summer break. He is like our best friend."

"Fuck that little piece of shit!" Brian raising his voice for the first time since stopping. "He's not one of us." The concern over the sounds or what Chris had seen somehow forgotten. "Sometimes I just wanna punch him in his face. Spoiled little rich kid... staying in that mansion. Relict Mansion, that's what my dad calls it. Rich Bitch Mansion is what I say." Brian began to pace in a circle, stomping his feet in the dirt of the cornfield with his face pinched in anger. Denny and Chris slowly backed away, each looking cautiously at the other. Neither had ever heard Brian talk or act this way in the past.

"God, I hate that snotty kid. His ass is grass!" Spittle flew from his lips as he spat his words out. "If he was here right now, we would fight. Him and me, right here and now. I just wanna beat him up once and for all. Show you guys what a..."

"You wanna fight me?" Rusty stepped from between the rows of corn. "Fine. Let's go." He put both his fists up. After hearing the harsh words

Brian said about him and his family, he was angry enough. "Come on then, you stupid jock!" The two boys began moving towards each other before Denny stepped between them with his arms stretched out. He started to say something, but never got the chance as Brian grabbed him by his shoulders and flung him down to the ground.

"Stay out of this, you little pussy."

"Leave him alone!" Rusty couldn't believe his eyes. "And empty your pockets. I know you have that pocket knife on you." Rusty was fuming and ready to fight, but not with weapons.

"What? You afraid I'll cut you? Stab you to death? You are so dumb. Stupid little spoiled rich kid." Brian shoved both his hands down inside the front pockets of his jeans. "I hate you!" He pulled the pocket knife out and held it in one hand. In the other, he held the carved beads, each now shimmering blue in the bright sunlight, along with the human teeth they'd found earlier that day.

As if torn between actually opening the blade up and using it or not, Brian smirked at Rusty, who was looking nervously down at the knife before adding, "You ain't worth it, rich kid." He tossed the blade on the ground. Then, holding the shimmering beads and white teeth in his bare hand, a surge of rage seemed to bubble up from within. In a fit, he turned and threw all the small objects into the air like a handful of gravel, grunting with exertion as they flew from his hand. Facing Rusty, he turned his palms out. "Satisfied, you little..."

Rusty closed the gap fast, running at Brian with both fists flying. He connected with a right and a left that sent Brian to the ground in a heap before they heard it. Something crashed through the cornfield to the boy's left, disturbing the perfect order of the rows. Rushing past the four, no more than five or six rows away from them. Whatever it was heading like a freight train across the field. The tops of each row of corn waving wildly enough the stunned boys could watch as it tore across the cornfield.

"Holy shit!" exclaimed Chris. "What was that? Let's get out of here!" He spun and hobbled in the opposite direction of whatever it was tearing across the field. Denny regained his feet and did the same, trailing after the limping redhead.

Rusty looked down at Brian, confusion and shock splayed across his features with blood dripping out of one nostril. He reached down and helped the bloody boy to his feet before pushing him in the direction of the other two. "Move it, man! We'll meet at the other side of the field!"

Brian, unmoving, looked at him dumbly. "What... what just happened?" He rubbed at his eyes as if he'd just woken up. "Why'd you punch me? Were we fighting?"

"Just run!" shouted Rusty back. "We'll split up. You follow them and I'll go the other way. It can't get us all!" When Brian finally seemed to recognize the urgency in Rusty's voice, he started after Chris and Denny.

Rusty turned and ducked his head, swiping at the leaves about his face as he crossed row after row of corn. Finally picking one row and sprinting down it as fast as he could. Glancing backwards every few steps, but seeing nothing, he cut diagonally through more rows. Slipping between green stalks, then hurrying up the next row before crossing over again and doubling back. Still running, Rusty started to cross more rows before realizing he had no idea where he was at in the cornfield. Or more importantly, where whatever they were running from was at. He stopped and shrank into one row of towering cornstalks, flattening himself tightly against them. The corn taking him in and hiding him. He hoped.

Rusty was gasping. His breath roaring in his chest while he pressed a hand painfully against the growing stitch in his side. He had to stop running, figure out where he was and where his friends were. He strained his ears for any sound and looked wildly from side to side for any movement. Long minutes crept slowly past.

Nothing.

He was deep inside the field where the corn held the worst of the sun's heat. Humidity and corn sweat radiating out on all sides of him. He was plastered with perspiration and felt like puking. The wind had completely stopped. Thin strands of cornsilk were wrapped between each of his fingers, and he picked at them absently while he waited and watched for any movement or sound.

Nothing.

He saw no birds overhead. A suffocating and an oppressive silence filled his head with doubt as he silently picked at the silken strands along his hands and arms. Bugs. Where were all those little black bugs? Or even the flies? They ought to be swarming all over him right now, but they weren't. With a slight shiver, Rusty leaned forward out of the row of rustling corn. His trembling knees barely supporting him.

Nothing.

Stepping out from his hiding place, Rusty took tentative steps forward before reminding himself how utterly lost he was in the expanse of the cornfield. He wanted to cry out for his friends, but not as badly as he wanted to stay silent. Looking up, he shaded his eyes from the sun to locate its placement in the sky. The late afternoon sun was setting in the west; the opposite direction he needed to travel back to the tent. Putting the sun at his back, Rusty began to slowly move eastward in the cornfield. Hopping randomly from row to row to maintain his direction, he pressed through the corn. Praying he was not delving deeper into the cornfield; unsure how close he might be to the edge of the field on any one side. Ten steps later, the field emptied into a sort of clearing. Wide swaths of cornstalks lying in a riot and covering the rich dark soil. Except for in one place where the earth had been gouged.

Something.

Rusty stepped tentatively into the open space for a closer look. Warily eyeing the surrounding corn, tensed, and ready to bolt if whatever made the indentation in the ground returned. He took three more steps before stopping once more.

Something.

To his left, down one long row, the cornstalks on either side were disturbed. The stalks on both sides of the row, though still standing, all bent slightly away. A few green leaves were lying on the ground and a couple of not yet ripened ears of corn had been broken off as well. Unlike the deeply scratched earth inside the clearing, the disturbance down the row was subtle, almost unnoticeable if you weren't looking for it. But to Rusty, it looked as if something big had moved down the row. The dry packed earth showed no footprints, but his eyes were drawn to the ground where he saw it.

Something.

He walked over and bent down. Eyes transfixed and focused, when behind him, the cornfield erupted in movement. The long silence broken by Rusty's scream as he turned to face what came for him. Still screaming, his arms raised in defense as he was enveloped in a... hug? Bewildered, Rusty looked down at Denny as Chris and Brian broke through the dense crops and spilled into the clearing in the middle of the cornfield. Chris was grinning at him, "spit and sweat," was all he had to say. Each of them understanding it was their own code words for saying they were inseparable. With Denny still gleefully patting him on the back, Rusty's relief slowly evolved and became bigger. Looking at his three best summertime friends, he felt for the first time like he belonged. Like he was part of...

Something.

When Denny finally released Rusty from his grip, Brian walked sheepishly over. He started to apologize, but Rusty waved him off, "Forget about it."

"But that wasn't me, man. I don't know why I said those things. I don't want to fight you. I just couldn't... I don't know, just couldn't get happy. I've never ever felt like that before. And I don't ever want to again either. I was so mad at you, but I don't know…"

Rusty, fidgeting and uncomfortable, stopped him again. "Don't have a cow, man. Just forget about it, alright?"

"You mean it? You're not sore?" Brian seemed on the verge of tears. His emotions like a rollercoaster veering from one extreme to the other.

"I wouldn't shit you," replied Rusty. Brian wiped at his damp eyes glowing with appreciation. "You're my favorite turd." He smiled and reached out to slowly punch him lightly on his arm.

"Lame joke, dickface."

"The lame ones are the only ones you ever get…" Rusty started to reply before Denny interrupted.

"Uh, guys. You might want to take a look at this." Denny was on his knees next to the upturned soil in the middle of the clearing. "Do you think whatever was chasing us did this?" He pointed as the other three boys crowded around him. "Whatever did this was big. I think it stopped suddenly here before turning around. See how the dirt is piled up on one side? Then over there," Denny pointed to a spot some five yards away. "Doesn't that look the same? I think whatever it was, spun around here."

"Yeah, I was thinking the same thing." Rusty pointed down the row that earlier he thought looked different. "I think it came up and down that row. See the broken ears of corn? And how the cornstalks all kind of lean away?"

Breathlessly, Brian asked what all four boys were thinking. "What around here is wide enough to do this?" He gestured at the flat area of scored raw earth. "Someone on a horse?"

Chris spoke up, "What I saw was big. We all saw how it tore across the field. Nothing I know is that big and fast except a grizzly bear."

"A grizzly bear? There are no grizzly bears in Illinois. Or Iowa either. Don't be such a…"

"Whatever it was, it's gone now. Hear that?" The other three boys stopped talking and listened, each looking questionably at Rusty. "Those are all bugs. Grasshoppers or cicadas, maybe."

"Yeah, so?"

"Earlier, when I was hiding. There were no sounds. No bugs, no birds flying, like that one either." Rusty pointed to a red-winged blackbird gliding gracefully across the blue sky above their heads. "I think whatever it was, has left. Maybe we scared it away?"

"Scared it away?" Brian was starting to look and sound like himself again. "It scared *us* away! Especially Denny, I bet you peed your pants when it charged across the field." But unlike earlier when he taunted Rusty, there was no malice in the teasing. All four boys began giggling.

"Me? I was the one helping Chris while you were acting all crazy and..."

"So why did it charge? It wasn't after us or it would have plowed us under." Rusty pointed to the trench-like mark. "It took off right when you tossed away your pocketknife," he nodded at Brian.

"Not the knife. It was the teeth. It was when I chucked away the teeth and, aw shit man, I lost the teeth and those weird beads." Brian dug his hands into his pockets as if what he tossed might have suddenly reappeared in them. "Sorry, guys, I threw them all away."

"Found one!" Denny picked something off the ground at the edge of the clearing in the field and carried it over. "Unless someone else lost a tooth out here, I think this is one of those teeth." He held it up triumphantly between his forefinger and thumb before handing it over to Rusty.

He looked down at it with a puzzled look on his face. "So, if this was here, we must have been over that way when Brian threw everything. We should spread out and try to find the rest of them and those shiny beads." The abbreviated search only lasted a few minutes before the discouraged boys slowly came together once more.

Empty-handed.

"Let's go home. I betcha that thing took them," Chris spoke up first, dramatically limping and clearly wanting to leave. Rusty nodded but stood rooted. His eyes moving across the field and strange clearing, deep in thought.

"Denny, where did you find that tooth at? Go stand there." Once Denny was in place, Rusty walked to where the ground was torn open in the middle of the clearing. "So, if we were over there," he pointed at a place behind them out in the cornfield, "and Brian threw the teeth and beads over this way," gesturing at where the boys now stood. "Those shiny beads were heavier than the teeth. So, if the teeth only made it that far," he pointed at Denny, "then the beads could have landed about here." He looked down at his feet. "Maybe Chris is right. Maybe it was after those beads."

Denny was nodding along. "And if it is as big as we think, when it turned it would have left some marks like that. Maybe took out this corn laying all over the place, too."

"Then took back off the way it came." Rusty pointed down the disturbed row of corn that had originally caught his eye. The row disappearing in the expanse of corn, but clearly leading back towards the lost graveyard. All four boys in unison said the same thing.

"It came from the cemetery."

MARENGO, IOWA
AUGUST 8TH, 1906

HE RAN HIS UNTRIMMED *nails ever so slowly along the bare wood floor where he lay. The purposely elongated scratching, he knew from past experience, could be both alarming and uncannily eerie. But also, just as easily dismissed as common background noise. It just depended on the listener. In the pitch black, where he lay for the last two hours under the sleeping children's bed above him, he smiled hideously. He could just make out the sharp intake of breath from above him. Good, he thought. At least one of them had heard. He wondered if it was the smaller boy or his slightly older brother. Both siblings shared a single bed in the tiny two-bedroom farmhouse. When no further response came from the mattress above, he exhaled deeply. Deliberately allowing the hollow sound of his escaping breath to echo ever so lightly around him under the bed. Again, the sound, open to the interpretation of the straining eavesdropper.*

There is no denying it when you don't know what lingers under your bed.

A hushed whisper above. It won't be long now... Pooling drool seeped out of the corner of his mouth. But still he waited. Silently toying with the creeping silence he now embraced, allowing it to percolate in the dark night. Above him, the mattress dipped low, whisking the tip of his nose. The homemade wood bed frame creaked. A second, more urgent whisper now. Followed by a groggy reply of assurance. Then nothing more. But still he waited. Savoring the delicious tension he'd created. Imagining the scene above him. The smaller boy, bedcovers pulled up to his little cute chin, eyes wide and sweeping desperately about the room. Possibly finding nothing, but likely staring in the darkness long enough to start seeing what isn't there.

He reached up and tugged once at the corner of a pillow with dirty fingers.

An audible gasp followed by a wild shifting above. He readied himself. The only question being which young boy would be brave enough to lean over and peep under the bed first. His mouth began to open. Wide! The boldest one dared the black under the bed. His soft hair followed by his forehead until finally the whites of his eyes shown. Wide! The cherub face exploded like a ripe tomato as the man came swiftly out from under the children's bed. The second boy, the older one, was barely able to raise his head from the pillow. Scarcely even able to get his eyes open, much less his mouth to scream. Not a sound escaped his tiny lips. Reading his last desperate stare before his skull was punctured, it was clear he'd thought the devil himself was descending upon him.

"Mmmmm…," said the man who rose from under the bed.

CHAPTER THIRTEEN

"Another saying of his is, 'any day on this side of the grass is a good one,' or something like that." Jenny laughed from across the small café table.

"Personally, I like the other one better. I may just have to steal that... what was it again? 'It's a good day as long as your elbows aren't touching pine,' was that it?" Jenny, still smiling, nodded as she crushed out her cigarette and took a drink from her glass of ice tea. "The pine meaning from the inside of a pine box coffin, right? Wow! That must be an old saying. Doubt pine coffins are actually used much to bury folks these days." Despite his earlier misgivings about having lunch with her, Secrist found himself enjoying the company. The historian's granddaughter engaging and gregarious.

"Paps, my grandfather, he's full of really old and quirky sayings like that. Sometimes I think he must be reincarnated or maybe a time traveler. Either that or he has written down every funny saying he ever heard and later on memorizes them." Jenny paused while the waitress dropped off their order. A cup of soup and salad for her while Secrist stared down a massive grilled cheese made of oozing mozzarella. The waitress caught his look of surprise.

"That's the house special, mister. Arlene's Café is famous around these parts for their Texas Toast mozzarella cheese sandwiches. Enjoy!" With that, she turned and headed back towards the swinging doors behind her.

Secrist pulled a French fry off the plate and plopped it in his mouth before asking, "So, who was this Laura Trace again? An older cousin? And what happened to her that was so strange and mysterious?" He picked up the thick grilled cheese and looked for a narrow side to start on before giving up and squeezing one corner into his mouth.

"Well, first off, you have to understand Laura was my absolute favorite. She was a lot older than me, more like an aunt than a cousin, and so funny and beautiful. I used to beg and beg to stay with her as a kid. Spending the night with her was some of the best times I remember from when I was a little. She'd make popcorn for us, and we'd stay up late watching old Vincent Price movies together. I just loved her to death..." Jenny blew on a spoonful of soup before daintily sipping at the steaming liquid.

"So, what happened? Walking over here you said that she just disappeared one day. I have to tell you, as a long-time detective, that's hardly an uncommon occurrence. Even in a small town like this. Now I'm not trying to minimize the loss or the likely tragedy if no sign of her ever turned up after all these years. But I want to be real here."

"Oh, I know all that. But when I got older, well I guess you could say I got bolder." Secrist, having taken another bite of the thick grilled sandwich and dealing with a strand of stringy cheese threatening to stay stuck in his moustache, gestured for her to continue. "I asked for an update on the investigation," she paused before continuing. "This would have been about 20 years after she first went missing. After I was an adult. But all I got was the runaround. It didn't seem to me like much was ever done to find her."

Secrist, defending local law enforcement, said, "I completely understand that it may have looked that way. But after 20 years, you have to understand how hard it is to carve out time to even discuss old cold cases like that. Every minute doing that takes time away from active or current investigations."

"I get that. I really do. I'm not badmouthing anyone. I just want you to understand why I started digging on my own, trying to talk to people and see what might have happened." Tears welled in her eyes as she continued. "I just had to know. Can you understand? Think of your favorite uncle, aunt, or cousin. The one in your family that you had that special connection with. For me, that was Laura." Jenny dabbed at her eyes with a napkin before adding hoarsely, "Oh, I promised myself I wouldn't cry!"

Secrist reached across the table and placed one hand on top of hers. "I do understand, really. I have a good friend who lost his big sister probably at about the same age that you lost your cousin. He's carried that loss and hurt with him his whole life. I know sometimes he still, well... when random things in life don't turn out, he blames himself. Thinking he's cursed or something. Which is crazy, but kind of a normal feeling. Time can heal, but sometimes it won't."

"Thank you. God, look at me blubbering. I'm sorry."

"No need to apologize. Go ahead when you're ready." They both took sips of their drinks before Jenny continued.

"Anyway," she blew out a long breath, "so here's the thing. I am kind of addicted to all those true-life crime shows. I'm sure, as a real detective, you must think they are a joke." Secrist nodded non-committedly as he chewed. "But I tried doing some of what those docudramas show investigators doing. Namely, I started looking into other disappearances from around the area at around the same time."

Secrist was impressed, that was a good start. "Smart girl," he smiled across the table at her. "What did you turn up, Nancy Drew?"

"Well, I started compiling a list of names, dates, locations, all that. You know, just to see if something clicked."

"Did it?"

"I think so, but I can't get any of the police I spoke with to take me seriously. That was part of why, when you said you were writing a book on mysteries along the Mississippi River, I kind of pounced on you. I was thinking, well maybe hoping, if you agreed and put it in your book, we might shine a light on this. Stir up some local interest. Maybe get some answers."

"Answers about what? What did you find?" Secrist could hardly believe what he was hearing. Stander had asked him to look into this Laura Trace, to find out what had happened to her. Clearly, he suspected some type of foul play as well. And here, seated in front of him, was a member of her extended family, also clearly suspecting something odd had happened to her. That was some coincidence, and he didn't believe in coincidences. "What did you discover, Jenny?"

"I know you are going to think I'm nuts. But I think I may have stumbled upon a serial killer." She leaned in despite the next closest customer being four booths away. "Within a 200-hundred-mile radius of Almore, there have been at least 15 disappearances and or murders since Laura vanished."

Secrist exhaled, a little let down, but still curious. Though she may not realize it, there are plenty of places where in a 200-mile radius you could find way more than 15 disappearances and murders spread out over twenty years. Hell, he thought to himself, likely way more than that just up the road in the Quad Cities alone.

"Huh? Well, that is interesting." Secrist kept his poker face, feigning more curiosity than he actually felt. He tried to let her down easy, hoping he wasn't saying some of the same things someone locally in law enforcement hadn't already told her. "But I'm not sure over 20 years that makes a mystery."

"But here is the kicker," Jenny lowered her voice even more. "Every one of the murders was done the same way: the victim was bludgeoned to death with a blunt object like a hammer, axe, or crowbar." Secrist cocked an eyebrow, maybe he had rushed to judgement. "And every single disappearance and murder that fits this pattern happened in late summer." Now Secrist sat up in the slippery plastic booth, thinking to himself OK, there just could be something to this. He at least would share this with Stander. "Plus, there is only one like that each of the years."

"Do you mean to tell me, every single summer around here, one person either is murdered or drops off the face of the earth going back 20 years? That is a mystery worth finding more about."

"Right. It does make you wonder, doesn't it?" Jenny was beaming, likely relieved that someone was taking her seriously. "And again, if you draw a circle around the area and ignore state lines – because these happened in Iowa, Illinois, and Missouri – right dab in the middle is here." Jenny sat back. Both of them letting what she said set in before she added. "I can bring you all the data I collected so you can fact-check it all. I'm not crazy or making this up. Who knows, maybe you'll find more."

Secrist nodded slowly. "And Almore is dead center..."

CHAPTER FOURTEEN

"A confetti farting unicorn?"

"Nope, guess again." Secrist shook his head, chuckling slightly.

"I give up. What am I not going to believe you found?" Stander rose unsteadily with glass in hand. Pulling down a nearly empty wine bottle from the fireplace mantle above him and pouring the remaining contents into his cup before placing the glass container beside its twin at his feet. Also empty. Silently he tipped his glass towards Secrist; the gesture an offer of sharing that Secrist declined. Rebuffed, he returned to his chair and sat down hard once more in it. The same wood chair he'd dragged over to the fireplace earlier that day.

"A family member of Laura Trace, her cousin, actually." When Secrist returned from his daytrip down to Almore, he'd found Stander facing the mammoth fireplace with only a glass and the bottles of wine keeping him warm. The fireplace, unlike Stander, wasn't lit. Despite the less-than-ideal condition he'd found his friend and boss in, Secrist recounted his entire visit into town and what he'd learned. Even playing Stander the recording he'd made earlier of the elderly town historian. Stander asked a few questions, but for the most part, just sat listening.

"Do you think there is any validity to Jenny's theory? Does this area have its own Jason or Michael Meyers running around hacking people up?" Stander laughed and let his head fall forward. "I'd believe anything is possible at this point."

"Why? What happened while I was gone that has you partying here alone?"

Stander raised his head and exhaled deeply. "I've always been a party of one, haven't I? Man, I wish Frazier was here... I miss my dog." Secrist ignored the cryptic comment, waiting patiently for Stander to explain. Soon he spoke again, taking his time to explain what Lucas had said and shown him on their video call earlier that day. By the time he was finished, he'd drained his glass. His bushy white moustache-tinged pink along the edges from the red wine.

"And the symbol here, this twisted, teardrop shaped parody of the Tree of Life," Secrist pointed to the clear carving above the fireplace mantle, "is the same? I wonder what the symbol is supposed to stand for." He paused, mulling over the revelations just shared. "There must be some scholar out there somewhere who can tell us. It looks Egyptian, but maybe it's Roman? The quarry was dug by Romans, right?" Stander shook his head doubtfully; Lucas had all but ruled that out already. "Or maybe it is simply a stone mason's mark? You know, like the makers marks they find on super old jewelry and other metal objects to identify the best craftsmen's work."

"Metal!" Stander, clearly having had plenty to drink already, raised both hands with the forefinger and pinky extended on each. Flashing a pair of devil's horns like you'd see by the thousands at any hard rock or heavy metal concert. "You wanted the best, and you got the best..." He was mumbling and soon his voice trailed off.

Secrist ignored him, trying to keep the conversation on track. "So, after I finished lunch, I called a buddy of mine that does some work for the FBI on multi-jurisdictional cases. He owes me more than a few favors, so I picked his brain about what I had heard. He had me send him an email with what Jenny had already researched and documented." At this, Stander raised his head, his eyes slightly more focused and nodding to show he was following along as Secrist continued.

"He has access to databases the Feds use that collates tons of data like that. Solved crimes, unsolved crimes, related evidence, witness statements, geography – you name it. He said they have software programs and computer algorithms that basically pull up and organize anything related to the data entered. Pulling information from tons of different resources. Not just official reports and police work, but even other areas of data sets pulled from old newspapers and things of that nature. The combination of the software and algorithm will then generate, if you know how to work the system like my buddy does, lists of like events or crimes."

"So how long until you get the results back?" Interest piqued; Stander sat up straight in his chair.

"I already have the results," said Secrist, smiling. "My buddy worked the data to eliminate a few false flags. And again, the results are pretty raw and in no way investigated yet."

"Quit stalling, Tommy. What the fuck did you find out?"

"I'll forward you the results so you can review them yourself when you, uh... are feeling a bit better. But the Reader's Digest condensed version is this: Jenny was right. There is a major anomaly happening in this area. It is pretty hard to make much sense out of the disappearances, like what happened to her cousin Laura Trace. Some of those could be related, but..." Secrist shrugged his shoulders, as if to say who knows? "Anyway, compared to other similarly sized and populated areas, there is way more of that than you would expect to see. But the real kicker is the number of murders involving head trauma. Specifically unsolved murders, where the killer used a blunt object to split skulls open." Secrist stopped, surprised at the lack of surprise registering on Stander's face. It was at that moment he realized Stander had never shared why he had such an interest in Laura Trace and her missing person's case. He made a mental note to revisit the topic when Stander was a little less intoxicated. "Anyway, this whole thing is way bigger than what Jenny stumbled upon."

"In what way? What do you mean bigger? Seems like she came to the same conclusion as the fancy ass computer program. Just took her a little longer." He swayed slightly in his chair, smiling up at Secrist.

"Jenny looked back at dates near when her cousin vanished and then traced similar activity from then until now."

"Yeah, so?"

"The algorithm data set had no dates entered. It was looking back as far as anything was ever recorded. Police reports, death certificates, old newspaper accounts, coroner's records, etc. Murders like these, blunt force head trauma in a 200-mile radius of Almore, have been reported regularly since at least the turn of the 20th century. Most unsolved and it's likely any that were solved, back before modern police work evolved and we realized serial killers existed, likely punished innocent citizens."

"How many are we talking?" Stander lowered his head once more and began massaging his temples.

"All together? I haven't added them up. But almost every single year, going all the way back to 1900 or 1901, there were at least one or two. In the early sixties there was a series of pretty gruesome murders up in the Quad Cities, as well. I guess they never caught the killer. But that murderer's M.O. was completely different so we filtered all those deaths out."

"The good ol' Quad Cities. Isn't that where you were born?" Stander looked up at Secrist with bloodshot eyes.

"Yup, Rock Island, Illinois. At least, that's what my birth certificate says. But I really have no idea. As you know, I was adopted and spent my childhood up in Michigan with my dad. Or the guy I considered my dad." Stander looked like he was going to ask another off-topic question so Secrist hurried to add. "Anyway, I'm willing to bet the years where no murder like this was recorded, there are missing persons reported. Like in 1980, when this Laura Trace vanished without a trace."

"Not without a trace…" Stander muttered low enough that his friend only caught the word trace. Thinking Stander was saying something about the woman named Trace who'd gone missing decades earlier, Secrist ignored the comment and continued.

"The question I have is this: Jenny's grandfather, the local historian, said the Norte settlers were wiped out in a flood that happened in 1900, but I am pretty sure he was lying about that. Jenny told me there is a copy of every single newspaper ever printed in this area stored at the Almore Historical Society building. She is going to meet me there tomorrow morning and let me in since the building is closed to the public that day. We are going to see if we can find if that flood really happened or not. If it did, it would have been huge news and certainly would have made the local papers." Stander was nodding, but Secrist couldn't tell if he was agreeing with Secrist's plan or beginning to nod off in a drunken stupor. When he answered moments later, the retired detective was pleasantly surprised Stander had actually absorbed everything he'd been saying despite the shape he was in.

"I bet it goes back farther. Maybe I'll, maybe tomorrow I'll do some research, too. See if there is any way to find out who this Norte was and where he came from." He paused once more with his eyes closed. For a moment, until he next spoke, Secrist thought he may have fallen asleep sitting in the chair he occupied.

"I admit, I'll be interested to know more about this guy who supposedly had such command of his followers. But there is no way the same guy could be doing what has been happening around here now. He'd have to be like 150 years old! But maybe there is some follower of his carrying on the tradition? Remnants of a cult handed down across generations?"

"Religion... what were we saying the other day?" Stander opened his eyes and looked up again. "You either pray how they want you. Or you become their prey... fickle fucking gods..." He shrugged.

Secrist looked down at his watch. "It is way past dinner time. You want to go grab a bite to eat? That little diner, Arlene's Café, has some great home cooking. I ate lunch there today. Jenny said Arlene's Mac & Cheese is a staple in the diet of the residents of Almore. What do you say?"

Stander rose to his feet and shook his head no. "I drank my dinner already this evening." A pause. "Man, Tommy, I'm drunk... Think I'll go have a little nap. See you when you get back." Swaying slightly, he headed out of the room back towards the direction of the bedrooms where they both were sleeping. Just before exiting the room, he called out once more over his shoulder. "Tommy, I might just go to bed instead. I'll see you in the morning, huh?" With that, listing slightly to the left, Stander headed down one of the long hallways of Relict Mansion.

A party of one.

CHAPTER FIFTEEN
1984

IT WOULD BE OVER two years before the boys were able to return to the forgotten graveyard Rusty had first stumbled upon as a ten-year-old. They'd made a pact with each other not to revisit the site until all four of them could go together. But conflicting parents' plans, various family vacations, and bad timing kept the four mostly apart that next summer. Rusty was only able to visit his great Aunt Madeleine's estate for a handful of long weekends that year. She'd taken several lengthy trips abroad and begged off watching Rusty over the summer. Outside of a few hours of play here and there, some barely legible letters and a couple of long-distance phone calls, the four boys were unable to dissect, or hardly even discuss what they'd seen.

Rusty had been crushed.

Even when he and his father were in town for a visit, he'd barely seen the other three. Instead, spending time with Izzy because his friends often weren't around or available. Rusty always meeting her at the same small lake they'd first met at, innocently swimming and talking. Exploring the lake, diving to the bottom together and coming up with different swimming races and new games to play together like their favorite one, Hot Lava. The two of them still jumping over creeks and ruts like they first had as ten-year-olds. Pretending if they lost their balance, they were consumed by lakes of streaming fire. Rusty sometimes found himself looking forward to seeing Izzy just as much as his three long-time friends.

When the "wolf pack" next met, the four boys were all almost fifteen years of age.

Yet despite the time apart, within minutes of all four getting back together, the childhood friends picked up right where they'd left off two summers ago. Horsing around and joking as before, easily falling into their roles and spending nearly every free minute together. By the end of the second day, they'd begun to plan their long-awaited return to the lost cemetery. Three days later, the four adolescents – full of the bravado and bluster that comes with teenage boys' desperate need to prove their manhood – pushed their way past the woods, pastures, and fields of crops. This time setting up their tent at the edge of the timber bordering the long-forgotten graveyard. Using the scorched ground where Rusty first found the melted shoes and burned purse as the site for their campfire. A full view of the weed choked tombstones and two broken stone pillars sprawled out below them. A noticeable gap among the cluster of trees at the far end where the rotted old shack once stood.

"Hey Denny! Help me string this up. Here, take this end." Rusty brought with him two lightweight mesh hammocks and, now that the tent was standing, he was busy tying them between neighboring trees. Denny pulled his end and used one of the knots he'd learned in Boy Scouts to secure it. "Yeah, that looks about right. This way, two people can be out here keeping watch while the other two sleep in the tent. We'll take turns staying up all night." Rusty continued talking, the three others nodding appreciatively at the portable and collapsible hanging beds. When they were done, the heads of both hammocks were tied to the same tree while the bottoms were tied on two separate trees at either end.

"Let's see if they'll hold us. That mesh looks pretty cheap to me." Chris lumbered over and the heavy-set redhead attempted to sit in one before it spun over and dumped him backwards on the ground, eliciting howls of laughter from the other three. As he regained his feet, Chris wiped the dirt and grass off himself sheepishly. "This is lame, man. I think they are defective."

"Nah, you just have to be real careful getting in and out of them. See?" Rusty pulled the two sides apart before cautiously sitting. Holding his arms out, he spread the constrictive white mesh and slowly laid down. Cocooning himself inside before pushing off, swinging back and forth under the shade of the trees the two hammocks and tent were under. "Now this is relaxing." He put his arms over his head contently. Denny carefully climbed in the other, nearly tipping over twice before righting himself.

"I think I'll just sleep all night in here," Denny reached down to push himself like Rusty, but the hammock spun over and he ended up face first on the ground like Chris. Again, the other three boys laughed and Chris reached down to help him to his feet. "How do Gilligan and the Skipper make it seem so easy?" Denny started to sit back down on it again, but this time more cautiously.

"Hey, Brian, bring that boom box over here. Let's hear some tunes now that our camp is all set up." Rusty felt like he was in paradise. A perfect summer day, back with his best friends and about to go on the biggest adventure his fourteen-year-old self could imagine. "What tapes did we bring?"

Brian disappeared inside the tent before climbing back out with a massive black cassette player and radio lined with silver knobs. Two chrome speakers dominated the face of the battery-operated stereo, and Brian set it on the ground between the two hammocks. Denny and Rusty swung back and forth between the trees while Brian and Chris sat on the ground combing through the myriad of cassette tapes the four boys pooled together before leaving on their camping trip. "Let's see. We got *Quiet Riot's Metal Health, Creatures of the Night by Kiss, Survivor, Helix, Y&T, Fastway,* a couple *Scorpions* albums... here is *Blackout*! I love that cover. Or how about *Axe*? Have you ever heard their song, *"Rock and Roll Party in the Street?"*

"Yes! Excellent! I love that fucking song, man! Crank it up!" Rusty began to play air drums after the song's piano intro. He sang along with the lyrics, his head bobbing in time.

Denny pulled out a partially crushed pack of cigarettes and lit one, nearly upending himself once more in the process. "Anyone want one?" The four boys sat together in the late afternoon sunshine mostly talking about sports, music, and video games. Smoking and listening to some of their favorite songs and albums.

"Hey, Rusty," Brian began during a lull in the conversation, a small smile playing across his features, "is it true what they say about your great Aunt Madeleine? Does she really walk around all day without any clothes on? My dad says he even saw her naked as a jaybird when he was hired to run some new wiring in her library. Said she wasn't bad looking for such an old dame."

"Ew! Isn't she almost 100 years old? I bet she is shriveled up like a raisin," Denny crinkled his nose up in disgust.

Brian countered with, "Get this. My dad said she has tattoos all over. And she actually looked a lot younger than what he..."

"Come on, guys!" Rusty groaned from his swinging mesh bed, "I don't want to talk about this."

"Ah Ha! So, she really doesn't wear any clothes at home then." Chris joined the conversation, showing Rusty the rumor was well-traveled within the local town of Almore as he turned to Denny with a, "I told you so."

Before Denny could open his mouth again, Rusty admitted what they all knew. "She doesn't walk around buck naked all the time. Geez! But sometimes she sunbathes on her deck, and, yes, in the buff."

Brian boldly asked what was obviously on the mind of all three of Rusty's best friends. "Have you spied on her before? What does she look like?"

Rusty rolled his eyes and let out a long-exasperated sigh. "All I'm going to say is this, and then I don't want to talk about it anymore." His three friends looked over at him expectantly. "First off, usually she has a swimsuit on. You know the Sports Illustrated swimsuit issue we all rush to buy when it comes out each year? With Christie Brinkley or Cheryl Tiegs on the cover?" The three nodded in unison, all intimately acquainted with the popular issues. "Well, it seems like no matter how old my great aunt gets, she can still hold her own against some of those so-called 'supermodels'." Rusty made quotation marks in the air when he said supermodel.

"Yeah, right... like Sports Illustrated would ever have a swimsuit cover model in her eighties." Denny sat back in his hammock, a look of disappointment on his face.

"Well, if they ever do, it would probably be a lively old gal like my great Aunt Madeleine. She is fearless and a bit of a rebel." Rusty felt some pride, happy he could defend his much maligned relative.

"So," Brian began once more, "since we are on the subject of lively gals. Tell us about your hot little girlfriend Izzy. Did you get in her pants yet?"

Though he had never tried to hide the time he'd spent with Izzy over the last few summers, Rusty still nearly flipped out of his hammock when Brian brought it up. "It's not like that, man. We are just good friends." He felt his face flushing, how could he explain what he felt for Izzy to his buddies? Or how it sometimes seemed like they'd known each other forever. Only he and Brian had ever "went" with other girls before. Neither Denny nor Chris had shown any real interest in the opposite sex yet.

"Ritchie Shockey at school says she isn't real. He says there is no family out this way with a daughter." Chris was looking up at Rusty inquisitively. "He says she must be a ghost."

"A ghost?" Brian laughed, "Well, if she is a ghost, Rusty and I are both haunted by her. I've seen her around town a time or two. I just wish she wasn't homeschooled or whatever. She has bigger boobs than any of the girls at Almore Junior High." He paused before adding, "I guess she has scared me "stiff" a few times." Brian guffawed loudly at his crude joke, but it sounded forced.

"Whatever, man. I bet that Ritchie dude just ends up with his underwear all stuck to him after seeing her. Probably doesn't know how that happens and thinks it is ectoplasm like in Ghostbusters. The only difference is some weird spirit slimed Bill Murray. Out here in the boondocks, you guys only slime yourselves jacking off." Rusty sat up in his hammock, anxious to change the subject. "Did we bring that *Kim Mitchell* album with '*Go for a Soda*' on it? I want to hear that one next."

"No, I didn't bring that one." Brian got up and replaced the cassette tape in his boom box with *Def Leppard's* album *Pyromania*, before pressing Rusty once more. "So, what is the deal then. You say you and Izzy are just friends? How come? Just because she lives here and you live up by Chicago?"

"I don't know. I guess that is part of it. I don't know." Rusty fidgeted, leaning out of the hammock and pulling several long strands of grass out of the ground under him. "I know it sounds strange, but hanging out with her kind of reminds me of being with my sister, Sherry. Girls just see and talk about different things than we do. Sometimes, when Izzy brings up something, it reminds me of how Sherry was. I don't know..."

"Gross! That's almost like dating your own sister. I can't imagine ever wanting to hang around with my sister." Brian stopped before adding, "You saying you two have never even made out? No kissing or anything?"

Rusty slowly raised his head, a big grin now on his face. "A true gentleman never kisses and tells."

"Well, if I see a true gentleman around, I'll remember that. But, right now, all I see is a chickenshit dude holding out on his friends." Brian tossed a thin stick at Rusty's head.

"Well," Rusty began, a smirk slowly replacing his grin. "Let's just say boys aren't the only ones who make ectoplasm in their pants and leave it at that." When he looked up, both Denny and Chris had their mouths open in shock. Brian hid his surprise better, a look of admiration clear in his features.

When the last song on the tape began, "Billy's Got a Gun," Brian stood up and returned to the tent. Coming out this time with his .22 rifle, a present from his dad last Christmas. "I'm bored. Let's go do some shooting. You know, get ready for the hunt."

"Cool, man. Did you bring those throwing stars, too? I want to practice with them before we start looking around." Brian nodded and pulled two out from the plastic package stuck in the back pocket of his jeans, handing them carefully to Chris. "I think I'll carry these and the nunchucks for protection." Chris and Brian walked a few feet away looking for suitable targets to practice on.

Denny asked, "What about you? You want to go shoot Brian's gun?"

"Not really… I am enjoying just lying here. Besides, I got my sling-shot." Rusty pointed at the ground where he'd laid it before climbing inside the hammock. "What about you? Did you bring your new hunting knife?"

"Sure did," Denny turned on his side and pulled a long knife out of the cheap brown leather holder strapped to his belt. The knife was serrated on one side with a thick grey handle. At the top of the handle was a small compass that you could unscrew and separate from the knife. The handle of the knife was hollow and Denny kept several wood matches, Band-Aids, and thread with a needle inside of it in case he ever needed to stitch up a wound. Just like Rambo did in First Blood, his favorite movie. "I'm always ready for anything." Rusty nodded appreciatively; the knife was about the coolest thing he'd ever seen. He still couldn't believe Denny's mom let him have it. The same way he couldn't believe Chris's parents had let him bring along some of their family's fireworks.

It was nice finally being a grown-up...

In the background, the two boys heard the repetitive pop of the .22 rifle going off. Rusty pulled himself carefully out of the hammock and put a new tape in the boom box, turning the volume up even louder. With the drum intro for the song *Metal Health* pounding out, Rusty played air drums along with it and Denny joined in on air guitar. Both boys lying in their hammocks and singing loudly until Brian and Chris returned.

Gaining their feet, Rusty asked, "The sun is starting to go down, you ready? We finally gonna go find out what that thing was?"

Brian seemed offended. "Not just find it. We are on a hunt, man. We are going to be famous! We'll bag it and send the pictures into The National Enquirer." He lifted up the small caliber rifle. "I'd like to see it run from us this time."

"Uh, hello! I think we did the running last time," Denny pushed his glasses up on his face. "I just hope we don't end up in that graveyard."

"Yeah, we should probably dig our own graves before we start." Rusty laughed as the other three turned to him with looks of astonishment. "What? You really think anything dangerous is still out here?"

"Well, if there is, we are ready for it. Right, boys?" Chris pulled the nunchucks out of his back pocket, two pieces of foot long polished wood strung together by a small chrome plated piece of chain, and twirled them in one hand before pretending to lash out at an imaginary target. The end piece snapping back and hitting the top of his arm. "Damn it!"

"You're such a spaz, Chris."

"Aren't you going to grab those fireworks you brought? You really think you want to get close enough to hit it with those?" Brian pointed to the crude weapon shaking his head. Chris retreated to the tent to retrieve his backpack loaded with assorted sized firecrackers, bottle rockets, cherry bombs, and Roman candles. When he reemerged, Brian continued, "Everyone got their flashlights? Good. Let's do a quick weapons check." He couldn't see Rusty rolling his eyes beside him.

"I got my knife," said Denny.

"I got fireworks and the Ninja throwing stars."

"What about the nunchucks?" Brian asked as he motioned to the .22 rifle slung across his back. "I got the gun and plenty of ammo."

"The only wood he's bringing is the woody between his legs..." Rusty snorted from behind. Denny laughed, but both Chris and Brian ignored his joke. "Anyway, one slingshot accounted for, Captain." He did a brief mock salute. "You leading us?"

"He's got the gun, don't he?" Denny commented as all four boys started down the hill. Wading through the tall weeds of the graveyard silently, making their way to where the queer wood shack stood before they'd torn it down two summers ago. All the nervous joking left behind them, along with their tent and supplies. The sun just beginning to dip below the surrounding tree line.

Pieces of the shack were still visible on the ground near the crater the strange building once hid. The old planks deteriorating and slowly being reclaimed by nature, grass growing between the holes and cracks in them. Down inside the trench, the story was much the same. Remnants of the torn down walls and collapsed roof lying in rot. Black mold and several doughy brown mushrooms the only newcomers to the sagging pile of dissolving wood.

One by one, with each teenager helping the other, the four descended into the dirt-walled cavity. The jagged opening, once hidden beneath the shack and behind a crudely crafted makeshift wood door, yawned widely. The planks that had covered it, all soggy and moss covered at the bottom of the cramped entryway where they'd fallen. The stifling stench, so overpowering their last time here, now subdued and tolerable. One by one, the four boys clicked on their flashlights and, with Brian still in the lead, they crowded into the underground chamber.

They found nothing.

No beads. No riot of hollow rocks, skulls, large eggshells, or whatever it was Rusty had glimpsed crowding around the weird statue or being last time. In fact, the effigy itself had disappeared as well. The earthen compartment filled only with four sweaty and pimple faced teenage boys. The tight, winding underground passageway Rusty saw two summers before lay past them. Uncluttered, still intact, and circling away from where they stood. Appearing to lead deeper in the earth, but angling to the left. Hiding its pathway, destination unknown. Each boy was wide-eyed and prepared, their respective weapons ready for anything. Except this.

Nothing.

"What the fuck..." whispered Rusty, more to himself than his three friends wedged in tightly around him. He waved his flashlight, peering intently at every nook and cranny in the cramped entryway.

Nothing.

"This is totally bogus. It was right here, I'm telling you. It doesn't look like anyone has been in here since us. But all the things we saw are gone." His voice trailing off, "I don't see..." Rusty couldn't say it out loud.

Nothing.

Denny, in a hushed tone, asked, "Maybe that was what chased us. Maybe it came back to life when Brian stole the beads."

"I didn't steal. They were just lying here, right here where we're standing now." Brian squatted down, rubbing his hand across the dirt floor, searching for more of the odd shiny beads.

Nothing.

"No, no that couldn't have been what was in the field. It was like the same size as me," countered Rusty.

"And," Chris added, "What I saw in the cornfield that day was huge. I'm sure. And the way it tore through the..." He stopped talking. They all did. They'd heard it. Exactly what it was unclear.

But something.

"Shhhh...," hushed Rusty. A series of sounds came that couldn't be passed off as the wind in the trees. It was not anything either of them had ever heard before, here or anywhere else. It was a mixture of a slow cough and a sharp bark. The boys could feel it as much as hear it. The sound was deep and powerful, suggestive of an expansive chest and wide mouth.

Something to be avoided.

Three sets of eyes now looked back at Rusty, wide, white, and round. Rusty could feel his own pulse pounding in his head. He suddenly felt small and fragile, defenseless against what was to come. Teenage bravado evaporating in an instant. Their fears, it seemed, like whatever was moving outside, had never left.

A sound came again. A puff of air snorted behind them. Outside. Something scraped like stone against rock out in the fading daylight. On the floor of the entryway, a shadow flowed. The silky motion followed by a long and horrible sound spewing from an unseen mouth. Rusty understood now: it had trapped them in the underground cavity. It may be too big to enter, but it had them cornered. But what was "it?"

Something unforgiving...

Denny stood rigid. His eyes locked on the jagged underground opening they'd entered. Though Rusty knew the crude doorway remained empty, he was tempted to look back, wondering what it was that spooked Denny so badly. Next to Denny, Chris had raised his arms out in front of him. But his movements were somehow indecisive, as if he were warding off something unseen before realizing the idea was hopeless, both arms left hanging in the air. His lips trembling like a small child or the boy he still was. Rusty's own breath deafened him, and Brian looked as if he wanted to scream and bolt. Anywhere. His panicked eyes jumping in his head, both pupils blown out. The unseen presence was immense, crowding them in the cramped space.

Something seized Rusty.

Like a drowning man, Denny had suddenly grabbed him, his white-knuckled hands clamped down. The sound from outside had changed. The grunting turning into a yipping that seemed almost like language. Was it communicating? The tips of the hair on the back of his neck whispered back, answering only to Rusty. Who cares? Run!!

In a desperate panic, he jerked himself free of Denny's grasp. Fear overtook him and he pushed past Brian. Bolting straight down the claustrophobic passage that led... well, he had no idea where it led, except away from whatever had made those awful sounds outside. And that was good enough for him. He scrambled along the underground tunnel, yanking his head around just long enough to confirm the other three were following. But the blonde fourteen-year-old also saw the end of a black shape trying to squeeze in after them before vanishing back outside.

Something black, dripping dampness for a mouth. That was the second time he'd seen it.

Rusty felt the dirt passage constricting around him as it veered slightly left. Both the floor and ceiling of the tunnel joined the conspiracy, compacting all four as they ran. Clumps of fallen dirt and rocks littered the floor under their feet, and the sides of the tunnel became more jagged the farther they ran. Long vein-like white roots hung down along the sides and from above. Their lengthy tendrils brushing along pallid faces and dragging through the teenagers' hair. Rusty swept them aside as best he could, his hand coming back wet and slimy. Fifty yards in, the ground began to rise higher, inspiring hope that the tunnel led back to the surface. But soon the ceiling drifted lower with each step as well. The four hunching over as they ran. Like soldiers running in a war-torn trench, heads down and legs pumping, dirt and desperation keeping pace on all sides. Ten more yards and Rusty was forced to drop down on all fours in a lurching scramble forward to keep from banging his head on the dirt ceiling. Another ten yards and he was forced to stop.

The underground trench ended unceremoniously at a wall of wet dirt. The four teenage boys, crammed together underground, reduced to wide eyes peering out from dirt-lined faces. Their flashlights shaking and pointing to the end of the line in disbelief.

Dead end.

BETHEL, MISSOURI
AUGUST 17TH, 1905

THE HOME, SILENT AS the tomb it was about to become, was little more than a shack. It sat not even 200 yards from a set of train tracks that ran alongside several other equally dilapidated buildings. He waited long minutes beside the window he'd entered the home from. Patiently taking in the meager possessions of the tenant and verifying the dog he'd slit the throat of outside didn't have an indoor companion. Glancing around the room silently, he located a single kerosene lamp sitting unlit on a crooked wood table. Taking tentative steps across the room until he'd reached it.

The axe that was in his hand, found outside by the wood pile, he left propped under the window.

Gently shaking the metal and glass lantern confirmed it still held fuel. He pulled a match from his front shirt pocket and dragged it across the table. It flared and he swiftly lit the lamp before hurriedly blowing the match out and turning the wick down. Only a small halo of dull light shone through the soot-stained glass chimney. Purposefully and unhurried, the next train wasn't due until near morning, he closed each open window despite the stifling, muggy condition of the sultry summer night. Pulling flimsy torn drapes across each of the home's dirty windows so the dim light of the fuel burning lamp wouldn't draw any suspicion. Doubtful as it was at 2:00 AM. When he was done with each window, and with a practiced hand, he glided to first the front door and then the backdoor. Securing each and placing a wood chair pulled from the table under each doorknob. As always.

"You can never be too careful," the man whispered under his breath, smiling.

Next, he moved methodically towards the single bedroom door. The door's handle was missing and it sat slightly ajar, as if expecting his visit. He pushed it open gingerly. On the floor lay a single dingy yellowed mattress, and in the air of the small room hung an oppressive smell that made him wince. Urine, sweat, and the obvious musky smell of a woman's sex mixed together in the foul air. An empty whiskey bottle lay on its side on the floor. He stepped towards the sleeping woman huddled on the filthy cushion, a corpse simply waiting to happen. Drool filled his mouth. When he began to open it, thick saliva dripped down his chin.

Unexpectedly, the woman rolled over. With eyes closed, she mumbled, "Thought you wasn't coming back, Henry." She pulled aside the threadbare sheet that covered her, exposing fleshy pale thighs and a matted bird's nest of black hair between them. Menstrual blood, clotting and thick, seeped between her legs as she spread them. "Hurry now," she sighed heavily, "I want you inside me again." Her eyes barely slits, she reached up and began to rub her heavy breasts. "Mmmm, come to me, honey..."

Granting her last wish, a man not named Henry descended and entered her. Opening her skull greedily. "Mmmm..."

CHAPTER SIXTEEN

The text, sent just before 6:00 AM, read, *Aren't you sorry you didn't drink with me? In a few hours I'll feel WAY better than now. While you'll feel just as shitty as you do right now. ALL DAY long.* The text from Stander ended with a sad yellow emoji puking green slime.

Still sitting at the side of his bed after waking, Secrist saw he'd received a follow up text right before 7:00. *Going out hiking. See you when you get back.* Secrist frowned. Before heading out this morning he'd hoped to talk more with Stander. Get some specifics about Stander's interest in the missing person from 1980, Laura Trace. Plus, an explanation about what actually happened to Stander when he visited this place as a kid. But for now, he guessed, that would have to wait. Secrist was meeting Jenny this morning at 9:00 back in Almore. He thought to himself, except for the supposed flood, what am I supposed to be looking for? Thinking a little clarity before spending all morning digging through all of those old newspapers and town records sure would be nice. He sighed wearily and rubbed the sleep from his eyes before rising from the bed.

When Secrist arrived at the Almore Historical Society building, the front door was unlocked. Walking inside, he'd found Jenny smoking a cigarette and sipping from a giant mug of steaming coffee, waiting for him to arrive. After a few pleasantries, they'd headed upstairs where the town's long history was archived. The building's entire second floor was lined with shelf after shelf of thick dusty books, old crates, and legal boxes dated crudely by hand. In the middle of the room stood a badly scarred, long, narrow wood table along with several equally battered chairs. A couple of deteriorating boxes and water-logged binders laid out on top.

"I couldn't sleep much last night so I got up early. I hope you don't mind," Jenny continued shyly, "but I already pulled out a few things I thought we could start with." Secrist nodded his head appreciatively. Without her help, he knew, this would have been like hunting for a needle in a haystack.

"Mind? Are you kidding?" Secrist smiled and clapped his hands together once, rubbing them expectantly. "What do you want to show me, Nancy Drew?"

Jenny blushed. "Well, I know you are focused on finding out any details related to the Norte settlement that lived down at the Mississippi. I knew there were still a few early newspapers and random clippings saved in here that go back that far, so I dug them all out. Plus, those boxes over there," she pointed at a small pile stacked at the end of one shelving unit, "are from when the train bridge collapsed. You know, when the teen was killed and Paps had told me their fractured skull reminded him of the Norte settlements' dead?"

"Oh yeah, right..." Secrist said distractedly. He wanted to primarily focus on the history of the settlement and the disappearances, not some dipshit pyromaniac teens from the past.

"While you start looking through all that, I'll pull the boxes from the summer of 1900 and see what I can find about Pap's supposed flood. The one he said washed away the Norte settlement and followers."

"Sounds like a plan." Secrist pulled up a chair and took a seat at the table. Slapping a legal pad and pen down beside him, he began flipping through the brittle and yellowing pages Jenny had laid out. Still unsure exactly what he was looking for, but feeling certain he'd know when he saw it.

A little over two hours later, he'd decided he was wrong. Scant details were revealed in the old articles and newspapers. He sat back in the hard wood chair and rubbed his temples before stretching out his legs in front of him and yawning.

"Hope you are having more luck than I am," said Jenny from across the room. She was sitting cross-legged on the floor beside the racks. "Every time I find an article about flooding, I get excited. But outside the reports of a few drownings, damaged homes, and lost livestock, there doesn't seem to be any mention of an event where a large number of lives were lost. I'm beginning to think I was right. Paps was lying." She looked across the room at Secrist. "But why?"

"Maybe someone told him the story and he's just repeating it. But I kind of doubt it. Last night, I was wondering if maybe locals ran them off. Or worse yet, orchestrated the settlements' demise. That might make townspeople hesitant to discuss the event. Even a hundred years later."

"Run them off? But why? For what purpose?"

Secrist turned his palms up and shrugged, the universal gesture of uncertainty. "Hard to deny racism was a major factor in how communities developed back at the turn of the century. History is filled with acts we don't want to admit or face. I suppose a clue might be how your granddad described Norte. Said he wasn't from around here, had an accent and all that."

"Yeah. So?"

"Well," Secrist looked down at the few notes he'd taken, "I did find a couple of articles that may have indirectly mentioned the settlement. One article I read was focused on the traffic going up and down the Mississippi River. It clearly disparaged the influx of people coming up from the south. I'd say the article had racist overtones, but that would be kind." He smiled grimly.

Jenny rose to her feet, "Doubt that is unique to Almore," she commented as she bent down to replace the lid on the last box she'd been looking through. She lifted it and began putting all the boxes she'd been rummaging through back in their spots on the crowded shelves.

"Agreed. I really only found one article I think we can be certain was referring to Norte and his followers. Part of the newspaper had gotten wet at some point in the past and pages were stuck together. But it said, and I quote," Secrist picked up his legal pad and read from it. "'In this enlightened section of the mighty Mississippi came the man. His boat followed by tramps living under the spell of extreme excitement. Their adulation of the man a slap to the face of every true Christian believer.' Blah, blah, blah…" Secrist skimmed over his notes, clearly looking for a certain passage.

"Ah ha! Here it is. This might give us a clue. 'A rigid examination of the dark-skinned immigrant found he wore clothes only of white. He spoke laconically of share and share alike, his disciples practiced in miscegenation and…'" Secrist stopped when Jenny sat down beside him with a puzzled look on her face. "What?"

"What does 'miscegenation' mean?"

"Yeah, I had to Google that myself," said Secrist, smiling. "Basically, it means the mixing of races. But I don't think it would have been black and white mixing, considering the article was written in the 1870's. So, coupled with what your Grandad said about his Spanish accent, I have to wonder if he had come up from Mexico. Or from Spain, or maybe even South America."

"But Paps said his followers were white. 'God fearing Christians' I think was how he described them, didn't he?"

"Yeah, that was what he said. But again, anything he knows would have been a second-hand account at best." Secrist shrugged. "But reading these articles has got me thinking. Sometimes, in law enforcement, it's easy to get caught up in all the minutia. Sometimes unimportant details can blind you to the obvious unless you take a step back."

Jenny nodded. "Hard to see the trees through the forest kind of thing?"

"Exactly," Secrist smiled, impressed by Jenny's intuitiveness. "So, if we know the Mississippi runs into the Gulf of Mexico, down in Louisiana, maybe this Norte settlement originated near there. The Creole people down that way, even back then, were often a hodge-podge of many races. Still are. That could explain how Norte had followers that looked white but spoke uniquely."

"I always thought Creole people were a mixture of French heritage and African heritage? Isn't the Creole language just a bastardized version of French?" When Jenny finished her question, Secrist just sat staring straight ahead at her. "What? What did I say?"

"That is... that would be, that would be quite a coincidence." Secrist blinked, bits of conversations with Stander racing through his mind. The recently inherited trust, clearly with origins in France based on its name. Stander's mom, an immigrant from France. His description of a dark-skinned, sun worshipping great aunt. The quarry in France that Lucas was excavating next to. Secrist didn't believe in coincidences.

"Coincidence? What is quite a coincidence?" Jenny frowned, "Hello?"

"Sorry, I mean yes. I think generally you are right. But it really is a huge melting pot. The people who identify as Creole often have French ancestors. But also from Portuguese, Spain, Haiti, and other island nations. Some of those are Spanish speaking." Secrist stopped again, distracted. "I mean, if we want to rely on your grandad's description of Norte as having a Spanish accent." He looked away again, once more lost in thought.

"Well," Jenny rose, "seems like we have gone about as far as we can go in here." Secrist grunted, nodding, but still staring into space. "And it seems like you may have other things on your mind. I'll just put this stuff back where I found it." She began to collect the aged papers.

"What? Oh yeah, done with these." Secrist stood and helped collect what he'd pulled out when his phone rang. Pulling it from his pocket, he looked down at the call and stepped away from the table. "Sorry, Jenny.

I need to take this. I'll help you put all this back in a minute." But Jenny just waved him off, smiling.

Secrist stood at the opposite end of the room, near the large windows that looked across the quaint downtown of Almore. He asked a few murmuring questions, but mostly listened. Ten minutes later, the call ended and he returned to the now empty tabletop where Jenny stood waiting.

"Sorry about that," he repeated. "But that was a friend of mine that works for the... he still works in law enforcement and is helping me run down information related to your cousin Laura's disappearance." Jenny's face instantly lit up, expectant and hopeful. "He thinks he may have an angle I doubt has been looked at before. Do you think there are any old local railroad maps in here? Not ones from around the time of her disappearance, but going way, way back."

"Oh, I'm sure there is." Jenny put a finger to her pursed lips. "Just give me a little bit to think where those might be at." She turned and looked back at Secrist. "But why? No trains run through Almore anymore. I'm not even sure they still did back in 1980. I barely remember any trains running on the tracks around here when I was a kid. How could that be related to Laura?"

"It may turn out to be nothing. That's partly why I didn't want to say anything earlier about drafting some help. But this friend of mine, well, I sent him over all the data you had compiled. We spent some time talking about everything yesterday afternoon. This morning, he found some other information that matched what you put together."

Jenny's mouth dropped, beaming. "Really? What I put together?" But then the smile vanished from her face and she exclaimed, "Oh my god! Did he find a clue? Is there a serial killer around here?" She looked around her as if the killer might be near.

"Clues are just questions until they become answers. Not sure this question will provide any answers or not, but it's worth a shot." He reached over and patted her on the back smiling. "But regardless, way to go, Nancy Drew!"

Her smile materialized once again. "Oh god, if there's even the slightest chance of finding out what happened to her…" Her eyes misted over briefly before she looked away. "What's this clue? Or question?"

"There may be a pattern. My buddy found a few old midwestern railroad maps just doing internet searches that lined up pretty eerily with a theory he came up with. But the information out there online is incomplete. You see, at one time, railroads crisscrossed the entire nation all the way into the early part of the twentieth century. Nearly every town back then, regardless of size, had tracks and stops that carried freight and passengers before the interstates and trucks made them almost obsolete. Put a lot of rail companies out of business. Railroad maps of rural areas like these were rarely saved once those different companies folded and their tracks were abandoned and later pulled up. So, he's hoping we can find some old local maps that show all the rail lines going in and out of here. If there is a map, and the local track here connected to one of the more major rail lines my friend uncovered, we may be a step closer to finding out what happened to your cousin Laura."

"If we find these tracks, what does that mean?"

Secrist nodded, continuing. "My friend thinks your cousin's disappearance could be related to a killer who rode the rails. One previously unknown. Using modern techniques and applying what we now know about how serial killers work, he thinks he may have even found his pattern, or M.O. if you will. Part of this pattern places multiple disappearances and unsolved murders along train routes."

"But how could that be? A lot of what I found was from long after the trains quit running. At least around here." Jenny shook her head doubtfully.

"Yeah, that is part of what makes me call this a question as much as a clue. See, when my buddy starting tracing this pattern it went all the way back to 1900." Secrist stroked his moustache with two fingers contemplatively.

"OK. But besides the close proximity of disappearances and murders to train tracks, what is this pattern? I mean, if railroads were what tied communities of size together back then, you'd expect more violence. More missing persons and more murders happen in towns of size. There are just more people. So...?"

"The one glaring commonality was how most of the victims died. The pattern, if you will, is that their heads were caved in using a blunt object. Often, back before fingerprinting was used as an identifier, this killer would even leave the murder weapon next to the bodies. The guy seemed to like using an axe."

"Well," Jenny stammered, thinking out loud. "That is also just how Paps described the deaths of the Norte settlement. He said their heads were caved in. That the local teen who died..." Jenny stopped and put both hands to her mouth, "Oh my god. He said the teenager who died had their head caved in just like the Norte followers. And that it happened at the old rail bridge that used to span the Mississippi and connect Illinois to Iowa!"

"That would be some coincidence, huh?" Secrist had already been thinking along those lines. Silently cursing the condition he'd found Stander in last night. Thinking how he really needed to speak with him. Clearly, he knew, or had at least suspected something like this had been going on around here. "Maybe while you look for those maps, I'll go over those newspaper reports from that teen's accident. Maybe, as crazy as it sounds, they are somehow related."

"But how could that be? How could a killer caving heads in back at the turn of the 20th century still be killing people the same way eighty years later?"

Secrist just shook his head. "Doesn't make sense, does it? But before we jump to conclusions, let's do some more research here, huh Nancy

Drew?" As Jenny turned to retrieve the documents, Secrist thought of Stander's comment the other day about what Lucas was discovering down the hole at the bottom of the quarry over in France.

Curiouser and curiouser...

CHAPTER SEVENTEEN

"JUST LET ME DIE..."

Everything swirled hazily around him. The bright light streaming from above was practically blinding. He wasn't sure where he was or how'd he gotten there. Like in many dreams, time itself seemed elusive and untrackable. Racing forwards and backwards in his mind, images and thoughts crowding his brain with confusion. Everything moved in slow motion. This had to be a dream. Or a nightmare.

Begging, he pleaded with the porcelain god he embraced for release. His head bowed reverently once again and eyes closed, he made his final offering shamelessly. But nothing came. Stander dry heaved into the toilet one final time before shakily gaining his feet. Feeling slightly better – at least the cool touch of the toilet bowl on his forehead stopped his sweating – he looked down disgustedly at the white tiled bathroom floor around him. Thankful Secrist hadn't entered the bathroom earlier and found him passed out. If he had, with the cascade of red wine he'd puked all over the white toilet and white floor, he'd likely have called 911. The bathroom, splattered red, resembled a bloody murder scene. Though a couple of wine bottles were all Stander had killed the night before.

After he'd cleaned up both himself and the bathroom, Stander found it impossible to go back to sleep. Or eat anything. With the early morning sun just beginning to rise, he'd decided a little hike would be the best medicine for his hangover. After texting Secrist letting him know he wouldn't be there when he woke, Stander slowly headed outside. At first only intending to walk along old hiking trails near Relict Mansion until he felt better. Taking paths remembered from his youth that crisscrossed the timber and led to a small body of water near the back of the estate's acreage. The lake, a glorified pond really, one he'd spent countless hours swimming and fishing on as a kid.

But after reaching the lake, he'd continued. Walking farther along more of the wooded lanes he'd traversed so often when visiting his great Aunt Madeline as a kid. Gulping down more water from the container he'd brought along as he went, his measured pace slowly picked up. The water and cool dewy air of the early summer morning slowly reviving him. Chasing the ache from his head and alleviating the regrets his overindulgence the night before had saddled him with.

He'd hiked for nearly an hour before realizing where his steps were taking him. Sighing, he strode along the outer edges of the fields and pastures he came across, avoiding entering any of them. His path was the same trail he'd taken alone as a kid, and several times with the best friends of his childhood. Towards the Mississippi River and the lost graveyard from his youth. As he closed the gap between the present to the past, his phone rang.

"Hey, Lucas," he said. "Hope your morning started off better than mine."

"Ciao! But my morning ended a long time ago. It's my day that I'm about to end now. I hear a bottle of wine calling my name." The archeologist, as usual, was upbeat and positive. While inside, Stander's stomach lurched at the thought of drinking any alcohol right now. "Sorry if your day started out poorly. You want me to call back another time with an update? I don't have a ton of news to share today. Just more of the same really."

"No, please go ahead. This is actually perfect. How far did you get today?" Stander continued hiking as they spoke, closing in on the burial ground of the Norte settlement. "Find anything new?"

"Not really. Slow going again. We found more bits of pottery that will help us zero in on a date. Thank goodness. Ancient pottery is like the plastic of the old world, it just sticks around forever. Anyway, we were able to excavate down a little farther around the face and, like I suspected, what we found is not just a head. The statue continues on down deeper." He paused, waiting for a question. When none came, he added, "I sent more pictures to your email. But there is something I thought you might not want to wait and see. Give me a second and I'll text it to you if your laptop isn't handy."

After receiving the image and reviewing, Stander asked several questions. "I assume that is supposed to be a necklace carved around the neck of the thing. Those little indents supposed to represent jewels or something?"

"Yeah, so that is the question of the day. Clearly you are right, carved right under the chin looks to be a representation of some sort of adornment, possibly a necklace. But, although I doubt you can tell from what you are looking at, there are crude marks around where the stones or jewels would be." Pause. "I think, kind of like the missing pupil out of the face's eye, there used to be something in each of those indentations. But somehow, or likely someone, popped them all out."

"And let me guess, just like the missing pupil, which we think was found in Michigan and is in my possession, the stones are nowhere to be found." Although Lucas couldn't see, Stander shook his head disgustedly.

"Believe it or not, we did actually find one of them. It wasn't still attached like the single black pupil of the eye, but when you compare the circumference and depth of the stone, it is a perfect match for the carved necklace. It was buried in the rock sediment and dirt we dug out. I'm hoping we'll find the rest of them as we continue to excavate deeper." Stander could hear the excitement in Lucas's tone.

"Did you take a picture of it?"

"Of course! It is in the batch I sent over via email. I am also having it tested to find out the composition of the material. No one here has ever seen anything like it. I'll let you know what we find out."

"OK, sounds good. I'll pull all those up when I get back to the house. I'm actually out doing a little hiking right now." Stander moved steadily as he talked. Past all the farmer's fields and now making his way into the woods where just beyond stood the lost gravestones. As he hiked, he filled Lucas in on what Secrist had discovered so far. Norte, the leader of the odd riverside communal settlement, its complete abandonment in 1900, and the town of Almore's alleged ignorance of the event. He also brought up the tenuous connection to more recent disappearances and the unsolved murders that had piled up over the years in the surrounding communities near Almore. When he brought up the pattern their contact at the FBI had proposed, along with the commonality of the victims' blunt force head trauma, Lucas interrupted him.

"What you are describing sounds very ritualistic. And you are on the Mississippi River, right?" Lucas, born and raised in France, had received his Doctorate in Archeology from an American university on the east coast where he'd lived for several years. "I mean, my geography of the US isn't great. But are you close at all to St. Louis?"

"Well, I guess it's relatively close considering the entire length of the Mississippi River. I'd guess St. Louis is maybe a couple hundred miles away." Stander was puzzled by the odd question. "Why?"

"It's just that what you are describing sounds a lot like what archeologists found at Cahokia Mounds. Which is on the Illinois side of the Mississippi River, right across from St. Louis."

"Sure, I've visited there. My dad took me one time when I was a kid." Stander paused, trying to recall what the site actually was, but mostly drawing a blank. "I just remember not being very impressed and bored when I saw it. All I really remember are some grassy hills. But that's an Indian site, right?"

"Native American," Lucas corrected him. "But I think eventually they figured out various ethnic groups claimed it as home over the centuries."

"What makes you think there is a connection to the Norte settlement? I mean, besides the Mississippi River."

"Like I said, what you're saying mirrors some of the conclusions drawn by archeologists who worked at Cahokia Mounds. None of this is my area of expertise or anything I studied in depth, but I know they discovered human sacrifice was practiced by some of the cultures that laid claim to the area. I remember hearing at one point they found some 30 or 40 men and women who had been clubbed to death in a mass grave. Their skulls split open, likely with a blunt object." He paused, "See why I said it sounds ritualistic to me? I'm more used to seeing this kind of thing buried underground. From cultures way back in history, not in such recent times."

"But right here in the Midwest? I always thought human sacrifice in the Americas was mostly an Aztec or a Mayan thing?" Stander had stopped hiking now, engrossed in the conversation.

"Human sacrifice, we now know, has been happening as far back in time as we can dig. And on every continent at one time or another. The Aztecs sacrificing people by cutting out their hearts made all the headlines, but, if you'll pardon my pun, there were way more heads lined up by other cultural offshoots. Just in your part of the world alone there were Incans, Mayans, Aztecs, and Native Americans. They all sacrificed huge amounts of victims to their gods. Often by bashing in their brains. Maybe you have some modern-day whackos emulating these practices?"

"Interesting... today I was planning on trying to trace where this Norte and his followers originated from. Your theory gives me something to focus on." Stander resumed walking once more. He was nearing the plot of land where he'd first, literally, stumbled across the graves of the Norte settlers. "Anything else you can remember about Cahokia?"

"Hmmm... I mean a little, but not much. I know the belief now is that the large earthen mounds at Cahokia, the 'grassy hills' you said bored you as a kid, served religious purposes. The tribal chiefs, who may also have been priests, used them to separate themselves from the common people. Show that they were closer to the sun, which, like many cultures did, they worshipped as the source of life. The chief or ruler called himself 'Brother of the Sun' and worked with other priests to honor the gods and spirits of the unseen world. The religious beliefs of the Mississippian peoples, as well as a lot of Native Americans, was called animism."

"Animism?" Stander had never heard the term before. "You mean the worship of animals?"

Lucas laughed slightly before correcting him. "Good guess! But no, animism is the belief that there is a complex supernatural power woven into every part of the natural world. Most Native American tribes made no distinction between the natural and the supernatural. In their minds, spiritual power was neither singular nor transcendent, but diverse and ubiquitous."

Stander pulled the phone from his ear and looked down at it shaking his head before placing it back against his ear to interrupt. "Whoa, whoa, whoa... you are talking way above my education level here, Lucas. Keep it simple and use words you think I can spell."

"Right. Sorry! Basically, their belief system was that the world's filled with an infinite variety of beings. All of them possessing varying powers. And that every single living thing in what we would call the entire universe is simultaneously spiritual and material. To them, supernatural power is found in every person, animal, plant, cloud, body of water – you name it."

Stander stood rooted as he asked. "What about rocks? Or jewels and stones?" He stopped and neither man said anything for a few seconds. "You know why I am asking, right, Lucas?"

"Oh, I know. Or at least I know what you and Secrist thought you saw, anyway. But sorry. I just can't subscribe to the idea that you watched some lady teleport using that unique black stone you found. Even if it does turn out to be the missing pupil of the statue we discovered buried beside the quarry. The laws of physics don't work that way." None of what Lucas said was new to either of them. They had both debated the plausibility of such a thing several times in the past.

"Whatever. I appreciate your skepticism. I wouldn't fucking believe it either if I hadn't witnessed it with my own eyes. But regardless, did they believe rocks held supernatural powers as well?"

"They, and for that matter plenty of ancient cultures, believed that everything – stones and rocks included – holds supernatural powers." Stander didn't respond right away and after a couple of beats Lucas added, "They also believed the world was flat, you know."

"Fuck off, Lucas." But Stander's voice held no venom, and Lucas was used to his crude vocabulary. "Do you think, excuse me did *they* think, these supernatural powers affected different people, or even separate areas, differently?"

"Hard to say. I mean it isn't a stretch to think that would be the case. Again, none of this is really my area of expertise. But plenty of ancient cultures across the world believed in mystic powers. Most believed some things had a greater concentration of this power than others. Also, that these mystical or supernatural powers affected people differently. Harming some, helping others. That certain people, or even races, were more or less tuned in to it, if you will. Of course, most of that was because they didn't understand diseases, natural disasters, insect bites, and..."

"Yeah, yeah, I know." Stander interrupted him. "Hey, I need to go. Let's continue this conversation later. Something just popped up on my end."

"Uh, well... OK. I'll talk with you later. Ciao."

"Hey and Lucas," Stander didn't wait for his reply. "Thanks for all this. I mean it, you're the best. Keep your team safe over there."

Pocketing his phone, he looked out across where the lost cemetery of the Norte settlement stood.

It had vanished.

Not a single gravestone was visible. The shack, torn down in youthful exuberance, and the underground cavity it had once hid was gone as well. Filled in. Stander stood looking out across a cornfield where the graveyard had remained forgotten for over a hundred years. The leafy cornstalks began to wave unhurriedly in the wind. A rippling movement that spread across the field not unlike when a rock is tossed into still water.

Stander turned on his heel. Still waters run deep…

PROMISE CITY, IOWA
AUGUST 22ND, 1904

The cloudy night threatened rain, and somewhere in the distance the low rumble of thunder menaced the windblown fields on either side of the house. No matter, she'd thought, now that she was here it could rain cats and dogs for all she cared. Afterwards, the cleansing water only made it easier for her. What was that saying of church goers? Washed by the blood of the lamb? She'd be bathing soon enough. She covered her mouth to suppress the laughter.

She crept along the side, her back pressed against the home's siding, ducking under the empty clothesline that stretched between the young couple's home and their outhouse. The outdoor toilet was one of the cleanest she'd ever hidden inside. For that, she was thankful. After jumping from the train just beyond the village city limits, she'd had to hide for much longer than usual. The young man had stayed up late smoking on the tiny back porch. But she bared him no ill will. After the way he had been fucking his young wife earlier, he deserved a little break.

And after all, she thought to herself. As loud as the woman had been screaming "harder" over and over again, she now knew there was no reason to worry about neighbors hearing when it was her time to pound them both. Perhaps she should thank the guy? Surely both he and his wife would be sleeping like the dead soon.

Her hand went to her mouth once more to stifle a laugh. Like the dead? Neither would ever wake again.

Reaching the window she knew opened to the parlor, she paused. Ahead in the distance, back where the train would later take her back, a flash of white lightning erupted. The brief illumination in the black night helped her see the loose corner on the screen. Sticking skinny fingers under it, she easily pried it from the window frame. Once out, she reached down for the hammer at her feet. In another moment, she was inside the quaint house.

The window shades pulled down one by one...

CHAPTER EIGHTEEN
1984

"What do we do now?" Denny put both hands on Rusty again, clinging to him in the dark underground earthen tunnel. His glasses hung crooked on his face, a streak of near black mud across his forehead that blended with the color of his hair. "I... I don't want to be here... what do we do?"

"That thing. What the..." Brian had the barrel of his .22 rifle pointed back down the tunnel. Both he and Chris pointing their flashlights the same way, eerily lighting up the winding underground tunnel. "Should I fire a warning shot or two?"

"No, don't do that. It might ricochet. Don't shoot in here unless you see it coming."

"Coming? It can't get in here, can it?" Denny still clung to Rusty; his face illuminated by the light of the four flashlights each of them carried. Repeating himself more urgently, "What do we do, Rusty?"

"Shut up and let me think." Rusty firmly, but gently, pulled his shirt out of the claws Denny had made his hands into. "Everyone just shut up for a minute. Do you hear anything?" The teenage boys' ragged and gasping breaths echoed eerily around them in the tight quarters. For long minutes, the four sat on their haunches clustered closely together. Brian never took his eyes from the opposite end of the tunnel, but the other three stared at each other in the dim, shadowy light. Each straining to hear any sounds. The only noise was the occasional drip of water above their heads, splashing down on the mud beside them.

"Brian, go down just far enough that you can see the opening. Make sure we are alone in here."

"No way, man! I ain't going back down there!"

"We can't stay in…" Rusty started to say.

"If you are so damn curious, why don't you go, huh?" Unmoving, Brian hissed back at him. "Here, take my gun." He pushed the small caliber rifle at him, now splashed with sticky clay and dirt. Rusty reached for it, but Chris quickly took the gun from Brian.

"I'll go," he said flatly. "But just far enough to see if the opening is clear so we can get out of here."

"I don't want you to go. I think we should stay here. Wait for help." Denny's eyes were red rimmed and his nose was dripping and damp. He still sat impossibly close to Rusty.

"No one knows we are here. There's no help coming," Chris stated this very matter-of-fact, like an adult. With that, he started back down the tunnel. The hefty boy, with the backpack of fireworks still slung across his back, barely squeezing past Brian on his hands and knees before suddenly crying out in pained surprise. "Ouch!" Lifting his knee slightly, he reached at a spot underneath it, using his fingers to dig out the hard object his knee had painfully landed on. Pulling it from the earth, he turned it over in his hand twice while playing his flashlight off it. Though maybe twice as big as the others – golf ball size versus marble size – it was clearly another strangely gleaming rock or bead. The same as what Brian had found the first time they'd discovered the hidden passage.

Like the three others they'd later lost, it was smooth as glass with a glittery, blueish hue at its center. The outside layer shaded in reds and browns under the beam of Chris's flashlight in the shadowy lighting of the tunnel. Chris tossed it over his shoulder where it landed in front of Rusty. The boy picked it up and shoved it down the front of his dirty jeans with barely a second glance, way more concerned right now with what was outside the cramped tunnel. Chris started forward once more, rising enough to get his legs under him as the tunnel expanded. His flashlight illuminated the cramped passageway ahead of him; the barrel of the gun pointed the same way. "I bet it was a big dog. Or maybe a bear," Chris mumbled mostly to himself as he moved farther away.

It was Brian that pointed to the scurrying first, though they all saw it at the same time. Farther down, maybe twenty feet from Chris and closer to the entrance, a thing dark and hideous crawled along the ceiling. Lanky, a slick blackness slipping in and out of the swinging beam of the encroaching redhead's light. Suspended, it seemed to jump in the darkness with each sway of the flashlight. Moving quickly on all fours down the passageway. Small but brawny, nearly the same size as the boys. Silent and scuttling upside down along the top of the tunnel like a cockroach. Each leg and arm gripping the dirt ceiling with an incalculable amount of digits.

The four shrieked in unison.

Chris tried to turn in the confining tunnel, but the wood handle of the rifle got caught on the shoulder strap of his backpack. When he tried dislodging it, the gun went off. A deafening blast that sent the bullet whizzing harmlessly into the dirt above his head. Startled, he dropped the weapon as he rushed back to his three friends. Horror etched on his features, a ringing deafness in his ears, and blind terror in his eyes.

Above him, at the sound of the gun's discharge, the ceiling crawler stopped and rotated its faceless head. Dropping it down and focusing on the bellowing teenagers crammed together at the end of the passage. Two horns, or antennae, Rusty couldn't tell what they were in the poor light, sprouted from the top of its head like limp feelers. Each hanging down like withered stalks in desperate need of water. It had no ears, nose, or eyes that were visible. Piercing mouth parts moved up and down and side to side simultaneously. A pasty fluid dripped and ran out on all sides while something pink swirled deep inside. Like it was licking its lips... When the ends of the hanging stalks swayed their way, Rusty couldn't look anywhere else. Staring, the ends of each fluttered once before opening wide and staring right back at him with steel-blue eyes. A cunning intelligence gleamed in each.

At this, all the sanity in Rusty was chased away.

Still screaming, he stood abruptly. No longer aware of his surroundings, his head banged hard against the low dirt ceiling. He went down in a huff. His body hitting the floor nearly as hard as his head had hit the roof of the tunnel. Barely conscious, he rolled on his back. A dark fog muddling his brain and a swollen bump rapidly enlarging near his hairline. He groped and touched it, rubbing the still forming lump before tittering with laughter. In his mind's eye, an image flashed of the cartoon character Elmer Fudd with a rising goose egg on top of his head, maybe after being hit with a frying pan or having an anvil dropped on him, trying to push it back down. Rusty tried to do the same, but his eyes filled with fresh tears. He squeezed them shut and re-opened them again. His gaze landing once more on the advancing black thing scuttling quickly on all fours along the ceiling. Rusty started laughing out loud at the bizarre image. It made no sense to him. It was something like seeing Bugs Bunny in person.

Above him, where his head hit, Rusty looked back and saw a slim piece of wood hanging down. Soggy, cracked, its slowly crumbling fragments fell down around him. Pieces of finished planking. His unfocused head spinning, and still practically deaf from the gun discharge, he sat up casually. Seeming oblivious to the surrounding chaos, he reached up and tugged at the splintered wood. It came off in his hand, slippery and moist. As it gave way, more dirt and wood followed behind it. A cascade of debris tumbling slowly out of an ever-expanding hole above him. More wet dirt and rotted wood rained down on top of Rusty. Covering his face and mouth with soggy rot. He leaned forward, spitting and wiping at his eyes. Clearing his vision just in time to watch a clothed, but fleshless skeleton, come tumbling down on top of him, joining the wave of rubble slowly burying the fourteen-year-old. When the skull landed in his lap, Rusty, still dazed and confused, turned to look up at Denny. "Hey look! Denny! Look, I'm getting head," before bursting into laughter.

Denny, who watched the entire episode slack jawed, ignored him. He'd spied daylight streaming down from the still widening hole. A single ray lighting the small trickle of water descending from near the surface. He screamed at Brian and Chris, both frozen and watching the advancing ceiling walker, now mere yards away from them.

"Light! Light! Come on!" The small teen boy reached up and found a firm handhold on a piece of dry planking, first standing before beginning to pull himself completely into the overhead cavity. Kicking his legs under him, he pulled himself up, only to find he was inside a musky smelling and soggy wood coffin. Half of it rotted away on both the top and bottom and full of slippery mud; the other half dry and empty, but close to the end of usefulness as well. Its previous occupant having just been unceremoniously jettisoned below.

Pushing his hands past the soft wood of the coffin's lid, he tore at the soggy soil above him. Chasing after the daylight. Pulling out huge clumps of dirt and depositing them inside the near empty coffin. Below him, Brian and Chris yanked the still laughing Rusty to his knees. Both intent on following Denny, they pushed and pulled until they got Rusty through the hole. All three scrambling towards the surface behind Denny, leaving the crawling black shape behind.

As Denny's hand pierced the surface of the ground just feet above them, hope bloomed. The top layer of soil was compact and hard, unlike the wet soil underground. He pulled himself up and out by clutching blindly at the long weeds surrounding the one-time grave, squeezing one shoulder out at a time. Caked in mud, he reached desperately for the tombstone as he pulled his legs and feet out of the hole. Before spinning and reaching back down inside the ground to help a slowly sobering Rusty out of the grave. Right behind him, Brian and Chris sprang out of the burial ground. All four spilling into the deserted cemetery, climbing out dirt covered and desperate. Each of them looking like starving zombies ready to ravage the countryside.

Behind them, deep in the abyss, something raged and stampeded. The ground under the teens' feet trembled as if fearing what was about to be released. The four looked down at the shallow, empty grave with unbelieving eyes. The black hole they'd escaped from a toothless mouth gobbling dirt and widening as each clump fell silently down into the chasm. From inside, a slender, shiny black claw of a hand, full of wiggling digits, reached into the bottom of the wood coffin. Grasping for a hold to pull itself up.

And out.

"Fuck you, you ugly motherfucker!!" Rusty, his senses regained, thundering back at whatever had come for them. "Help me!!" he screamed as he reached for the grey headstone that once named the bones below. Together, the teens toppled the flat marker, slamming it down across the jagged opening like a stone age toilet lid before they took off running. Not caring which way they ran, only caring that their legs took them away from the black thing in the ground below them. They raced towards the river.

At the water's edge, the four were forced to stop, the natural boundary separating them from the state of Iowa and fencing them in. Bent over, gasping, and hands on their knees, surprisingly only one of them puked. Chris spilled the contents of his stomach loudly. His groans barely covering the messy splash of his puke across the rocky shoreline of the Mississippi River. Next to him, Brian babbled. "My gun, my gun, my gun! Aw hell, man. Guys! My gun is back there! My dad is going to kill me!"

"Kill you?" Denny rasped. "Your dad... is going... to..." He was shaking his head as he tried to calm his breath enough to speak. "Who gives a shit?" He finally managed to spit out before adding, "Lot of good it did us anyway."

"It would have if fumble fuck over here hadn't dropped it." Brian jabbed an accusatory finger in Chris's direction. The redhead, still bent over and spitting over and over, answered with only his middle finger.

"Don't be a twat," Rusty, bent over and dizzy, spoke as he rubbed his head. "We all blew our cool in there." He pulled his hand away and it came back bloody. Wiping it on his jeans, he stood straight once more. "We just need to leave..." He gulped down another mouthful of air. "Get out of this place. It's starting to get dark now."

"But how do we get back home? I'm not going back down there!" Denny pointed back the way they had just ran from. "I am never setting foot back inside of this..."

"Oh god! Mommy, no... no!" Chris stood straight up for the first time since arriving at the river's edge. Vomit, clingy and thick, dripped from his chin, but unnoticed by all four. Their eyes focused on where he pointed, even though each understood what he saw without having to look.

They did anyway.

At the edge of the tree line, it lingered unmoving, low to the ground. The stalk-like eyes moved independently of its blank faced head, rotating and taking everything in. Seeming to weigh the risks of coming out of the shadowy forest where it blended in so perfectly among the darkness of the timber. It made no sound. Nor did anything else within earshot. The rushing water of the river at the teens' backs the only noise and, possibly, the only movement. The figure was motionless, thoughtful even, before it began to transform.

Becoming unspeakable.

For Rusty, the motion was a reverse of the first time he had seen it. Instead of slinking down among neglected, overgrown vegetation, as he'd seen as a ten-year-old some four years before, the lanky figure of darkness rose in height. Unabashedly showing itself, the hunt over, no longer feeling the need to stalk its prey. The thing appeared to savor the reveal, moving in a casual, almost sensual manner.

Inviting scrutiny.

The black shape flared out, expanding until it grew both taller and wider than either of the teenage boys. Its head raised, the terrible shape long and ragged. The ends of its eyes, once closed on the ends of limp horns of a sort, were now clear and attentive. Each perched on the top like twin periscopes out of a submarine, taking the shape of an upside-down L. Both blue, bright, and focused. It grew larger still, expanding outward, gaining bulk and menace.

Poised.

Chris was crying, and behind him, Rusty could hear Denny whimpering until Brian's high-pitched squeal cut it off. Rusty reached out and grabbed Brian's arm, spinning him around. "Run!" he screamed as he pushed him up the shoreline away from the black thing at the edge of the woods. He did the same to Chris and Denny, pushing them after Brian before following behind. He cast a hurried backwards glance, only to find the creature's tube-like eyes following his friend's path. Rusty couldn't be sure, but he thought he saw pleasure in the gaze before jerking his own eyes back around.

The four sprinted along the shore line. Unencumbered by the trees and brush of the woods, they dashed across the broken bottles and sun-bleached cans littering their path. Softball sized rocks threatened to turn their ankles and upend them with every desperate stride. Water logged branches, leafless and without bark, lay about like faded fleshless bones baking in the sun. The fast-approaching nightfall cooled the air along the shoreline, but the stretching shade felt like a ticking clock. Rusty tried not to think about what they would do when darkness completely fell.

After minutes of desperate escape, Brian, the fastest runner and still in the lead, began to babble and point. Each boy grunted in approval of the plan, no words needing spoken. Dead ahead of them lay the abandoned tracks of a long defunct train line. Stretching out across the water, a hulking rusted steel bridge loomed unsteadily above the river. It looked as if the last train to use it was likely decades ago. The opposite way, to their right, the tracks stretched out endlessly back across the flat lands of Illinois.

I bet it heads to Chicago, right through Kankakee where I live, thought Rusty. As scared as he was, Rusty thought he could run all the way home. Leave this monster behind. Unable to catch his breath and knowing Brian was too far ahead to hear him anyway, he chanted to himself, "please go right, please go right, please go right." Willing Brian that direction; back home to safety.

One minute later, Brian climbed the slight incline, scrambling up dirt and gravel to reach the elevated tracks. He made a sharp right at the weed choked railway and tore down the middle of the twin rails. Rusty breathed a sigh of relief, feeling triumphant. Only the best of friends could psychically communicate the way he, Brian, and the others did. Since it worked, he felt a surge of hope. He was part of something good here. A wolf pack! Since they were the good guys and good guys always win, he knew they were going to make it now. They just had to get to the train track.

Twenty yards down the line, just as Rusty, Denny, and Chris crested the rocky incline the track lay across, Brian skidded to a stop. His feet sliding out from under him as he tried reversing his direction. The faceless thing, black as night, sprung from the shadows of dense vegetation that lined the side of the tracks. It was huge now, bloated or puffed up and easily twice the size of teens. Fully exposed in the fading light of dusk, its skin appeared smooth, oily, and whale-like. Misshapen bumps, or a barbed ridge lining the middle of its back. The behemoth had cut across the woods unseen, instinctively pursuing the retreating teens at an angle to cut off the most obvious route back to civilization.

Whatever it was, it was smart.

Brian turned and faced the other three. All four boys frozen on the deserted railway, three together and one alone farther down the track, eyes locked on each another. Four best friends, a wolf pack and blood brothers, inseparable for life.

The thing pounced like a great cat, enveloping Brian and easily dragging the flailing teen back to the edge of the tree line before abruptly halting. Seeming with purpose, it staged a dramatic execution. Not unseen in the wooded timber mere feet away, but in clear view of the other three. Daring them to turn away. Knowing they would not. Brian's tortured pleas ending as its mouth latched hungrily onto the top of his head. His skull split and pierced; it rummaged around inside with careless impunity.

Its busy mouth working.

Disturbing, wet sucking sounds filling the space emptied of nature's usual cacophony. Mother Nature hushing her charges as if stunned by what she was witnessing. Nothing seemed to move except the shuddering corpse, now convulsing and twitching under the shadow of what feasted on its brains. The lifeless body now merely a shell. A suit of flesh drained of content. Brian's light extinguished before he'd barely begun to let it shine.

When it was done, the black thing turned and faced the three remaining boys. The tubular eyes trained on them, unflinching. Brian's body still held in its grotesque hands, multitudes of digits massaging his cooling skin as if enjoying the texture. Kneading the flesh. Somehow, the groping seemed more offensive than the meal it had made of Brian's brain. A single baseball-sized hole in his head dripped gore. The only signs of the violent demise. Casually, the bloated black creature cradled

Brian's body, owning it. Then it came for them. Unforgiving in its advance.

CHAPTER NINETEEN

THE THREE 14-YEAR-OLDS TURNED and bolted in the opposite direction. Their feet trampling dry weeds and spewing gravel out from under the rotted railroad timbers. Frantic, they ran towards the rapidly setting sun. Chasing after the dwindling light and sprinting down the abandoned train tracks together until Rusty pulled ahead of the other two. Easily outpacing the lumbering Chris while his long strides slowly increased the distance between himself and Denny with each step.

Reaching the rusted and crumbling steel railroad bridge first, Rusty dared a backwards glance. Denny and Chris had fallen behind him, but they were still ahead of the nightmare chasing them all.

But it was closing the gap...

Rusty pleaded with both to move faster. Urgently waving and calling out to follow him across the tenuous bridge stretching across the Mississippi River. Hoping the black creature wouldn't, or couldn't, follow across the decrepit old railway bridge. Darting along the edges, it didn't take long before the poor state of the rotted boards and corroded steel trestles forced him to stop running. Major portions of the bridge were missing or hanging with little or no support. Small pieces dropped and fell off the bridge around him, splashing into the river water below. Though it may have been his imagination, Rusty thought he could feel the bridge swaying under his hurried feet as well. He stopped once more and twirled, no longer confident in his escape plan.

Back at the beginning of the bridge, Denny continued running, but like Rusty, he soon encountered trouble navigating past the rotted gaps, and his progress became a less than artful dance. A slow one, forcing his body to slow and battling his mind with each step. Just behind him, Chris stopped at the edge of the railroad bridge. The terror of what chased them now battling his fear of heights and danger the long-neglected bridge presented as well. Indecision, often the most crippling horror of all, seduced the redhead. He stood rooted as the black locomotive of a monster behind him chugged down the steel tracks, still clutching Brian's corpse. Chris looked up at Rusty gasping and spent; resignation in his eyes and feet still unmoving. Spellbound, Rusty couldn't pull his eyes from that face. Chris sank to his knees, crying, then laid down on his side on top of the tracks. Pulling his knees in tight against his chest, his lungs heaving, he closed his wet eyes. Spit and sweat mixing together on his face.

"No, no, no, no..." Denny was screaming, but unlike Rusty, he turned back for Chris. Scrambling along the bridge the way he'd started across, racing back for Chris while fumbling for the knife at his side, finally pulling the long blade from its holder. Reaching Chris, he raised the knife high above his head screaming. Rusty, his paralysis broken, stumbled back for Chris as well. Like Denny, pulling the only weapon he had on him out of his back pocket.

His slingshot.

As Denny reached Chris, beating the hideous black mass now mere yards from the prone redhead, he dove forward, plunging the knife down. Burying the end of it in the soft wood of the bridge, nearly scalping the redhead in the process. Then, crawling across his schoolyard friend, he yanked the backpack full of fireworks off him. He tore the zipper open with one hand while dragging the handful of tipped wood matches he'd pulled from the hollow handle of his knife across the closest rotted wood railroad tie. The matches flared, and as they did, Denny tossed them inside the backpack.

Rusty could see small wisps of smoke coming out of the bag's opening at the top. It was going to blow! Denny grabbed Chris and together they rolled twice along the ground before dropping down the side of the railroad tracks. Sliding on their butts, they disappeared below the rail into the thick, untamed brush under the bridge's train tracks at the water's edge. Gone. Both Rusty and the monster stopped and watched the brazen escape, a mere 20 feet separating them.

Callously, the thing tossed Brian's body on the ground. The corpse slid down the side of the railroad embankment in a mock parody of a chase. Following the same path Denny and Chris had just used to reach the ground below at the river's edge. The lifeless body landed in a heap at the lapping water, one leg sticking up grotesquely in the air, the hair on its head wet and shiny.

Rusty, still standing on the bridge, barely noticed. He watched the backpack expectantly while raising one hand to shield his eyes. But the grey smoke coming out of the top waned, then vanished completely. Nothing happened. Rusty, slingshot hanging limply at his side, tore his eyes from Chris's backpack and looked up. The thing from the cemetery was already moving towards him once more, a purposeful finality in each step. Rusty turned and looked across the expanse of rotting bridge stretching across the Mississippi, then down at the muddy water below him. With the creature baring down on him, he makes his decision. As he raises a foot to jump down into the churning river water, he pauses, the Doubting Thomas inside him raises a question. What if it can swim?

The question goes unanswered.

Abruptly, flares, explosions, assorted pops, bangs, and whistles explode in the still quiet of the dusk. Bright flashes of light brilliantly bathe anything nearby in a blinding array of vivid colors. The fireworks inside the backpack ignite all at once. Surprised, Rusty barely rights himself before almost toppling over into the water below him. He looks back to the beginning of the bridge just in time to duck as a cluster of bottle rockets screams past him. Whistling in the air before igniting over the river. Roman candles pour smoke and flame out of the bag, and rapid-fire explosions like gunfire echo down the long steel bridge. What seems like a thousand firecrackers go off in rapid succession.

Rusty stands unmoving, warily eyeing the end of the bridge, hoping to see the stalking black mass running away. Or better yet, going up in flames. He didn't get the pleasure of seeing any of that. The thing was gone. A slight smile lifts the corners of his mouth. If there is one thing any monster movie, TV show, or book agree on, it's that every nightmare beast fears fire. Under his breath, he says, "Just burn. We torched you, so…" He chokes up, smile dropping from his face. Brian is dead. Rusty's head swims and he reaches out to steady himself on the bridge railing.

Brian just died here.

He looks up again as the fireworks, now mostly spent, begin to peter out. A small fire burning where the knapsack first ignited. The wood railroad ties were so weathered they're practically kindling for the burgeoning flames. He watches as the fire quickly spreads across multiple wood railroad ties. Grease and oil, spills that long ago seeped down into the railroad ties, aiding the budding flames along with the dry brown weeds that cluttered the abandoned rail line. Soon the fire catches one of the wood trestles supporting the end of the railroad bridge and begins to meticulously climb. Brightening the early evening and sending billowing black smoke into the sky. Rusty warily eyes the growing blaze. With the blasphemous thing from the graveyard no longer on the tracks or bridge, he picks his way back towards land, giving the growing flames a wide berth. When he reaches the end of the bridge, he hears Denny and Chris below, shouting out to him and waving. Relieved they are safe, he waves back. Hurt smiles on the three faces. Happy to be alive and happy to see each other.

But Brian was dead.

As Denny and Chris climb up the side of the river's steep embankment, Rusty, still above them, watches from the railroad tracks. The fire now burning brightly and eating away the wood of the long bridge. Pieces of flaming material begin to drop down from the bridge and into the river water below. Heavy steel beams shift and groan as the support pieces around them weaken and burn. Rusty jumped down from the tracks, a growing concern for the expanding blaze now eating the dormant railway bridge. He cautiously makes his way down the ridge and into the surrounding weeds, nearly falling several times on the sharp grade. Hiking down to meet his friends, unsure what to do since... since Brian was dead.

A heavy splash from the muddy river as more falling debris hits the water. The ripples glimmering in the glow of the bridge fire. Rusty watches the waves spread out, joining with the currents on the river. Behind Chris and Denny, water laps the shoreline more urgently. Rusty watches the next approaching wave in the growing light, the undulating water turning over on itself. A crash from above him, another portion of the bridge collapsing in on its self, steals his attention. When he looks back down into the river, a larger wave approaches the shoreline. Rusty thinks to himself, *whatever made that sure was big* before the rush of water rose even higher, gaining speed and momentum. The rippling water was not diminishing in size as it approached the shoreline, but rather growing. Moments later, the water cascades outward and, dripping wet, the monster from the graveyard charges out of the river. Crawling on all fours as it had along the ceiling in the underground cavern, it hurried up the shore in pursuit of Denny and Chris. Gleaming in the firelight and snapping its multi-hinged jaw open and shut as fast as a buzzsaw.

"Behind you! RUN!!" Rusty called out, yelling at his exhausted friends, imploring them on. "Move it! Move it! Move it!" But it was no use. Chris could barely pick his feet up, and Denny slipped in the weedy field. Neither of them looked behind them. They didn't have to. Rusty's desperation making it clear what closed on them.

Rusty, too far away to help either of his friends in time, watched helplessly. His heart crawling up his throat even stopped his warnings. When the thing stood moments later, rearing up on two legs, the dripping visage was hard to look at. It simply didn't belong here. Not in this world. Crying now, Rusty nearly threw the slingshot in his hand at the thing from the graveyard, desperate to try anything to keep from watching it eviscerate another of his friends. But eyeing the slingshot, he instead quickly reached into the pocket of his jeans. Pulling out the golf ball-sized bead Chris had dug out of the ground of the tunnel. He expertly loaded the slingshot, burying the oversized bead inside the soft leather pocket before pulling it back by its two long rubber tubes as far as he could. The rubber quivering under the strain.

Taking careful aim at the large black target, he muttered to himself, "Sharp. As. A. Marble." Then he let it fly, firing his one lone and last shot before falling to his knees. His legs no longer able to support him, he fell at the feet of Denny and Chris. What he'd aimed for only steps behind them.

The sound was like the puncturing of a beach ball. The whoosh of air what you imagine in your head when the wind is knocked out of you. He'd hit it. What followed was an eerie, hurt sound, but a tone the teens' ears could hardly register. Neither of them saw what happened next. Rusty lying face first on the ground, a nose and mouthful of long weeds stabbing at him. The other two still racing away from the water's edge, neither daring to believe Rusty could actually turn it back. But they all heard the heavy splash as it returned into the water. Then silence.

It was gone.

LOCAL TEEN BOY MEETS TRAGIC END

ALMORE, IL-A TEENAGER WAS pronounced dead late yesterday evening in rural Almore. Mercy County Sheriff Charles Milner said 14-year-old Brian Naylor suffered fatal injuries after falling from an abandoned rail bridge near the small town of Almore, Illinois. The Sheriff said a group of youths had decided the dormant bridge would make a good launching point for their own private fireworks display. One firework shell entered and became lodged in a bridge mechanism left over from the bridge tenders shack and exploded. The ensuing flames then set the grease on the bridge mechanism on fire. The fire eventually caused the lift span to fail and drop into the Mississippi River. Three other local youths were able to escape the flames by jumping to safety. The fourth was not so lucky. The Sheriff went on to say the exact cause of the tragic accident was still under review pending further investigation.

The accident is expected to block river traffic for several days until the US Army Corps of Engineers can safely remove the collapsed 220-foot vertical lift section. The Almore Bridge was a vertical lift bridge that carried a single railroad track across the Mississippi River between Lewis County, Iowa and Mercy County, Illinois. The now damaged bridge replaced a previous Iowa Central railroad bridge, constructed in 1884 by the Phoenix Bridge Company, that crossed at the same location. A new bridge was built in 1908 on new piers alongside the old bridge. The bridge had consisted of 9 truss sections, plus the 220-foot-long vertical lift section, and a short truss section on the Illinois side. The Iowa Central was bought by the Minneapolis & Saint Louis Railroad on January 1, 1915. The Minneapolis & Saint Louis Railroad was later purchased by the Chicago & Northwestern on November 1, 1958. The C&NW closed this rail line in 1972.

CHAPTER TWENTY

"So anyway," Stander finished hoarsely, "now you know what happened." He pointed at the copy of the newspaper article Secrist had returned with. "I was never questioned about any of what went down. I'm not really sure where the local Sheriff quoted in that article got his information from. My guess is that Denny and Chris must have come up with this story. Or, if they did tell the truth, maybe none of the grownups believed them and the adults in charge just guessed." He took a sip out of his coffee cup as he gazed out the open window. Cicadas buzzed noisily from the trees surrounding Relict Mansion. "Can't say I blame them."

"But how were you never even questioned? You were there, accident or no accident. Monster or no monster, you were a witness to the tragedy." Secrist, having returned that afternoon from his second trip to the Almore Historical Society building in as many days, shook his head ruefully. "What kind of Sheriff doesn't even bother to investigate?"

"I doubt the Sheriff in that newspaper did anything besides take the word of the local policeman." Stander turned from the open window and leaned his back against the wall beside it. Facing the table where he'd been sitting much of the afternoon talking with Secrist after returning from his failed hike to find the now vanished graveyard. "And he was only a small-town, part-time kind of rent-a-cop dude. I remember my buddies said everyone in town made fun of him behind his back. Chris always used to say the guy was as sharp as a marble. Looked like one, too."

"Sharp as a marble? Is that who you picked up that saying from?" said Secrist, smiling. "And as much as I hate disparaging any fellow law enforcement officers, I know what you mean. You get out in the boondocks like this and you find mostly a lot of Barney Fifes, not Andy Griffiths."

"Yeah, this guy was a real piece of work. Shaved his head bald, trying to look like a tough guy. This was back when the only bald guy you ever saw was Telly Savalas on TV."

"Sure, Kojak. 'Who loves you, baby?'" Quipped Secrist, still smiling.

"Exactly. Wore a handlebar moustache, too. Like some circus strong man left over from the 19th century. Strutted around the town like he owned it. You know the type, shaved head, loud talker, all that. Probably just compensating for a dick about the size of this." Stander held up the pinky on his right hand.

"Sure. Guys like that are a dime a dozen. They just don't usually get to wear a tin star." Secrist paused. "But still, how could he not have even spoken with you?"

"Oh," Stander laughed. "Well, like I said, he strutted around town playing the big tough guy. But I know he was scared shitless of my great Aunt Madeleine." He paused, his eyes looking at a spot above Secrist's shoulder, but not really seeing anything. "Everything was such a blur afterwards. That night, I mean. So, I may not be remembering everything exactly how it all happened. But it seems like my great aunt showed up right about the same time as the dipshit cop that night. I never figured out how she managed that. Maybe she saw the nearby smoke and drove over to investigate. Who knows? But the three of us were still huddled together. Around... whew, this is hard." Stander dropped his eyes, now looking right at Secrist. "I haven't really thought about that night for a very long time. Sorry."

Secrist nodded, "Take your time, Russ."

After a minute, he started once more. "We were huddled together. A little semicircle around Brian. His eyes were still open and I remember being too scared to reach down and close them like you always see people doing in the movies. I... I didn't want to touch him. So he went on staring, staring but unseeing. God, I'll never forget that awful blank stare... Denny, he was crying hard and Chris, Chris just wanted us to leave him there." Stander walked back over to the table where Secrist still sat, pulling back the chair and sitting down across from him again. "Not that he wanted to leave Brian, you see. But he was scared. Terrified that thing was going to come back at any moment. I was scared too, but also numb. My arms and legs felt like they were filled with lead. I'm pretty sure I was crying as well. But before we could really discuss anything or decide what to do next, we heard the sirens. It was a firetruck. The bridge was burning pretty good by that time. Thick black smoke was billowing up in the air and someone must have seen it. Called it in."

"I bet. Black smoke like that in the woods would be a huge cause for concern. Especially out in the middle of nowhere like that." Stander nodded, not really hearing him.

"Seems like the firemen, again just local volunteer guys, they covered up Brian's body and must have had us walk back with them to their truck. I remember there was a little gravel side road farmers used to get their equipment back and forth from the nearby fields. But, as soon as we got to the firetruck, my aunt's Bentley pulled up."

Secrist's eyes got wide. "Your great aunt drove a Bentley? Around here? In bumfuck Egypt?"

Stander nodded his head. "Yup, it was her car, but she never drove. Harold, her groundskeeper, he usually drove it when she needed to go somewhere. He was driving that night. I remember that because he was wheezing in the front seat like Darth Vader. I think he had allergies or something or other. I don't really remember. But anyway, they pulled up and made me get inside. I remember at the time being really embarrassed. The couple firemen, the way they looked at her and the car made me cringe. My old great aunt, the weird car, and Harold. Who I already knew was thought of as a bit strange by the people in Almore. So back then, when the firemen saw them pull up, they started pointing and talking amongst themselves. Their faces contorted. I was sure they were making fun of me, of us. Laughing. Only much later did I understand."

"Understand what, Russ?"

"The cop, the Kojak looking one, he pulled up along the dirt lane and parked halfway down in the ditch. The little gravel path we were on wasn't even wide enough for two cars. When he saw my great aunt, he had the same look on his face as the firemen. Pinched and contorted. But neither he nor the firemen were making fun of me, her, or Harold. Or even the car, for that matter."

"No?" Secrist questioned. "Did he say something?"

"Nope. He took a quick look inside the backseat of that big car and saw Madeleine sitting there. She had her window rolled down and spoke to him briefly. Real icy, authoritatively like. Then Kojak, he just waved us off, told Harold to get the car out of there so the other rescue vehicles would be able to make it down the lane and get closer to the blaze." Stander was staring down at his hands now as he spoke.

Secrist shrugged, "Well, I guess that kind of makes some sense. Getting the area clear. But he still should have spoken with you."

"Yeah, you would think, huh? But, as I sit here now, I recognize what the look on his face was. And the look on the firemen's faces. None of them were laughing at us or making fun of us. That was just my own personal little teenage insecurities. They were spooked, scared of us. Plain and simple." Stander looked up and met Secrist's eyes. "Naked fear."

Secrist nodded without really knowing why. But the clues, or the questions waiting to become clues, were starting to line up. "And the little small-town cop, Kojak, he never came back and questioned you later?"

"If he tried, I never knew about it. As soon as we got back here," Stander gestured around the inside of Relict Mansion, "I started to lose it. I was never much for dramatics. But, as you know, I lost my big sister Sherry when I was just a little kid. And got virtually no explanation or closure when it happened. By the time of all this," Stander pointed once more to the photocopied newspaper article on the table, "I knew my mom was never returning from her trip back to France, either. I mean, I didn't know she was lying dead on top of a charnel pit of ancient bones in some fucked up medieval mass grave at the bottom of that god damn quarry. But I knew she was dead." Stander, shaking his head, stood once more. He began pacing as he dragged the deep waters of his childhood memories. Recollections he'd buried as dead until just recently. But now those depths were giving up all their dead...

"And just when I finally began to feel normal again, making friends and hanging out like kids that age are supposed to be doing, all this happened. Some... some demon or... or monster comes out of a graveyard? Are you fucking kidding me? Kills one of the best friends I ever had? Man, I just lost it."

"What does that mean, you lost it?" Secrist had a hard time imagining Stander ever being out of control. Even as a kid.

"I ran, man. I just fucking ran. I threw the biggest fit you can imagine. I was scared to death, Tommy. I mean, what was that thing? I couldn't handle it. I started throwing shit, breaking stuff, screaming at Aunt Madeleine. I told her if she didn't take me home, far away from this fucking place," again Stander gestures around Relict Mansion, "that I would kill myself."

"Jesus, would you have?" Secrist paused, "Bad question. Dumb, sorry. At almost fifteen, who knows what we'd do. So, forget I asked. But what happened next, Russ?"

"That seemed to get her attention. My threat of self-harm or whatever suicide is called these days. She called my dad to come get me. Kankakee was only like a three-hour drive away. After that, I remember she made me something to drink. Tea, I think. She tried talking to me about what had happened. That it was going to be okay, and I was just being tested. I remember her saying how my experiences here would never let me go. I don't know if she meant what had just happened, or in a general way because of my age." Stander sighed audibly. "Anyway, I barely remember anything after that. Next thing I knew, I was back home in Kankakee, where I grew up, in bed. I lost several days, maybe a week even. My dad, he barely spoke of it. What happened, what I saw, Brian…" Stander went back to looking out the window. "What the fuck, Tommy. I'm a fifty some year-old man now. All this was over thirty years ago. Yet it all feels like it happened yesterday." He turned to face Secrist once again. "Feels so raw. Sorry, man."

"What happened to your buddies? The other two survivors. Did they say they saw the same thing as you? How did they explain it?" Secrist wondered how, if he'd been the responding officer, he would have reacted to a story like this. Would he have taken the boys seriously? Written down their account in the official record? Doubtful.

"Madeleine died that next winter. Until this trip now, I barely ever came back here and I never spoke to either of them about it." Stander looked down, clearly embarrassed. "Actually, to be honest, I never spoke or saw either of them ever again. It's like I told you, I ran. Been running from all this shit ever since. Brian, Sherry, my mom, my wife… Hell, what you and I both saw happen to Liz. But hiding up in Michigan playing barkeep for the last ten or so years didn't work. Here I am, poor, pitiful me, huh? Found my mom, found Sherry, and found my dad was keeping a lot of shit from me."

"Found out you're stupid rich too. You know this ain't all bad." Secrist offered.

"Yup," he sighed, "that's what I mean. Poor pitiful me, right?" He paused, "I found Frazier, too. God, I miss my dog. But anyway, I know now what I need to do."

"And what's that?"

"Go find Chris and Denny. Talk with them. See what they remember. Hell, see if they remember me, for that matter." Stander lifted his cup and drained it.

"You need me to start looking them up? See if they are alive and where they live?" Secrist pulled his pen off the top of the legal pad he'd been using for notes.

"Way ahead of you, Tommy. I already know where they are. Right here. I'm going to have a beer with Denny in," Stander pulled out his phone and looked at the time, "about an hour and a half. I couldn't track down Chris, so I'm hoping Denny will know where he is."

"Wow, well okay. What do you want me to do then?" He clipped the unused writing instrument back to the top of the pad of paper.

"More research. After hearing everything you've found out, what your contact at the FBI theorized, and what Lucas mentioned this morning, I have an idea." Stander walked back over to the table and turned his tablet back on. "I want you to start looking at all the North American cultures that practiced human sacrifice. Regardless of country. Look up in Canada, down in Mexico, and maybe even Central America. Come up with some timelines and work it backwards."

"So, what is the catch? What am I looking for?" Secrist took the electronic tablet Stander handed over to him.

"Not sure. But start with the Norte settlement arrival and work it backwards through time. See if there are any similarities or stories out there. I'd like to know where they came from."

"OK, but what about that thing? The black monster, or whatever it was that killed Brian? Wouldn't you rather have me work it from there up to present day? See if you killed that thing or not?"

"We'll get to that. I just want to understand what we are up against first. I also am hoping Denny or Chris may be able to help with that part. Let me talk with them first before we go modern day monster hunting." Stander smiled grimly. "I'm not running anymore. I want that motherfucker's head mounted on my wall above the bar. Right next to my slingshot..."

CHAPTER TWENTY-ONE

"GOING INTO CHRIS' BATHROOM was like walking in a rain forest after a nuclear war. Damp and smelly, with layers and layers of dust and grime caked on everything. Like nuclear fallout. Weird colored mossy things growing in the corners and on the walls. Dead vines twisted and gnarled coming up from the floor. The shower curtain was barely hung and half melted, so I couldn't help but glance down in the tub. It was black rimmed with rancid water pooled down near the bottom. The bathroom window wasn't boarded up, but you still couldn't see out of it. Dead flies everywhere... ugh! Thank god the toilet seat at least was up. Doubt I could have found the strength to touch the lid as slimy as it looked." Denny pushed a few strands of his barely greying black hair away from his face, squinting in distaste as he spoke. "So don't be surprised if Chris doesn't show. Meth rules his life now."

"Wow... I would have never guessed. I mean that Chris would end up like that." It hurt Stander to hear the conditions Chris was now living in. It was tough to reconcile with the hilarious, electronics whiz he'd been as a kid. Stander had always imagined Chris working with computers somewhere. Or maybe designing video games out in Silicon Valley.

Stander looked across the table at his childhood running mate. At one time, the two had been closer than brothers. Spending countless summer days playing, riding bikes, and fishing together. Denny, or Dennis as he now went by, was one of the few people Stander had ever really allowed to get close to him. But now, as two grown adult men with more than 30 years between this conversation and their last one, they both struggled to carry the awkward meeting forward. Now it seemed tough to even get a good read on his old friend. Of course, it didn't help that Denny had left his sunglasses on when they'd entered the bar together. Stander wondered if Denny was embarrassed to be seen with him. "So, then you never really see Chris anymore? I mean, after that last time. He's changed that much with the drugs and all?"

"The Christopher Bond that lives alone in the broken-down mobile home at the far edge of town is a nutcase, Russell. Everyone in town knows it. He abused alcohol and various drugs for years, really since high school. But now lately, Meth has taken over his life. His brain, it's worthless." Dennis seemed about to say more, but instead tipped his beer bottle back.

Stander let his eyes rove over the few scruffy patrons of the roadside bar. Their hushed conversations with the bartender were the only sounds in the dreary tavern. The bartender, a large man of maybe 40 with a long braid down his back, sat solemnly on a single stool. He'd barely risen or spoken when Stander had bought the two beers he and Denny were drinking.

The Almore Y, as the bar was known by, sat at the intersection of state highway 12. If you hung a left just outside of town on Route 12, you continued on among endless fields of corn and beans. But if you hung a right, the single lane road off the highway led you into Almore. The two merging blacktop roads split in a "Y" that became the small bar's namesake. The white painted building looked plain and drab from the outside. The flashing neon beer signs in the two windows providing the only clue as to what the establishment was. Clearly a tavern that catered only to its regulars. Outsiders, it seemed, like Stander, raised more eyebrows inside than any of them ever stuck around raising beers. Nothing about the place made you want to stay. A single TV along the back wall, unwatched, droned on mutely. One dartboard with a crudely written out-of-order sign sat unplugged and silent in the far corner. A wood legged pool table with a badly marred maroon surface stood unused in the middle of the brown paneled room. The only two beers on tap were Budweiser and Miller Light.

"Was he surprised I was back in town? I wasn't sure either one of you would even remember me." Stander leaned back and looked at the front door tentatively, no longer sure this little reunion was such a good idea. "Did Chris say anything? Been a long time, man." He looked back at Denny and forced a smile.

"I didn't talk to him. I just messaged him." Denny shrugged indifferently. "I wouldn't hold my breath expecting him to..."

"Goddamn it! What have I told you about coming in here? Christ! Get out of here or I'll call the cops again on your squirrely ass!" Both Stander and Denny turned in time to see the barkeep rising from the stool where he'd been somberly planted the majority of the time since they'd arrived. "Or worse for you, maybe this time I won't!"

The thinly veiled threat was aimed at the tavern's newest arrival. A redheaded man with thinning hair stood in the doorway. He was missing at least his two front teeth and was shockingly gaunt in appearance. His jeans were dirty and he wore mismatched slippers on his otherwise bare feet. The walking skeleton stopped just inside the entrance and flipped his two middle fingers up in greeting before bowing forward at the waist dramatically. "I'm here on official business meeting two," he raised his head and lifted his arms to the sky with both middle fingers still raised, "fuckers raised from the dead. Modern day Jesuses with a guilty conscious daring to touch this leper. For as unclean as I may be now, once upon a time, my good man, I saved their lives. Was a veritable hero! A man among men, though in fact, and this is oh so very important, I was but merely a boy. A child who..." But despite the speed of his chatter – the redhead spoke very quickly – the newcomer was unable to finish his speech. The bartender met him at the doorway, clearly relishing the violence he intended to hand out.

"Ah, my good man, I think not." From behind his back, the bar's newest patron pulled a gun. Though he didn't point it, the sight of it stopped the barkeep in his tracks. "For as mighty as thee might be, even you don't want what's in this."

The hulking bartender stood a few feet away from the newcomer, scowling and blocking the entryway. "You crazy son of a bitch. Now I am calling the cops. You of all people can't bring a loaded weapon in here. Freaking whacko!"

Across the room, Denny quickly rose to his feet and Stander followed suit. Denny called out, "Chris! Chris!" He waved urgently to get his attention. "What are you doing?" Unmoved, the redheaded man blinked once and reached down with his free hand to scratch a spot near his chest.

"You know this freak?" The bartender never took his eyes off him, throwing the question over his shoulder. "He isn't allowed in here. You want to talk with mush mouth here, you do it outside." Denny, followed close behind by Stander, started to make his way to the entrance.

"Mush mouth? My dear man," Chris shook his head dramatically, "that sounded much like an insult. Clearly it is not I needing my mouth cleaned out, but you." Chris raised the gun now, pointing it directly into the face of the sullen bartender. "Bang, bang, bang," he said as he pulled the trigger. Splashing the shocked features, he emptied the water pistol's contents.

Five seconds of dead silence followed. Denny and Stander stopped walking forward, briefly stunned into paralysis. The only other two customers of the bar – both had ducked beneath the counter when the gun was first pulled – peeked out tentatively. One of them still held his beer and he slowly lifted the cup for a drink. His eyes trained on the bizarre scene unfolding. As the soaked bartender reached up to wipe his wet face, Chris calmly pocketed the plastic water gun.

Stander took advantage of the brief reprieve. Moving quickly to diffuse the situation, he strode forward and moved between Chris and the gradually reddening barkeep. As Chris spoke cheerily, "Hi, Rusty. How have you been? Wow! What a bushy white moustache you have. When did you grow...?" Stander placed a hand on his bony chest and gently pushed the chattering redhead away from the towering inferno of a man clearly about to erupt. With his eyes, he motioned Denny should get Chris outside as he turned to face the now sputtering bartender.

"Sorry about that," he started with. "Bad joke, huh? Squirt gun! Geez," Stander shook his head deferentially, "good thing a little bit of water never hurt anyone." The big man glared straight ahead, a full head taller than Stander, his red face inscrutable beyond his barely restrained rage. But, Stander thought, it was a good sign the man was still keeping himself under control.

Was.

From behind him, Stander heard Chris call out as Denny shoved him back outside. "Water? Nah... I got thirsty walking over here and drank it all. That was my piss in there, not water." The big bartender roared and lunged for the door, catching Stander off guard and unbalanced. The two big men scuffled briefly. Stander, barely able to maintain his footing, reached out to keep the man inside the bar by clutching at his shirt collar. No longer restraining himself, in response, the bartender grabbed a handful of Stander's t-shirt as well, ripping it as he took a swing at his head.

Stander rolled with the sucker punch, and it barely clipped him near his ear. Instinctively, the muscle memory of the former prize fighter kicked in. He ducked under the lumbering man's second punch and drove his own fist deep into the bulky side of the bartender. The shot stunned the big man. Gasping, he tried to wrap Stander up in his thick arms. Stander pivoted just out of his reach, leaving the bartender holding only the torn sleeve off his black concert shirt, and threw a second punch. The blow landed squarely in the middle of the barkeep's face. The bulky man flopped backwards. His nose broken and streaming crimson before he hit the floor.

He didn't move again.

The two regular customers rose in unison. The boldest one, nearly as thin as Chris and wearing skintight jeans and pointy red cowboy boots, advanced quickly on Stander. He tossed his glass of beer at Stander's head, trying to distract him while lashing out with one foot. The kick, aimed for Stander's crotch, was easily blocked. When the skinny man followed up his attack by swinging a wild punch, Stander grabbed his thin forearm with one hand before it landed. Holding the man's arm out straight, Stander turned and drove his free fist down onto the outstretched arm. The audible snap of the attacker's dislocated elbow was followed by the bar patron's howls of anguish. He dropped to the ground at Stander's feet next to the unconscious bartender, grabbing his newly bent arm and wailing.

Stander turned to the third and last man standing in the bleak tavern. Rolling his shoulders back, Stander snorted once. His right fist was slick with blood and he was missing the sleeve off his shirt on the opposite arm. His rippling muscles, covered in bright tattoos, were tense and quivering. Snarling, he challenged the man. "Come on then, motherfucker!"

Without a word, the lone patron meekly returned to his barstool. Sitting down, he reached over the bar and filled his partially empty glass directly from the unmanned tap. He didn't look at Stander. Instead, his gaze meandered over to the local weathermen mouthing silently from the flickering TV on the back wall of the bar. With the short-lived skirmish apparently over, Stander turned and exited the bar. Leaving to a streaming chorus of profanity being spewed out by the man whose arm he'd likely just broken.

"Where is Chris?" Stander blinked in the light of the setting sun, gravel from the tavern's parking lot crunching under his feet. "Is that him running back towards town?"

"Yes," Denny answered. He stood beside a newer model pickup truck and clicked the key fob in his hand to unlock it. He casually opened the door and donned a green John Deere ball cap before turning to face Stander. "I saw what you did in there. I'll have to be sure to remember that." He paused before adding, "You should probably get out of here as well. I'll stay and try to smooth things over."

"Thanks, Denny. Sorry about that, but I was just defending myself and..." Denny waved a hand in the air.

"I wouldn't worry about it. Not sure those guys are going to be eager to involve the police anyway. All three of them are on parole and probably not even supposed to be drinking." Denny shrugged, and, after another beat passed he asked, "Where did you learn to fight like that?"

"Huh? Oh that? I, uh... I used to fight professionally a long, long time ago. But in there," Stander jabbed a thumb at the entrance to the bar, "that was just luck. That big guy could have killed me!"

"Fought professionally? Were you one of those MMA guys? King of the octagon or whatever?"

"No, no, I did tough man tournaments back in the day. Boxed some, too." Stander turned to watch which way Chris was headed; he didn't want to lose him. But his old friend had stopped running and was bent over by the side of the road panting dramatically and clutching at his side.

"Boxed? Really? Fight anyone I might have heard of?"

"I like to tell people I held my own against Mike Tyson." Stander, smiling now, waited a moment for the usual shocked reaction before adding the punch line. "But when I do, I'm lying." Denny, unlike most people, barely reacted to either statement. Not a fight fan, I guess, thought

Stander. *The two of us really are strangers after all this time.* He fumbled for something more to say, something to reconnect the impenetrable bind they once shared. Something they had in common.

"You ever go back. To that old cemetery we found, I mean? See if that thing…"

"No. I never think about that place, and I never went back. Why would I do that? Besides, I heard it all got washed away back in '93 when the Mississippi flooded. Doubt I could even find my way back. Or that anyone could ever find a trace of it after all this time." Denny's voice sounded flat, unemotional. Maybe that was how he'd dealt with Brian's death. His version of running. But before Stander could give it more thought, the sound of puking interrupted his thoughts. Roadside, ahead in the distance, Chris retched violently into the ditch that ran alongside the blacktop road.

"Ugh. I better go see if I can help him." He turned and shook Denny's hand. "We'll try this again soon. We didn't really get to talk much at all. But I'm going to be in town a while longer, and I'd really like to sit down with both you guys."

"Where are you staying? Surely not your aunt's old place?" Somehow, these questions sounded real. The few earlier ones Denny asked had sounded more like bored conversation, just feigning real interest.

"The one and the same. The place has been a little neglected, but it'll do for a few days." Stander turned towards his Jeep, intending to pick Chris up by the side of the road where he shakily stood. "I'll be back in touch soon."

"Russell?" Stander thought his name sounded funny coming out of Denny's mouth. He'd always just been Rusty before, another thing that time had changed between them. "Don't believe most of what Chris might say. No one around here does anymore. Chris is crazy, so you need to be careful around him. He is not the same kid you knew before." None of us are, Stander thought as he watched Denny, or Dennis now, turn and walk back into the bar.

After climbing in, Stander drove the fifty yards or so to where Chris was still bent over by the side of the road. He inched forward with the driver side window down, trying to convince Chris to climb in. After a few minutes of back and forth, much of it nonsensical ramblings by the redhead, Chris reluctantly agreed. By the time they pulled up the long lane that led to Relict Mansion's front door, Chris had fallen asleep. Stander carried him inside and laid him on the couch in front of the massive fireplace in the mansion's sitting room. He kept one eye on him as he prepared a small dinner for them both.

BUSHNELL, ILLINOIS
JULY 31ST, 1903

THE CLAPBOARD TWO-STORY HOUSE stood proudly on top of the small hill rise. Only a few years old now, its white paint gleamed and the wood wraparound porch offered gorgeous views of the picturesque valley below. At the very bottom of the valley ran the long steel tracks and wood railroad ties that connected small Midwestern farming communities like Bushnell to other similar rural villages. On either side of the tracks, green fields of corn and beans spread out as far as the eye could see.

Set aside from the house stood a red barn, one of three outbuildings built by Mr. Billings and his two grown sons. Inside the large barn, the straw strewn about the hayloft stirred. Though it was the dead of night, the witching hour, as some would say, a tall skinny man was just waking. He stretched contently and petted the barn cat who'd sought him out earlier in the night. When he'd first arrived at the Billings farm. The cat purred under his touch, urgently pushing its head against the comforting hand. The feline's mate was a bulky tabby that seemed skittish, keeping a distance. Eyeing the stranger in the barn.

"Here kitty, kitty, kitty." the man cooed softly.

The Billings family, successful farmers going on three generations now, had purposefully constructed their new farmstead several miles away from the town of Bushnell. Their previous home taken over by the oldest son, Walter, who'd married just last year, had been just at the edge of town. The elder Mr. Billings telling his wife Edith at the time he just hadn't been comfortable with many of the decisions of the village. Saying he preferred the company of strangers to their nosy neighbors.

A saying about to come back and haunt him.

The stranger swung his legs over the side of the hayloft. His feet finding the wood rungs of the homemade ladder nailed to the loft. He descended silently. Walking to the opening of the barn, he stood long minutes staring out at the grand, dark house in front of him. Only moving once again after he'd wiped the saliva that began to spill out the corner of his mouth with the back of his hand.

The specter of an unknown stranger would haunt generations of Billings to come...

CHAPTER TWENTY-TWO

"LET'S JUST SAY HE was full of more hot air than the Wizard of Oz at his most bombastic and leave it at that." Secrist plucked the last potato chip off his now empty paper plate before wiping his hands on the paper napkin in front of him. "So, you owe me for putting up with the arrogant professor. But I think you'll agree, what he shared is very intriguing."

Stander nodded, anxious to hear what Secrist learned now that they'd finished eating. "So, how did you hook up with the guy? You just called his office and started talking? I'm surprised he took the call without scheduling ahead for an appointment."

"I found his name online after I spent half the day looking things up myself. He was quoted in a couple of articles and, when I found out he was tenured just an hour away at the University of Iowa, I took a chance. Over the years, I've dealt with enough college faculty to learn that especially in between semesters, like now, charging straight ahead is the best way to get answers. Otherwise, you just get the runaround. Regardless of the university. And lucky for me, this guy was in love with the sound of his own voice."

Secrist stood and pushed himself away from the circular table where both men had taken to eating their meals while staying at Relict Mansion. Clearing off the trash from dinner, he walked to the black garbage bag lying on the floor at the opposite side of the room and deposited it inside. Walking back towards the table, he pointed to the abrasion along the side of Stander's face. "So, did you get that mark on your face the same time you tore your shirt? Fall down during your hike? Or is that a souvenir from your drunken stupor the night before?"

"You mean this?" He rubbed the pinkish mark by his ear. "It's nothing. It was just a little rough getting Chris over there into the house." Stander motioned to the sheet covered couch in the next room to where the bony redheaded man, mouth wide open, snored loudly. "It took some coaxing on my part to pry him out of the bar we met at." He turned his hands up as if to say, what can you do?

"No offense, Russ. But I could barely eat smelling him. I know he is a friend of yours and all, but he looks like a homeless guy. Actually, I'm willing to bet he is a meth head judging by the way his mouth looks. You sure you know what you're doing bringing him here?" Secrist cocked one eyebrow questioningly.

"No, not really. But I couldn't just leave him. Like I said, he was one of my best friends growing up. Maybe I can help him past this rough spot, get him back on his feet again." Secrist nodded, but looked on doubtfully.

"Guess you ruined your shirt there, too. That leaves you with what? Only another 788 black concert t-shirts? Better rush out and get a replacement right away, huh?" The last sentence dripped with sarcasm.

"I'll have you know this shirt is irreplaceable. It was the first time I ever saw Stonesour live. I got this shirt in Wisconsin at a big rock festival they played at a few years back. These guys," he pointed down at the band's image on his chest, "kicked ass. So, this shirt is super meaningful to me. Maybe I'll just cut the other sleeve off, probably still look good. Don't you think?" He rolled up the lone remaining sleeve to show Secrist.

"Sure, shave your moustache, cut your hair, get a new face, and you could be a model, Russ." Secrist rejoined him at the table. "These guys have any hits? Anything I would know?"

"With your piss poor taste in music, I doubt it." Stander paused in thought briefly. "Maybe *Through the Glass*? Goes like 'I'm looking at you through the glass. Don't know how much time has passed. All I know is that it feels like forever when no one ever tells you that forever feels like home sitting all alone inside your head..." Stander looked for any sign of recognition on the retired cop's face but, as usual, when it came to music, their tastes were so divergent that none came. He hummed a few more bars before giving up. Instead, snickering a bit as he added, "Oh well, country music is more your speed, right? Someone like Shania Twain maybe?"

"Heck yeah! She is beautiful and talented." Secrist leaned back in his chair, smiling.

"Can't argue with that. You know, I think Lucas is a big fan of hers as well. Next time we get together you should mention you dig her music. Might give you guys something to bond over since you both hate most of the music I listen to." Stander tried to shrug nonchalantly and hide his smile. "Maybe watch some videos together. I bet Lucas would be 'excited' to do that." Stander did his usual air quotes.

"Okay," Secrist said slowly, picking up on the sly tease, but ignoring the urge to question it. He was about to start relaying what the University of Iowa professor had said when Stander's cell phone went off.

"Speak of the devil. It's Lucas. Here, I'll put it on speaker and we can talk with him together." Both men turned and looked down at Stander's phone as he set it on the tabletop while answering the call. "Hey, Lucas, didn't expect to hear back from you again today. Something happen over there?"

"Ciao, Russ," a pause. "Am I on speaker or do we have a bad connection again?" Lucas's slight French accent came over clearly.

"I think the signal is good. But Tommy is here with me, so I figured we could have a discussion together. Go ahead." Stander reached out and raised the volume on his phone.

"Ciao, Tommy. Hope I am not interrupting anything."

"Nope, we were just talking music." Stander winked at Secrist who had no idea why. He ignored him.

"Ah… well anyway, I thought I'd try you before I turned in for the night. I found out an interesting little tidbit I thought you'd want to hear about right away." Stander nodded and Secrist raised his eyebrows as the French archeologist continued. "You know this morning when I told you we found a piece of the statue that had fallen off. A piece out of the carved necklace?"

"Sure, yeah. You were having it tested. Did you get the results back already?" Stander looked over at Secrist and covered the microphone, "I'll show you the pictures Lucas sent of it later."

"Didn't have to wait for the results. Though to be 100% sure, I'm still having it tested to verify. But the professor of geology I took it to knew exactly what it was as soon as he saw it. He says it's iridium. Can you believe it?"

Both Stander and Secrist exchanged puzzled glances, but it was Secrist who asked. "Sorry, guess I'm stupid. But what is iridium, Lucas?"

"Iridium is a super dense, really rare metal sometimes found in the earth's crust. It is one of the most corrosive resistant metals known to man. It is super valuable." The excitement in Lucas's voice was palpable, even over the phone.

Again, Secrist asked the question on both he and Stander's mind. "What do you mean by super valuable? Is it worth as much as gold?"

"Gold?" Lucas responded with a laugh. "Iridium is usually worth about three times more per ounce than gold. Partly because it is used in many different ways. Spark plugs, high-temperature containers, compass bearings, and in a lot of modern day heavy-duty electrical contacts. But also, because it is about ten times rarer than gold, or even platinum."

Stander spoke up next. "Could that be part of what the quarry was used for? Were the ancient Romans mining this stuff?"

"Extremely unlikely. I think it is just a weird coincidence that we found iridium in the land surrounding the quarry." Stander turned to Secrist and read his mind. He knew the retired cop often stated he didn't believe in coincidences.

"But if it's a natural mineral, it has to be mined, right? And you found it digging beside what was once a functioning mine." Stander shook his head no as Secrist spoke. "Excuse me, a quarry. Mine, quarry, hole in the ground, whatever... but yet you don't think it was being mined? Why?"

"To start with, while it is a sometimes naturally occurring metal, that is not where most of it comes from. Iridium is found in meteorites in a much higher abundance than in the Earth's crust. Iridium is a space rock, guys! Tossed down from the gods above."

Stander, who had seen the jewel-like carved image that once adorned the necklace around the buried statue's neck, spoke next. "So, you think ancient man stumbled upon this weird rock, this piece of iridium, and used it to decorate the massive stone image you are trying to recover?"

"Just stumbled upon it? Maybe, but considering the size of the piece, I would place a wager on your ancient man watching it fall from the sky for them to have used it in such a unique way. The fact it came from the heavens is what would have made it valuable to them. They would have had no way to understand its properties or values. Or know it likely was what wiped out the dinosaurs millions of years ago."

"Wait a minute. You mean the asteroid that hit the earth and killed off the dinosaurs was made of iridium?" Secrist looked doubtful. Stander quietly stood up and retrieved his tablet from the next room where Chris still lie sleeping. He powered it on and began typing as Lucas continued.

"I think iridium was part of the meteorite, yes. The earliest traces we archeologists ever found iridium was in native mined platinum crafted by South American cultures near modern day Columbia. The Chicxulub crater is an impact crater buried underneath the Yucatán Peninsula in Mexico. That is where the meteorite that killed off the dinosaurs landed."

Stander interrupted Lucas, reading from his tablet. "Hey, Lucas, I think you may be right. I did a quick internet search while you were talking. Listen to this. 'The unusually high abundance of iridium in the clay layer at the Cretaceous–Paleogene boundary gave rise to the Alvarez hypothesis that the impact of a massive extraterrestrial object caused the extinction of dinosaurs and many other species 66 million years ago...' Blah, blah, blah... Oh! Down here it says 'Iridium has been used as the base indicator of quantifying the amount of deposition of interstellar matter, such as asteroids and meteoroids, which make their way through the Earth's atmosphere to deposit in the sediments.' Ah, let's see what else does it say here?" He kept reading to himself while scrolling, "Boring, boring, boring..." He muttered before turning to Secrist, "Well fuck me, rocks from the gods!"

Lucas started again, "Exactly. Native platinum used by ancient South American cultures always contained a small amount of iridium. And platinum itself didn't reach Europe until arriving in some of their most ornate and decorative pieces of what we call platina."

"Platina?" Stander interrupted once more, "I think you are going over our heads here again, Lucas."

"Right, well think of silverette or crude silver. Items made of platina were first reported to be found in modern day Columbia in the 17th century by the Spanish conquerors. Around that area, iridium is relatively common in all meteorite pieces that are unearthed."

"So, what about in France, where you found the piece? Is it possible you found a piece of the naturally occurring form of iridium? Instead of a 'rock from the gods', as Stander here put it?"

"We are way outside my area of expertise, guys. I'm really not the best one to answer these questions. I'll speak with the geologist at the university in Caen when he contacts me with the official results of the testing. But, as I understand it, there has never been a large deposit of iridium found in France. Natural or otherwise. I think nearly all of it is found in South America, Australia, and Russia."

"Russia!" Exclaimed Secrist, shaking his head. "Guess the gods rained their stones down over in that part of the world as well. Wonder what ancient man over there thought when they saw meteorites screaming down from the sky. You think they used it to decorate statues, too?"

"More than likely, they created their own legends, beliefs, and folk tales around it. Just like the South American cultures did. Probably inspired more than a few nightmares."

"Of gods and monsters, right?" After Stander replied, all three men fell silent briefly.

"Anyway, like I said," Lucas added right before ending the call, "I just thought you'd want to hear what the geologist's initial opinion was. I'll keep you updated as I learn more. Ciao!"

"Ciao, Lucas." Stander pocketed his phone with a wry smile. "Makes you wonder what he'll unearth next, huh? But anyway, back to this university professor. What all did he have to say? You said it was intriguing. How so?"

"Right. So, I used the same line I've been using around here. Told him I was a retired cop looking to launch my writing career. Said I was looking for an angle on human sacrifice that I could use in a book and asked him if he could shed some light on the subject. Told him what Lucas mentioned to us about indigenous people in the past practicing ritualistic killing here in the Midwest and asked for details. Specifically, if he knew of any similar occurrences to what went on at Cahokia Mounds at other locations in North America and if or how they might be related." Secrist paused and grabbed his glass, swallowing the last of his drink from dinner.

"Nice. Were there?"

"Yes! He talked a lot about Cahokia at first, since that was what he was most familiar with. According to him anyway, that site is actually the largest archaeological ruins ever found north of Mexico's pre-Columbian cities. And it's just outside of St. Louis. Crazy! But he also mentioned some place in Wisconsin called," Secrist flipped over a couple pages on his yellow legal pad and read the name, "Aztalan State Park. He said that name is actually a misnomer because the native folks who built it weren't actually Aztec at all. But I guess, just like at Cahokia Mounds, early archeologists attributed the site to Aztecs because of the similarity to known Aztec mounds. Plus, back then, archeologists didn't believe ancient native North Americans were even capable of building the structures. They now know none of that is true. But despite modern archeology defining the differences between the Aztec culture and what he called," again Secrist flipped through his pages of notes, "the 'Native Mississippian culture', there were a few striking similarities that even now they are still trying to piece together."

"Like what?" Stander sat forward, absorbed by the brief account of early Native American practices.

"Well, the one thing that is really intriguing is that, at least for a brief period of time, both the Mississippian culture at Cahokia and up in Wisconsin carried out ritualistic practices that mimicked the Aztecs. Specifically, human sacrifice." Secrist looked up expectantly at Stander, believing he'd delivered just what he'd been looking for, a link to the Norte cult follower's beliefs.

But Stander wasn't having it. "I mean, that is interesting, but just because this 'Mississippian culture' did human sacrifice at Cahokia and at the site in Wisconsin, that doesn't explain why the Norte cult ended up with their heads bashed in centuries later."

Secrist, referring back again to the pages of notes he'd taken earlier in the day, pressed forward. "By itself, I agree. But here is where things get intriguing. Remember what Lucas said about Cahokia mounds? That they found human remains from ritualistic killing? Well, the professor I talked with added some more color. He said one mound alone had the remains of almost 300 people, most of whom were sacrificed. He said in total, at Cahokia, more remains of sacrificial victims were found there than in any other place on the entire continent north of Mexico. They uncovered one incident alone where almost 40 men and women were executed on the spot, and that these victims," Secrist flipped another page over, "where did I write that down...? Ah, here! He said it was 'likely the victims were lined up and clubbed one by one, splitting their skulls open.'" He looked up at Stander, "Sound familiar?"

Stander perked up, nodding along. "That sure does sound like what supposedly happened with the Norte cult. I've got to give you that."

"Exactly! Now get this. Up in Wisconsin, at the Aztalan State Park site I mentioned earlier, he said 'they uncovered,'" again Secrist read from his notes, "'remains of over 50 people who were sacrificed simultaneously for reasons unclear. Analysis of their teeth indicated they were local and likely not victims of capture, prisoners of war, or otherwise criminally punished.' And guess where this spot was? Right along the Mississippi River!"

"No fucking way, Tommy. Now I see why you said it was intriguing. Counting the Norte cult that would be three mass sacrifices along the Mississippi River. Each one only a few hundred miles apart, all with their heads caved in." Stander sat back in his chair and whistled. "And right here in North America! How do we not know about this?"

"I'll get to that in a second," replied Secrist, "but here is the really crazy part. The mass burial ground at Cahokia was dated at around the years 1000-1050. The one up in Wisconsin was dated some 300 hundred years later, at 1300. The kicker is that in both cases, the sites, which were hugely populated, were then abandoned a short time later for reasons unknown."

"Reasons unknown? The professor guy said that?"

"He said the common belief, and this is what I also found just looking the sites up on the internet, is that the mass exodus of people who made these locations home was due to climate change. Maybe a drought or famine, or maybe flooding. You know, environmental swings that put pressure on their leaders. He said there is some evidence of that, but that he personally has his doubts."

"Why does he think it was something else?" Stander reached over and dumped the last couple of ice cubes from his cup into his mouth, crunching them loudly with his teeth.

"I asked him that, too. The guy was a little vague, but he said the abundance of shell beads, which obviously would have come from far away oceans, would likely have been very rare and precious to the cultures. Yet many of the victims of sacrifice were adorned with clam shells. Meaning the communities must have still been prosperous at the time. He reasoned that if all the sacrifices were in response to an ongoing natural catastrophe, or political upheaval, that items like sea shells would have likely already been traded for food or resources. Instead, they were part of the sacrifice. Which, according to him, normally is a sign of a very prosperous community." Secrist paused, trying to recall the entirety of the conversation before continuing once more. "He did confess that his opinion was in the minority, mumbling something about other archeologists taking the easiest hypothesis instead of really deciphering all the contrasting clues unearthed at both sites. He was kind of complaining that some archaeologists pussyfoot around the question of human sacrifice on the North American continent. But to him it is clear that up in Wisconsin, and at Cahokia, the populations theatrically performed human sacrifice as part of some community-wide religious ceremony."

"So, a couple of guys think one way, but most think the other. Maybe this guy was just venting, you know, sour grapes and all that..." Stander looked over his shoulder at Chris who stirred briefly in his sleep.

"Yeah, could be. But something he said stuck with me, and I think it makes a lot of sense. He said the most compelling argument that it wasn't a natural disaster, or lack of resources, was the simplest."

"Which was what?" Stander questioned him. "What was this simple explanation?"

"He said it is undeniable that both sites were massive cultural centers with huge native populations. Plus, he said, it's obvious from all the varying finds that the people who created the Cahokia mounds and the Aztalan mounds were part of what they now call the Mississippian peoples or culture. You with me so far, Russ?" Stander nodded that he should continue.

"These same Mississippian peoples, he said this was indisputable, were the ancestral communities from which the majority of the American Indian nations and tribes descended from. At least the ones later living in the same regions here in the Midwest anyway... Yet in the end, neither site appears in any North American tribe's folklore. Nothing, no mention. He said for those places not to have been spoken about, or part of the stories handed down to the generations that followed, means, and I'll quote him, 'whatever happened at Aztalan State Park and down in Cahokia had to have left a very bad taste in the native people's minds.'" Secrist looked up again from his legal pad.

"Boy, that sure sounds familiar, huh? No one here in Almore today knows about the lost Norte settlement or graveyard, either. Probably only a handful of residents, like Jenny the historian's daughter, ever even heard of the community that once lived just a few miles away from Almore. Kind of like that professor said, must have left a 'bad taste' in their mouths as well."

"That was exactly what I thought, Russ." For the first time, Secrist sat back in his chair, clearly pleased with what he'd been able to find out earlier that day.

"Did he mention anything else? Were there any other things that struck you as odd, or that both communities had in common related to human sacrifice?" Stander drummed his fingers along the tabletop in thought.

"No, I don't think…" Secrist sat back up in his chair and flipped over the notes he'd written. "Oh yeah! I almost forgot; thought you'd find this interesting. He said at both sites there was a small number of burnt human bones dug out of a fire pit." He looked up at Stander, "Guess I was thinking about the burn pile you and your buddies found when you were kids. Probably a stretch, but you did say you found human teeth." He shrugged and flipped another page on the legal pad. "Let's see, did I mention the statue? Looks like I didn't write that down."

"Statue? No, you didn't! Jesus Christ, Tommy, don't tell me they dug up some huge monolithic stone carving like what Lucas is working on in France…" Stander looked over expectantly, a what-now expression plastered on his face.

"No, no, no. Nothing like that. He just mentioned at both sites a statue of a birdman was found buried in the ground." Secrist looked away from Stander, his brow furrowed in thought as he tried to recall exactly how the college professor had described the finds. "A figure with some kind of weird, beak-like face and wings. I think he said the statues were both about four feet high. Roughly the size of a young child. But I'm not sure I'd bet on that meaning much."

"I would bet on it." Stander recounted in greater detail the strange mounted deity or figure he'd found underneath the wood shack. The statue only revealed after he, Denny, Chris, and Brian had torn down the strange building that sat next to the graveyard. As he spoke, a disturbing shiver crept slowly up his back, raising the hair on his neck and setting his teeth on edge. As he noticeably shook it off, Secrist cocked an inquisitive eyebrow. "Don't know…" Stander shrugged. "What's that old saying? Feels like someone just stepped over my grave." He smiled sheepishly, dismissive of his own explanation.

"As long as it doesn't feel like someone stepping *out* of their grave, I'm fine with that." Secrist laughed, but it came out sounding forced and strained. In his mind, he was trying to compare Stander's description of the strange effigy he'd seen as a kid with how the university professor had interpreted what his peers pulled out of the earth. Both accounts were undeniably similar. Eerily so. He'd have to check later and see if he could find any pictures of them.

From behind them, in the other room, Chris spoke for the first time. Startling both men still seated across the table from each other. "We saw something step out of a grave, didn't we, Rusty? We all saw it, not just me. NOT JUST ME!" The emaciated redhead's challenging eyes were rimmed red as he shouted the last sentence.

Stander turned in his chair and looked back at Chris. "We sure did. Came right out of the graveyard."

Chris's challenging stare fell, relief breaking across his body. "We did see it. We did... we did see. It WAS real..."

CHAPTER TWENTY-THREE

"Believe me, I've watched plenty of documentaries on meth before. They are way more entertaining that way." Chris, his hair still wet from bathing and swimming in the baggy clothes Stander let him borrow, deadpanned. Two beats passed before either Secrist or Stander reacted. It was Secrist who got the joke first, but he wasn't laughing or smiling. He'd seen the insidious drug steal too many lives to be entertained. He stood and walked away from the table all three men had been sharing. Muttering to himself as he crossed the room and leaned against the far wall.

"Give it up and save your breath, Russ. He hasn't hit bottom yet. When he does, maybe he'll even survive. But I doubt it, they rarely..."

"Wah, wah, wah." Chris interrupted before Secrist finished the sentence, pretending to cry into his two fists as he rubbed at his eyes. "You don't like how I live, just look away and hate me. Stupid cop."

Stander, still seated across from Chris, spoke next. "Hate you? You know I, us, I mean, we don't hate you. Hell, I barely know you. It's been so long. But seeing you like this, man, that's hard for me to swallow. You know what that shit is doing to you. Your insides are..."

"Poisoned. My insides are poisoned. I know all that, see? But guess what, Rusty? That's what keeps me alive. Poisoning myself. You don't know what it's like around here now." Chris, after waking and cleaning himself up, had spent the better part of the last hour talking. The two childhood friends trading old stories and catching up while Secrist mostly listened. Only in the last fifteen minutes had the subject turned to his obvious drug use.

Stander started again, "I know I can't begin to understand what you've..."

"Understand? Rusty? Understand? How could you?" Chris spoke very fast. He continuously interrupted and spoke over the other two. As if he didn't say the words that popped in his head, they'd run away forever. "You bailed on us. Couldn't be bothered, right? Hell, even with all this social media and Facebook junk nowadays, I never heard a word from you. You left me all alone."

Stander winced. He knew every word was true. He had run away. He'd wanted to run away. He couldn't stand the sound of his own voice when he heard it say, "I was just living, man. Got busy and..."

"Well, I was busy too, Rusty. Busy warring with myself. Maybe you can tell, I lost. I'm a loser."

Secrist spoke, his shoulder still leaning against the far wall. "The only thing that makes you, or anybody, a loser, is that crystal meth you keep pumping inside yourself."

Chris turned. His eyes were tired but his face was slowly turning red, on its way to matching his thinning hair. "Told you already. That is what keeps me alive now. Without it, I'd lose my head. Or at least what's inside."

Stander spoke, but his words seemed like they came more from a hollow PSA, not like the caring advice of the friend he used to be. Was trying to be again. "You may think you'd die without it. But you won't. The drugs don't..." Once again, Chris didn't let him finish.

"You just don't get it, Rusty. Do you?" He laughed without joy. A sound as sad as any Stander ever heard. "This town is soiled. People move away and don't come back." Chris pointed at Stander, challenging. "Like you did." When Stander tried to object, Chris cut him off again. His speech got faster and faster as he spoke. His words running into each other.

"People just disappear. Guess I can't blame them. If I had the money to leave this place, I would too. But I lost my car, my license, and I'm..." As his voice broke, Stander could feel his own heart breaking inside. "I'm so ashamed of myself, Rusty. But I... I hear things. Feel things. So, I hide, stay away from people. Hard to trust anyone and it makes me so tired. I'm so tired, Rusty."

"What about Denny? You still have..." But again, Stander was cut off by Chris.

"Denny? He's changed. Just like you. Like everyone, I guess. But I don't see him anymore. I try to avoid him if I can. His eyes, his eyes aren't his. They aren't kind anymore. He looks at me like I'm a bug or something. Besides, it's not like I can invite him over to my place again. Denny barely stayed long enough to finish his beer last time. Couldn't wait to leave." Chris looked straight at Stander, smiling. "Not that Denny ever really liked beer. Remember?" For a brief moment, it was like they were kids again. He recognized the Chris he once knew, and everything was right in the world.

But the moment was fleeting.

"You know where I live now, Rusty? Way outside of town. Like a hermit or something. I live in an abandoned mobile home that isn't much to look at. But hey! I couldn't beat the price! It was free and you know why, Rusty? Because the couple who lived there before me disappeared. I thought they were my friends," his gaze narrowed as he looked across the table, "like I thought you were once upon a time. But I went over one day to smoke a bowl with them, and they were gone. They didn't have much, but everything they owned was in that crappy trailer. When I got to their place, it all was still there. It was like they'd been abducted by aliens or something. Vanished without a trace. I waited all day. Nothing. Woke up the next morning on their couch. Nothing.

I've lived there for over a year and," Chris cast his eyes skyward briefly in thought, "or has it been two years? Anyway, still no sign of them."

"Did you contact the authorities? Maybe they fell victim to foul play?" Secrist spoke authoritatively from where he remained across the room. "Maybe from someone who would have benefitted from their disappearance. Like, say, someone who got a free place to live."

Chris fairly leapt from the table. Catching both men by surprise, he grabbed the poker from the nearby fireplace and charged at Secrist with it raised. "Don't you say that! Don't you say that! Don't you ever say that!" His mouth wet, spittle flew from his lips. He swung the heavy piece of iron, but Secrist deftly avoided the blow. When the end of the fire poker struck the wall, the sharp end of it became lodged in the plaster. Chris had missed caving in the ex-cop's head by less than a foot.

"You crazy SOB!" Secrist jerked Chris's hand free from the poker and pinned him against the wall using his body weight. Outweighing him by at least 150 pounds, Secrist held Chris firm until Stander could corral him with both his arms.

"What the fuck, Chris! You could have split his skull open with that thing!" He spun him around and marched him back over to the table, shoving him back down into his seat, but keeping both his hands firmly on the redhead's bony shoulders. "You have those cuffs, Tommy?" With a scowl and a nod, Secrist disappeared, walking back towards the room where he slept and kept his belongings. But by the time he returned, Chris's rage seemed to have been spent. His eyelids were slits, and a single drop of drool fell from his bottom lip.

Secrist laid the cuffs down on the table close by in case they were needed. He pointed one finger at the redhead as he retook his seat across from him. "You're lucky Russ is here. Otherwise, you'd be on your way to jail right now instead of rehab." At the mention of the word rehab, Chris tried to regain his feet once more, furious nonsensical objections ringing out. Stander easily pushed him back down in his seat a second time and held him until his resistance waned and finally stopped.

Panting and sobbing, Chris begged to be released. Repeating over and over that he couldn't go to rehab. Stander eventually began interjecting questions, trying to take his mind off the facility and stop him from talking in circles.

"Don't you remember how you lived before you started taking that junk? Why did you ever even start? You had to know that stuff would kill you?"

"Rusty… it's that thing. Don't you see? It's still out there. What we found at the cemetery, it's still here." Secrist and Stander shared a brief look.

"Don't listen to him. You said your other friend, Denny or whatever, he even said so." Stander nodded his head, understanding what Secrist was advising, but wanting to hear Chris out.

"OK. So, it's still here. How does filling your body with drugs help that? If that was true, wouldn't you be safer escaping for real? Not just in your head?" He kept one hand on the back of Chris's chair as he sat beside him.

"Not just in my head?" Chris laughed loudly. "The head is what it's after. But it won't touch me like this. Not with what you keep calling poison running through my brain. It won't touch me…" Chris's eyelids began to droop again. He seemed on the verge of sleep once more.

"Are you trying to tell me the thing we saw as kids is still around here? Where does it live? Hell, how does it live?" As Stander asked more questions, he could tell Secrist was openly dismissive of anything Chris was saying. But the retired cop stayed seated, begrudgingly listening just the same.

"It lives in the same place, Rusty. Down by the river in the graveyard. It's lived there forever." Chris spoke with his eyes closed. The pace of his words finally slowing to a more normal cadence.

Stander leaned back in his chair, defeated and exhausted by the endless ramblings. It seemed obvious Chris was not right. Whether from years of drug abuse or an untreated mental illness, he couldn't be sure. Hopefully, the treatment center he'd arranged to take Chris in could figure all that out. The most important thing was to get him help.

"Chris, it can't still live at the graveyard we found as kids. I was just there. The place has been plowed over now. It's just row after row of corn."

"Yeah," Chris answered distractedly, his voice a low monotone, almost a whisper now. "Denny bought all the land down that way. He farms it each season. Told me, he told me he sacrificed a lot on that patch of land. That's why the crops are so plentiful."

Stander rolled his eyes at Secrist, "You mean he sacrificed a lot *for* that patch of land." It wasn't a question. He just corrected the slurring Chris.

Chris' eyes flew open momentarily before quickly closing once more. "That's, that is not what he said..." His head slumped forward, a snore the only sounds to follow. Stander slowly stood; thankful Chris had fallen asleep again. He needed to collect his wits, and maybe even rest for a bit, before leaving for the treatment facility about an hour away in Davenport. He silently motioned for Secrist to follow him, and both men slipped quietly into the kitchen.

"What did you think of all that?" Stander turned, "Did you catch what he just said?"

"Said? That guy nearly brained me! If we are looking for some crazy person cracking open heads, he should be at the top of our list. If it was up to me, he would already be in the back of a squad car." Secrist sighed once before adding, "I could barely hear him anyway, and he was half asleep. I wouldn't pay attention to anything your good buddy out there has to say."

"But don't you think it's odd? Denny told me earlier today he'd never returned to the place. Said it was all washed away in a flood. But Chris,"

Stander gestured at the doorway separating the two rooms, "just said Denny owns the land."

"You're chasing ghosts now, Russ. Whatever you saw as a kid, you saw with both those guys." Secrist moved forward and placed a hand on Stander's shoulder. "It took a toll on all of you, and each of you dealt with it differently. The guilt, I mean. You 'ran away', as you put it, Chris turned to drugs, and it's likely Denny buried it in his past. Probably did buy the land. Maybe just so he could physically bury any sign of what was an unexplainable and horrible experience. You were just kids, Russ. Things that happen at that age linger."

Stander sighed, nodding. "But why lie about it? Why say it was all washed away?"

"Maybe metaphorically that is how he views it. Didn't most of the land down this way flood back in 1993 when the Mississippi swelled so much? He probably bought the land afterwards dirt cheap and just plowed over anything still left standing. Owning, washing, and burying it all away to find his peace. When you showed up out of the blue, after being gone for years, his knee jerk reaction was to deny everything. What you all saw, Brian's death, even the memory of the place." Secrist dropped his hand back down. "I don't blame him. To be honest, he likely dealt with it better than either of you." Secrist glanced back through the open doorway of the room they'd just left. His shoulders sagged, "Oh no."

Stander, as he turned to follow Secrist's gaze, asked "What happened?" But there was no need for a reply. The table and chair where Chris had just been sleeping, or feigning sleep, was empty. Chris was gone. The door leading outside still standing open. "Dammit," he said simply.

"We better go after him. But it's dark outside now, and I doubt we'll be able to track him down very well." Both men walked together and looked out the kitchen doorway. "I'd bet money he's running back to his place. Probably needs to get high. Let's drive over and beat him there."

"I don't know where he lives." Stander stood, unmoving for a moment, before pulling out his phone. "Let me call Denny and get directions. Hold on," he placed the phone to his ear. After a brief pause, he spoke, "Hi, Denny, it's Rusty. Sorry I missed you. Can you give me a call back when you pick this message up? I was getting ready to take Chris to a treatment facility over in the Quad Cities when he bolted on me. I think he likely headed back to his home but I don't know where that is. I'm afraid he might do something drastic. Please call me back ASAP." When he was done, he pocketed the phone.

"No answer, huh? Hopefully, he'll call right back." Secrist walked over to the table where Chris had been. "Oh great! Looks like he took my handcuffs with him. Probably thinks he can sell them for a few bucks. Fiendish bastard..." He turned back to Stander, "Hope your friend calls back real soon. If Chris goes and gets a hit, we could have a really hard time with him."

For the next twenty minutes, both men waited for Denny to return their call. Stander tried twice more to reach Denny again, but both times his calls went straight to voicemail. He also sent him a text urging him to reply as soon as he saw it.

After he'd changed his shirt and another five minutes passed, Stander began to get antsy. It had now been almost half an hour since Chris had disappeared out the kitchen door. "What do we want to do? Seems like Denny isn't returning my calls. Maybe his phone is turned off, or he's someplace where he can't talk. But I don't think we can wait any longer. By now, Chris might have been able to walk home for all we know." Stander felt helpless, responsible somehow, and thinking the worst. Silently cursing his decision not to take his old friend straight to the treatment facility. What if something happened to him now? It would be all his fault.

"Right. Of course, if Chris was looking to get high one last time before rehab, he could have called someone to come pick him up. Hell, if so, he likely called his local drug dealer. He could already be lighting up right now if that was the case." Secrist shook his head pessimistically.

"Should we drive into town? See if someone at the diner knows where he lives? Or maybe that crappy bar. They seemed to know him there." But Stander knew it would be very dicey for him to enter the local roadside dive bar again.

"Maybe. But here, let me try Jenny first before we do that. Kind of a shot in the dark, but..." Secrist pulled out his phone and scrolled quickly before putting the phone to his ear, mouthing silently "she answered" before beginning to speak. By the time he'd ended the short call, Stander stood by the door with his car keys in hand.

"We'll pick her up at Arlene's Diner. It's on the way. Jenny said she knows where Chris lives, but not the actual street address. She said it's really hard to find, so she'll ride along so we don't get lost." Secrist disappeared down the hall briefly, returning with his licensed sidearm, readjusting his belt after sliding the holster behind his back. Seeing Stander's concerned look, he said simply, "You never know."

Both men hurried to Stander's Jeep and soon had Jenny in tow. After a brief introduction to Stander, she hopped in the backseat where she began giving directions as he drove. Just minutes outside of Almore, she had them turn down a dark, twisting, one lane road, leaving the flat farming fields that dominated most of the countryside behind. Less than a quarter of a mile later, she had them turn once more onto an unnamed gravel road where three unpainted and dented mail boxes sat clustered together on a single wood pole. Both the mailboxes and the dusty road were surrounded by towering trees.

Stander did his best to avoid the gaping ruts and potholes along the route, but all three of them were bounced around pretty good inside of the Jeep. In the rearview and side mirrors, big clouds of dust – eerie in the red of the tail lights – billowed out behind them. They passed no other cars or people down the lonely lane, and ahead of them no lights identified a clear destination. After cresting a small rise, a large barn seemed to leap into the beams of the headlights, materializing to their right out of the gloom without warning. The doors on the old barn were missing, and it sat empty, unused, and weathered to near rot. Beside it, but on the opposite side of the road, an abandoned farm house missing half its roof loomed unlit. In its front yard an old pickup truck without wheels sat idly on four cement blocks. The front windshield shattered in the shape of a spider's web and the hood missing.

Jenny motioned just beyond the junk truck, to a flat clearing beside the dirt road where they should park. "Chris lives in a trailer at the end of the Gladwell's land, down by the gully." She pointed out the front windshield, but made no move to exit the vehicle. "If you don't mind, I think I'll stay here. This place gives me the creeps." She drew her arms close to her body and crossed them.

"Probably better if one of us stays with the car anyway," said Secrist. "We'll lock the doors. Just blow the horn if you see Chris and we'll come right back. Sound like a plan, Nancy Drew?" He smiled reassuringly at Jenny and she nodded, clearly relieved to be staying put.

Both men slid out of the vehicle, and Stander hit the automatic locks before closing his door. Meeting at the front of the Jeep, and standing in the overgrown remnants of the gravel driveway, they looked down the slight hill ahead. Off in the distance stood a mobile home. Though the sky above held some clouds, at the moment the nearly full moon illuminated the dilapidated residence. Long tall shadows, created by the surrounding trees and deserted buildings, stretched out around them.

"Maybe we beat him here after all," Secrist offered. "There's no lights on."

"I'm not sure that means much. I don't think, from what Denny told me, Chris has electricity." The night was warm and the sound of buzzing cicadas filled their ears with white noise. Swaying weeds, waist high, crowded the sides of the lane and stretched out between them and the mobile home. The only breaks in the sweeping grass were various pieces of abandoned farm equipment exposed to the elements.

From where they stood, they could make out a couple of the bigger pieces. A lone tractor, more rust than metal, stood silently beside a grain wagon turned on its side. Nearby a hulking, combine harvesting tractor without rear wheels and a wrecked front end loomed out of the darkness. Its front row of crop dividing pincers left upturned and badly damaged from a violent collision. The remaining jagged and torn metal pieces stabbing the air as if to fend off an attack from the sky above. Other assorted pieces of farm equipment and several barely visible old automobiles littered the grounds like a junk yard. Stander suspected plenty more obstacles were hidden underneath the unkempt weeds. They'd have to pick their way carefully down the hill in the darkness. He thought back to when he'd first seen the thing that killed Brian. How he'd watch it sink below the tall grass of the graveyard. Where it could scuttle under the wavy brush like a ravenous shark swimming silent and unseen under the ocean waves. Before closing fast on its quarry and breeching the waves. He shuddered as he looked out across the bleak field. Anything could be under all those weeds.

Waiting for prey.

"Shit!" Stander whispered, "I left the flashlight I always keep in my Jeep back at the house. We were using it that first night we got there, and I never brought it back out." He shook his head, annoyed with himself.

"Why are you whispering?" Secrist looked over questionably, his tone normal. "If Chris is somewhere inside, he already heard us pull up. The headlights alone announced our presence, probably a quarter mile back. If he wanted to run, he already would have, and if he actually is here, he's likely either super messed up or passed out. Let's just go up and knock on the door. If the door is open, and he doesn't answer, we just walk in. See if he is here."

Stander nodded in agreement. "Guess if we need light once we are inside, we can use our phones." Secrist turned and began to walk normally down towards the mobile home.

"Just watch where you're stepping," Stander breathed out a warning, catching himself flinching as Secrist took the lead. "There is probably a ton of junk lying under all this. You step on an old nail and you'll be bouncing around on one foot howling like a stuck pig." Stander followed behind him, trying his best to walk in the path he'd cut through the tall grass weeds. "Though I guess it would make a good story later on. After the tetanus shots."

"I know, I know. What do you think I am, an idiot?" Secrist moved forward steadily with Stander just behind, carefully placing each step. Deeper in the weed choked field, more lost items revealed themselves. Half a rusting barrel, a badly corroded plow, a riding lawn mower missing its steering wheel. It was like walking through a battlefield of warring farm equipment carcasses. The unwanted machineries' remains, skeletal-like in the moonlight, left behind and no longer of use. Broken glass glittered in the moonlight all around the ground like snow.

Together the two men pushed through weeds swishing along their pant legs. Closer now, they could see a set of three rickety wood steps leading up to a front door that stood half ajar. The trailer, last painted white perhaps decades before, hardly seemed livable from the outside. Along one side of the mobile home, closer to the back, a second door hung wide open. Leaning from it a small hot water heater, the pipes attached seemed to be all that kept it from falling completely out. In the distance, a chorus of frogs competed with the cicadas. The combined sounds nearly deafening and, if you closed your eyes to the junk strewn land on either side, civilization seemed far, far away. Not just a few miles down the road. The entire farmstead, even in its heyday, was extremely isolated.

Reaching the warped stairs, Stander stepped ahead of Secrist, climbing them tentatively. Leaning forward he rapped his knuckles against the front door. The unlatched door swung inwards, creaking loudly on its hinges. Stander poked his head a few inches inside.

"Chris! Hey Chris, you in here? It's me, Rusty." No reply came from the black interior. Stander couldn't see inside farther than a few inches. "Chris?"

MORRISON, ILLINOIS
July 30th, 1902

The walk along the dirt field was pleasant enough. After riding the rail in a stinky boxcar all evening, it felt good to be out among the fresh air of the countryside. Behind her, the small town where the train stopped was still visible. The clustered roofs huddled in tight under the bit of pale moonlight punching through the cloud cover above. Ahead of her were the two homes that caught her eye when the train had first begun to slow. Both seemed promising.

"Eeny, meeny, miny, moe..." she whispered to herself. The two houses were nearly identical, both small and shabby, but big enough to potentially house a family inside. She loved children. Breathlessly, she whispered once more to herself. "They're delicious."

Her approaching footsteps were light as she made her way across the farmer's field. Though she'd been cautious as she'd disembarked unseen from the train, you could never be too careful. Even out here in the middle of a field. She weaved herself in and out of the cornrows expertly. The green stalks several inches taller than she was, perfect for clandestine traveling. Much like the anonymous trains she used to move the great distances needed to avoid suspicion.

Somewhere ahead of her and to the right, a lone dog began barking loudly. The still of the night broken by the incessant yapping. She stopped in case it was somehow the sound, or her movement, in the dark field that alerted the four-legged guardian. Not her scent. But, as long minutes ticked slowly past, the enthusiasm of the canine never wavered, and no one came out to silence the dog. Eventually, she turned and began to retrace her steps. Walking away from the homes she'd intended to visit.

She hissed, "Damnable mongrel!"

Back across the field, on the opposite side, stood a single house. Though barely more than a shack, the crooked wood fence surrounding it held a donkey and a lone milking cow. It was likely occupied. As she parted the stalks of the last row of corn, she spied two sets of worn leather shoes sitting on the front porch. But no shoes the size of children. Though saddened by the turn of events, her resolve remained as strong as her hunger. With morning just hours away, she made her way swiftly to the side of the house. There, wedged deep in the top of an old tree stump, was the homeowner's axe. Grasping the handle, she wiggled it free from the dead log. The smooth wood handle felt good in her grip.

The warm summer breeze blew across her face. She wiped at the wetness pooling about her mouth.

CHAPTER TWENTY-FOUR

Jenny picked at the dry skin around her nails, alternately chewing on the ends of her fingers and tearing bits of flesh off them. It was a nervous habit she'd had since she was a little girl. When she was at her most anxious, she sometimes picked and chewed at the ends of her fingers until they were raw in places. Sitting all alone like this, in the backseat of Stander's Jeep, she was certain she'd have at least one bloody sore by the end of the night. She peeked out the vehicle's side window at the old Gladwell farmhouse. The looming home was dark, an ominous sight under the light of the near full moon. The house had been empty for as long as she could recall, and the entire farmstead was supposedly haunted. Kids on dares practically the only visitors the place ever got now.

Well, except for Chris, the town "crazy."

Jenny turned to face the front windshield once more. In a squeaky voice, she said to herself, "Come on, guys. Where are you?" She was beginning to regret her decision not to walk down to the old mobile home with them. Sighing, she reached over and opened her door, stepping quickly outside and quietly closing it behind her. She pulled out a cigarette and her lighter, hoping a quick smoke would calm her nerves. Maybe save one of her fingernails as well.

"Hi Jenny, fancy meeting you here, huh?" Startled, Jenny flung herself backwards against the side of the Jeep. The voice from out of the darkness was so unexpected only the sudden intake of the harsh cigarette smoke saved her from screaming out loud. Instead, she started coughing, looking up as Mr. Reiner, Dennis Reiner, moved out from where he stood behind the Jeep.

"Sorry," he said, "I didn't mean to startle you. I thought the car was empty."

"Oh my, oh dear. You just about gave me a heart attack, Mr. Reiner." Jenny looked up and saw her own face staring back at her. Mr. Reiner was wearing his customary mirror sunglasses, even after nightfall. Probably thinks he looks cool. What a dick, Jenny thought to herself. "What are you doing out here?"

"I was about to ask you the same thing. But judging by this," he motioned to Stander's Jeep, "I'm guessing you're here with Russell." Jenny nodded as she took a long drag, wondering how long he'd been standing behind the car. Had he been watching her? "So, where is he? Close by or...?" Something about the way he asked the question gave her the "willies" as Paps, liked to say. Chris may be the town crazy, but Mr. Reiner was the creepy one. She'd heard the two men were friends as kids.

Figures.

"Just down the hill looking for Chris. They didn't know where he lived so they asked me to tag along and show them. I guess they're going to admit him into a hospital or something." Jenny hated not being able to see his eyes behind the dark lenses.

"They?" Mr. Reiner stepped closer, now just an arm's length away.

"He has a friend with him." The second sentence she blurted out as fast as the thought came to her. "He's a retired cop." It felt good to remind herself of that. It felt even better saying it out loud to Mr. Reiner, the creep. She repeated her first question. "Why are you out here?"

"Same thing as you, I guess. Russell phoned me, but I missed his call. He left a message saying Chris took off when they tried to take him to rehab. Asked if I could help track him down. So, here I am." He shrugged nonchalantly, then leaned against the side of the Jeep next to Jenny.

"Scary out here, isn't it, Jenny? You'd kind of hate to meet a crazy out in the middle of nowhere like this." He turned the eyes Jenny couldn't see on her. "Or a creep." Jenny felt icy little fingers of fear trailing up her spine. The man had always made her uncomfortable. He stood very close, too close, to her.

"Oh, yeah, for sure. That's for sure." Jenny stammered, maybe she should get back into the Jeep. The Jeep. Where is Mr. Reiner's truck? Out loud, she asked the same question. "So how did you get down here? I didn't see or hear your truck at..." But her breath was cut off. Mr. Reiner's strong hand, warm and calloused, closed over her mouth and nose. She felt his second hand reaching under her blouse, groping and crawling up her skin.

She struggled without success and screamed without sound.

"Chris! Hello! Where you at, man?" Stander stood just inside the door of the mobile home. The floor underfoot sagged slightly under his weight. A horrible odor was all that met his entrance. The smell foul beyond measure. A little chill reached out and touched him some place uncomfortable. He really didn't want to enter this narrow, unlit trailer. He was simply afraid.

Behind him, a white light flared, and Secrist moved past him. Entering the living room of the small trailer first, an empty TV stand stood alone on the far wall. A sad slouching couch, covered by two brightly colored Afghan blankets, the only other furniture. He held his phone out in front of him, sweeping the bright light back and forth exposing the insides of the mobile home for what it was.

Empty.

After unsuccessfully toggling the light switch on the wall several times, Secrist moved to his right, walking past the living room and towards the cramped kitchen of the trailer. Passing a lopsided table as he moved silently over to the stove and refrigerator. Neither appliance appeared to have been functional for quite some time. He opened and shut the freezer door once before moving to the kitchen sink and flipping up the handle on it. Discolored water cascaded out briefly before he turned it back off; his attention drawn to the bottom of the sink. Reaching into it, he pulled out a dripping, handheld claw hammer. As Stander walked up behind him, Secrist shined his phone light on the end of it. The heavy head of the hammer was mottled, patchy bits of hair and blood visible.

"Fuck me..." Stander whispered from behind him. "Is that what I think it is?"

"Blood for sure. But I'm not certain from what." Secrist spoke in a normal tone of voice. The sound booming in the small enclosure. "We'll leave it here for now and see what else we can find. But it needs to be tested to confirm where the blood came from." Grimly, he placed the hammer down into the sink before turning back around. Holding his phone out in front of him, illuminating their path towards the back of the mobile home, he said, "After you, Russ."

Both men walked slowly past the door they'd entered Chris's home by. A tight hallway led to the back of the trailer, two closed doors on the left and a single open doorway at the end. Stander grasped the door handle as they reached the first door. Twisting it, he pushed the door open wide and stepped inside, nearly tripping over a stack of magazines piled on the floor just beyond the doorway. Assorted periodicals lay scattered in bunches all around the room. Otherwise, the room was empty.

Stepping in behind Stander, Secrist waved his light around the room before bending over to inspect the magazine titles. "I suppose this is his stash of porn, huh?" But as he shifted through a few of the titles, it was clear he'd rushed to judgement. Each magazine was full of technical jargon on network hubs, routers, and servers. The glossy pictures on the covers might excite someone working in a corporate IT department, or supporting a help desk at Microsoft, but they did nothing for a retired cop and small-town bar owner.

Together, they ducked back into the cramped, wood paneled hallway and made their way towards the last two rooms of the trailer. The next door, again on the same side as the first, was the bathroom. The inside looked as bad as Denny had described it to Stander earlier, and an awful smell seemed to ooze out of the walls themselves. Retreating quickly from the stench of the empty room, they made their way down to the end of the small hallway to the last doorway.

They found Chris.

His back was to them, and he sat cross-legged on the floor facing the back wall of the room. Secrist placed one hand on the gun he was carrying. In the other hand, the light from his phone still shone brightly. A yellowed mattress took up the majority of the floor in the back bedroom of the trailer. Books were strewn here and there, many of them missing their covers. Silently, both Stander and Secrist stepped past Chris; the light revealing his wet face.

"Chris, why didn't you answer us? Are you alright?" Stander squatted down in front of him, nearly face to face.

"I had to come back here," Chris spoke the words hoarsely, not looking up. His face was streaked with tears, and under his nose, snot and drool dripped down into the folded hands on his lap, mixing with the tears flowing from his eyes. Clasped in his hands, clutched tightly, he held a stone the size of a golf ball. Like his hands, it was wet and shiny. He lifted his head and held it up, offering the stone for inspection, but not loosening his grip on it. "You recognize this, don't you?"

Stander barely glanced down at the shiny rock. "No, sorry, Chris. I don't think that is mine..."

"It's not yours. It's mine." Chris looked up at Stander then, wiping his nose with the back of his hand before continuing. His face looked like a glazed doughnut, smeared with snot and spit like a teething toddler. "No one believed us after Brian... after it happened. Me and Denny, we both tried to tell everyone, warn them about what we'd seen. But none of the adults would listen to us. They tried to convince us otherwise. That maybe we didn't see what we saw. Didn't see what fed on Brian. Told us we were lying. Denny," Chris barked out a short laugh, "he caved right away. Wavered even that same night. Started to say that maybe he wasn't so sure or hadn't seen it. The more I insisted, the more I looked like I was stupid, or crazy, or something. Denny changed his story and then stopped talking about it. Wasn't long before he stopped talking to me too... and you? You were already long gone." Chris looked over at Secrist a little subconsciously before continuing on.

"My stepparents, the pastor at our church, even that chrome domed cop. They made me go back days later. I didn't want to! But they made me. Kept asking questions about where I stood, you stood, where Brian..." Chris stopped talking and looked back down at the ground before speaking again. "Anyway, I started to doubt myself. I mean, I was just a kid and all these adults were telling me I was wrong. Ganging up on me, trying to convince me I hadn't seen the thing. That it was just a freak accident. But then I saw this," again he raised the stone, "buried in the soft bark of a dying tree. I knew right away what it was. None of the adults at the time would even look at it, much less listen to anything more I said. So, I pocketed it and just shut my mouth. I never gave in and said what they wanted to hear, though. I just quit arguing and that seemed to be good enough for them. The whole town thought I was crazy. They still do."

Chris kept the rock aloft in one hand while he spoke. "You must have shot this right through that thing. Sharp as a marble, huh? I found it lodged in the middle of that old tree, so I used my pocketknife to dig it out. I've kept it ever since. It's my good luck charm." He wiped one arm across his entire face again, managing only to transfer the snot and tears from one side of it to the other before looking up at Stander. His eyes were clear and sober. Earnest and sincere even. The eyes of friendship and perhaps even love. "You know, I never thanked you for saving my life, Rusty."

The conversation was completely unexpected, a total surprise. Even the cadence of Chris's voice was normal now. For the first time, Stander recognized in his tone, and especially in his eyes, the childhood friend he'd long thought lost. Emotions rolled unchecked inside him. Stander's eyes welled up, catching him completely off guard. His earlier fears stepping into the decrepit trailer evaporated, replaced by a tenderness and fierce need to protect his long-lost friend.

One he'd abandoned before.

Stander stumbled over his words, the turn of events head snapping. "I... uh... well, I guess, thanks then, Chris. Er... I mean you're welcome I guess..." Stammering, at a loss for words, he pointed down at the rounded rock still held in Chris's hands. "So, this is the one, huh? This is the rock we found underground? The one I shot that ugly fucking thing with?" He kept talking now, avoiding the swell of feelings bubbling inside. "Why did you keep it? I mean, after all these years you kept hold of it? Why?"

Chris held the stone aloft once more, higher than before and letting it bathe in the light from Secrist's phone. "See all these weird colors in the bright light? Beautiful, isn't it? But when you look at it in the sun, or even in just normal low light, it's rust colored." Chris looked directly into Stander's eyes, forcing him to meet them. "I kept it because it looks rusty. And my best friend during the best time of my life was named Rusty. I like to sit holding this and remember him."

Chris smiled as he spoke, sneaking a quick peek over at Secrist and addressing him directly for the first time. "He ever tell you what we called ourselves back when we were little kids?" Secrist shook his head no. "No? Well, we were a Wolf Pack. Me, Rusty, Denny and Brian. Silly now, I know... but it felt so important once upon a time. To be part of that gang. We went together like spit and sweat! I'd give up anything to be back together with all of them again. Maybe even drugs and alcohol. You know, it's scary even thinking I could ever really get off them after all this time. But with Rusty and this," he held the stone aloft, "I just might be able to dream enough about it to make it real. So, see," he turned back to face Stander once again, "I had to come back for this. Promise me, Rusty. Promise me that I can take this with me to rehab. Promise me!"

"I promise, Chris, I promise." Stander paused before impulsively blurting out, "Wolf Pack Rules!" Lifting his chin, he howled like a wolf, tentatively at first until he heard Chris chime in loudly. Both men howling and laughing together as Chris clambered to his feet. Stander reached out to Secrist, slapping him on the back and encouraging him to join in as the three men exited the sad mobile home. Shaking his head but smiling, drawn in by the infectious nature of the boyhood chums, Secrist let loose a howl. Three fifty plus year old men, all sober no less, howling up at the moon above and shocking to silence the cicadas and frogs of the surrounding timber.

Halfway back to the Jeep, Jenny suddenly stumbled out from behind a grain wagon, staggering forward, her steps unbalanced. She lurched into Secrist's arms, pale and wild-eyed, her blouse torn and tattered, held up only by her gore-soaked arms. As she sunk unsteadily to the ground at his feet, Secrist was left holding only her blood in his hands. "Oh my god, Jenny! Are you...? You're hurt!! What happened?" He wiped his bloody hands across his shirt. "Did someone do this to you? Jenny!"

"It was Mr. Reiner. He attacked me, came at me out of nowhere." She reached up to the back of her head, and when she pulled her hand back, it was slick with fresh blood. Matching the carnage splashed across her front. The fresh red blood appearing black under the shimmering light of the moon. "He slipped in the grass otherwise he would have... I don't know why... why he was trying to hurt me!" Jenny began sobbing loudly, burying her head in her bloody hands before she pointed back towards where they had parked earlier. "He was up there and chased me down here. When he heard you three, he took off. Back up that way. I never even saw him pull up, but he must have parked somewhere back on the road." Jenny began to shake uncontrollably.

"Denny? Denny did this to you?" Stander couldn't believe what he was hearing.

Chris piped up, "See? I told you he wasn't right. His eyes, his eyes are different."

Secrist cut him off, pulling out his gun, "Come on, Russ! We'll go see if we can find him. Chris," Secrist looked over at the redhead, "Stay here with Jenny. We'll be right back. Don't leave her side." Both men turned and began to run back up the hill, weaving their way past the junk strewn field. Back towards where they'd parked earlier.

The Jeep remained where Stander had parked it, untouched. But there was no sign of Denny anywhere. Together, both men crept farther up the gravel roadway, back towards the road. The light of the moon was bright enough that they were able to see clearly around them without using their phones. After a few more minutes of walking, with no sign of Denny or his truck, Secrist decided they should turn around. Each man walked back along either side of the lane, eyeballing the surrounding woods and tall weeds sprouting up from the ditches that ran along both sides of the road. There was no sign of Denny to be found.

Once the Jeep was back in sight, Stander jogged over to it. The two front doors were still locked, but one of the backdoors was unlocked.

Stander opened the car door, but found nothing inside out of place. Silently, he cursed himself for not checking out the car when they'd first walked past it. Had Denny been hiding inside until the coast was clear?

He turned to share his suspicion with Secrist who, after holstering his weapon, was carefully inspecting the ground near the rear tires. "He could have hidden in here until he saw us go by. Maybe we missed him and now he's taken off."

"Maybe. But check this out," Secrist motioned him over to where he squatted, looking down at the ground. He pulled out his phone and activated the light once more. "This is an awful lot of blood and it looks like..." Suddenly he stood once more, walking slowly, his light trained on the ground. The gravel had been kicked up and turned over as if to cover the trail of blood he was following. The telltale signs of something being dragged across the ground were only obvious to Stander when he pointed it out. "Way too much blood to have come from just Jenny. Maybe she fought back." He looked up at Stander briefly, "Fought back hard, I'd say."

"But what's with these marks? Did Denny drag himself away? It almost looks like someone was trying to cover up the trail of blood." Both men continued to follow the disturbed and uneven ground, following the visible splotches of blood that led deeper into the high grass. A few yards later, the bloody trail ended just below the driver's side door of the broken-down farm truck left to rot in the weeds of the deserted homestead. Recognizing the significance at the same time, both men stopped in their tracks. Secrist put one finger to his lips to silence them, then pointed at the door handle. Clearly just wiped, the clean chrome car door handle stood out like a sore thumb against the rest of the neglected, dust caked truck.

Pulling his gun once again, Secrist ducked low and inched towards the door. Silently, he motioned for Stander to watch him. Holding up three fingers, he mouthed a countdown from three without words, three fingers becoming two, then one before yanking open the unlocked truck's door.

Something inside had gone terribly awry.

What was left of Denny, formless and pooled on the floorboard, slowly spilled out the door's opening. A seemingly boneless pile of flesh, bloody and raw, splashed onto the ground at Secrist's feet. Soaking his shoes in loose guts and twisted entrails. The ghastly scene stunned both men to silence. Long seconds ticked slowly past as the horror of what they saw slowly seeped into their reality. Stander's breath stopped, clogging his throat with nothing, yet somehow no longer allowing anything up or down. It may have saved him. He knew, if he started screaming, it likely wouldn't have ended until his throat burst. Denny's mirror sunglasses, surrounded by a mop of his greying, but distinctive black hair, was the last of the abomination to slide out of the old pickup truck. The twin images in the lenses reflecting Stander's own disbelieving eyes staring back at him in revulsion.

Neither man uttered a sound. They didn't have time. A shrill scream exploded in the night. The desperate screech close by, back down the hill in the direction of the mobile home. Secrist tore his eyes from the mass of flesh first, sprinting toward the tortured sound.

"Come on! That's Jenny!"

CARTHAGE, ILLINOIS
JUNE 30TH, 1901

THE MAN FROM THE train jumped lightly out of the slowly moving boxcar. As he stepped unhurriedly from the train tracks, he didn't hear the whispered conversation from the railcar he left behind. The three traveling companions he'd spent the night with — all nomadic hobos riding the rails and likely running from something in their past — were also anonymous travelers. Men he'd met only nine hours before when climbing aboard the otherwise empty rolling wood box. They'd spoken sparingly, but shared both drink and smoke casually among them. The lone native of the land, dark-skinned, dressed uncomfortably in stiff bib overalls and a long sleeve shirt despite the stifling heat, moved away from the other three riders. Propping himself up with his back against the wall in a far corner. His long grey hair falling across his face. He spoke not a single word to, or about, the man from the train during the long ride. But once he'd left, the old Chippewa tribal medicine man uttered a single word. Not trying to hide his obvious revulsion as he spat it out.

"Skinwalker."

The man from the train walked leisurely around the small town. He gazed in the general store's front window, but didn't enter. Instead, he strolled up and down several of the streets, nodding pleasantly at those who acknowledged him. Once he'd spied the small schoolhouse at the outskirts of town, he slowed his pace. He watched the front entrance of the one room school carefully as the children were dismissed. When he saw two girls, obviously sisters, peel away from their group of friends, he fell in step behind them. He noted their patchwork clothing and dirty knees.

When the smallest child, perhaps age eight or nine, sat down along the side of the road and took her shoes off, he walked right on past them. Pleasantly greeting and smiling at both of the pretty red-haired girls, but continuing to walk the same direction they had been heading. Down a long lonely stretch of dirt road that split two cornfields in half. In the distance, he could see a single black shingled roof, but no other houses for miles either way. He slowed his pace.

After a few minutes, he stumbled. Feigning a twisted ankle, he hobbled over to a tree that stood beside the lane and leaned heavily on it. As he knew they would, the girls rushed to his aid. Asking if he was alright or if they could help. He smiled back at them amiably. Saying he was fine, but maybe a little parched. Asking if they knew if the house ahead was occupied and if the owner might let him draw some water from their well. The girls laughed and told him the house was theirs, and that, of course, he could get a sip or two.

The three of them walked together, the barefoot girl even reaching out to hold his hand. She informed him that their mother made the best rhubarb pie in town and asked if he would like to try a piece.

"Well, aren't you sweet. Both you girls look so delectable. Maybe I'll stick around and have a bit to eat." The man from the train smiled down warmly at them.

He wiped a hand across his drooling, wet chin.

CHAPTER TWENTY-FIVE

THE HYSTERICAL WAILING DIDN'T let up until Stander and Secrist finally reached the origin of the desperate screams. Jenny, flailing wildly, was handcuffed to the side of a hulking tractor chassis barely visible above the tall weeds and brush. One end of the cuffs – obviously the pair Chris swiped from Secrist when he'd run from Relict Mansion – was locked in place along a steel bar that ran the length of the rusting farm equipment. The other end was clamped tightly around Jenny's wrist.

"Get these off of me!" Jenny screamed at the dumbfounded pair. "Hurry up before that stinking mongrel comes back!" Standing, she pulled hard against the shackle over and over again. Her tightly pinched wrist bleeding and torn open from the exertion. When neither man immediately stepped forward, she began to curse them. "Release me, you stupid pigs! Right now, you ignorant fools! GET THESE OFF OF ME!!"

"My god, Jenny," Secrist began. "How did... where's Chris?" Putting his gun away first, he fished around in his pockets. "I have the key. Just hold on and calm down." He patted and reached down into the front pocket of his pants. Pulling his hand out, something twinkled in the bright moonlight. The key! "Got it! Here it is."

Abruptly, Jenny fell to silence. Lifting her chin, she somehow sensed Chris before he appeared. Exclaiming, "Look out!" just before he came around the corner of a nearby overturned grain wagon. He was running, and he made a beeline straight towards Jenny without acknowledging the two newcomers. In one hand he carried a hatchet, and in his other hand a red metal can swung wildly back and forth. The contents splashing out of the small opening on the top and soaking one side of his shirt as he ran. The distinctive and unmistakable smell of gasoline dominated the night air around them.

"Chris! No!! What are you doing?!" Stander started after him, taking an angle that would cut off Chris before he reached the shackled woman. "Stop! Chris! Have you lost your fucking...?" The last words were cut off as Stander toppled down face first in the weedy field. Landing in a huff less than five yards from Chris, tripped up by the scores of neglected trash that dotted the hillside. He watched helplessly as Chris reached Jenny.

The redheaded man stood over Jenny; a crazed look of desperation stamped on his features as he began dumping the contents of the gas can over her head. Jenny gagged and sputtered, frantically waving her free arm back and forth in an attempt to deflect some of the noxious fuel. Soaked in seconds, her efforts made little difference.

"Stop! Now!" Secrist yelled from behind Stander. He'd pulled his gun and was aiming it at Chris as he tossed the empty gas can at his feet. "Chris! Stop right now and back away from Jenny!" His voice was loud, commanding. "Whatever you are trying to do needs to stop. You don't want to do this. Talk to us!"

Chris froze, indecision mixed with sheer terror stamped across his features. "Look at her head. The back of her head!" He turned with pleading eyes, looking back and forth between both Stander, still sprawled on the ground, and Secrist, who continued pointing his weapon at him. "It's the monster. Can't you see? She's the monster!"

"Chris", Stander spoke firmly in what he hoped was a calm voice. With his heart pumping wildly, he couldn't be sure how good the deception was. On the inside, he was frantic; the scene spinning way out of control. Clearly Chris was damaged, unable to think clearly. The important thing now was to keep him talking and distracted until Secrist could free Jenny from the set of handcuffs. "You don't want to hurt Jenny."

"That's not Jenny!" Chris cried out loudly, his eyes boring into her. "No one! No one ever believes me!" He turned slightly and looked down at Stander who'd only risen to his knees. "Can't you see, Rusty? She's the monster, the one who killed Brian. Why won't you believe me?" His eyes welled with water, and the tears made streaky lines down his dirty face in the moonlight. He sagged slightly. His shoulders falling forward. "No one ever believes me..." Stander felt his own heartbeat slow slightly, a small measure of relief as the volatile situation began to diffuse. He looked back at Secrist who, gun still raised, hadn't moved.

"I think you can put that down, Tommy," Stander said as he motioned with one hand. Slowly, Secrist began to lower his weapon. Jenny remained silent. Her wide, fearful and untrusting eyes were still trained on Chris.

"I'll show you!" Chris suddenly leapt forward. Raising the hatchet in his hand and screaming, he swung it in the direction of Jenny's head. At the last moment, she was able lash out with her foot, throwing Chris slightly off balance while twisting her head violently to the side. The blade of the hatchet just grazing one side of her face before it clanged off the metal tractor chassis she was handcuffed to. Her startled cries of pain matching the intensity of Chris's scream of rage.

A gunshot silenced them both.

Pushing himself up, Stander froze with his hands and knees still touching the ground. Silently, he watched Chris collapse into himself. Lurching on halting legs, he turned and looked back, mouthing "Rusty" as he staggered to the ground. A red dot rapidly expanding on the front of his already soaked shirt. Chris pulled at the collar, tearing the thin fabric down the front as if to search for where the blood was coming from. The tattered t-shirt reduced to rags in his clenching fingers. Rolling over onto his back, he turned his head slightly to look back at Stander. In his eyes, the dawning realization that neither man had believed him. Failure molded his features until a darker emotion drew its black shadow across them. Regret.

His eyes slowly closed.

The silence that followed was brief. Replaced by Jenny's continued demands to be released. Her voice rising, vulgarities that made little sense in the aftermath of the tragedy. She was still cursing loudly when Stander felt a hand land on his shoulder. Looking up, he saw Secrist had put the pistol that shot Chris away, and he was reaching down for him. He gently pulled Stander to his feet, and both men stared at each other for long moments. An indescribable mix of emotions carving the face of each. They dropped their eyes at the same time, not a single word passing between them. In unison, they turned to face Jenny. Her dripping face wrenched in agony and despair.

Secrist took a hurried step towards her before Stander reached out and stopped him. He pointed at Jenny and repeated what Chris had said moments earlier. "Look at her head. God damn, Tommy... look at her fucking head!"

The hatchet's blade, though missing its intended target, had scalped a large slice of flesh from the side of Jenny's face. One ear and most of one cheek were now completely gone. Jenny had her free hand pressed to the side of her face trying to cover the wound the best she could. But she couldn't hide the lack of blood. Or the slick, oozing blackness showing through the patch of missing flesh. There were no cheek or skull bones revealed. No fresh blood or tender pink flesh freshly flayed. Only blackness, like the hide of a shiny wet seal surfacing out of water.

"What the fu... Tommy! Check out her wrist, the cuffed one!" Stander gestured wildly as he moved a few steps closer towards Jenny. "Behind the bones of her hand. Under the cuff! Look! All black... what the hell?" The same slippery blackness spilled out from the torn skin and flesh of her wrist. The constant gyrations as she'd struggled against the handcuffs had ripped the flesh all around her wrist. Her skin had rolled down from the wound, revealing white bone at the top of her hand. Stringy threads of black visible at her torn wrist, five of them running down towards each finger.

Both men alternately looked from her wrist to the side of her face. Each trying to make sense of what they were seeing. Neither was sure if they could believe their eyes or not. Jenny, or whatever the thing pretending to be Jenny was, fell to silence. Her eyes roving from one man's face to the other, seeming content to size the situation up before speaking.

Secrist moved first. Stepping forward, he stood beside Stander, barely a yard from Jenny. He pulled his pistol back out and leveled it at her damaged face. "If you don't want to swallow a bullet, you better start explaining. What is all this?" He waved the end of the pistol, indicating the black showing on her face and wrist. "What the hell are you? Are you... were you Jenny? All this time?"

Jenny remained silent, coolly contemplative until she finally dropped her hand to her side. The long flap of skin she'd been pressing to her face slid slowly down like a slice of freshly carved deli meat falling from a butcher's blade. Exposing nearly one whole side of her head, everything underneath was black and glistening.

"The sentiment you share with others of your kind never ceases to amaze me... even after all this time." The voice was undeniably Jenny's, but the words coming out of her mouth sounded all wrong. She'd never spoken this way in the days she'd spent beside Secrist, researching Almore's dark past. "But to answer your question, no. I'd only just slipped her on. Most of her bones I discarded back up by the top of the hill if you want them. Along with the remains of your companion Dennis Reiner. I've been using his husk for quite some time."

"God, this thing was inside of Denny? Pretending to be Denny!" Stander turned to Secrist pointing back up the hill towards the deserted farmstead. "That's what we found inside that truck! What was left of

Denny. How... how is any of this possible?" Though he didn't say it out loud, briefly he wondered if Chris had somehow slipped him some drugs. LSD maybe? How could he believe what he was seeing and hearing was real?

Jenny, or whatever was using her body like a flesh suit, reached up with her free hand to the top of her head. Grabbing part of her loose scalp, she pulled down on the slack hair and skin. Freeing the rest of her head and neck from its fleshy disguise. Revealing more of the slick surface underneath, exposing more of its true self. The black face slipped free from the confines of the human skin as the thing unmasked itself completely. No skull, grinning or otherwise, popped free. But rather, underneath was a smooth blankness suggestive of human features. Undistinguished, it was like a poor imitation or smudged carbon copy of Jenny's face. The substance beneath her skin was smooth and oily, a black whale-like surface slick and dripping. Two long feelers, or queer horns, emerged from the indentations where her eyes should have been. They seemed to stretch straight out, as if just wakened, before retreating slightly in a casual manner and flickering open. Cold blue eyes peaked out, curiously sentient, and appearing to squint. Below them, the black thing's mouth was also exposed. Like the projectile eyes, a stabbing beak that moved in four ways emerged from a cavity meant to mimic a human mouth.

"You gotta be kidding me." Secrist spoke softly, almost reverently.

"That is one ugly motherfucker," Stander added as he peered closely. Though the thing was like nothing Secrist had ever seen before, Stander recognized the strange being. It was the monster that had made a meal of Brian. Split his head open with that beak and sucked his skull dry. It took every ounce of his willpower to keep from destroying the foul thing right then and there. If he had carried a lighter or had a match on him, he'd likely have torched it. Yet the very sight of it, clearly not of this world, was strangely compelling. With its elongated eyes and razor-sharp beak, it was vaguely reminiscent of an octopus. That was as close as it came to anything else found on earth. Something that apparently could move easily among humans, cloaked and hidden within the features of man.

"You are equally as hideous, as I'm sure you must realize." The four-part moving beak clacked open and shut as it spoke in Jenny's voice. Both the sight and sound absurd. "But I can't resist your kind. You taste exquisite."

Secrist, his gun still drawn and pointed squarely at the thing's moving mouth, answered slowly. "The... the taste of... us?" He looked down briefly at the hollow and deflated face of Jenny, still hanging limply across her chest and dripping mottled blood. His voice rose. The pistol, still aimed, shook slightly. "You killed that woman! And for what reason? How could you possibly..."

The clacking mouth opened wide; a wet puff of air blew free followed by a yipping sound that may have been laughter. "Have you not ever hunted for your own food? Caught fish out of a lake or stream to eat from time to time? Do you not use bait? Worms from the soil or minnows from a pond? Do you cry for those beings as you do for this, Jenny? Simply put, I needed her for bait. This one," the tube-like eyes rotated over to where Chris lay unmoving on the ground, "no longer trusted Dennis and needed dealt with."

"That's not the same thing! This was a person! A woman and a mother that..."

"So sentimental. There is no difference! Life is life. The energy that guides you, drives every other living thing on this pitiful rock. All I did was let her energy move on. Freed her from this stiff shell." Jenny, or what had taken her over, gestured down at herself. "Even now, she is likely being reborn."

"Energy? You mean her soul?" Stander couldn't stop himself from asking, jumping back into the bizarre conversation. "Are you trying to tell us reincarnation is a real thing? Jenny is being reborn right now in some hospital somewhere?"

"Your kind is so self-centered... hospital? Maybe. Maybe somewhere in your oceans or waters as well. But maybe deep underground or in the back of a cave. Or maybe," the short burst of its yipping laughter came again, "maybe in a barn somewhere. Think of that the next time you fry up some chicken or eat a burger. You might be eating this, Jenny. Will you cry out then as you do now?" Stander and Secrist exchanged a puzzled look as the thing continued.

"The soul, as you like to call it, though not a unique concept among the vastness of life, is just energy. Her energy has moved on. While I do regret wasting the tasty meat she could have provided me, your kind has no problem making plenty more. After all, that's why I stayed here so long. This planet is... what is it you say? Ah yes, this planet is a veritable smorgasbord, and it has served me well." The yipping resumed from the pointed beak briefly before it continued. "That is, at least until you began poisoning your home and yourselves. Now it's hard to find pure and untainted nourishment anymore. This planet reeks of impending doom, as does Chris. His polluted brain is now just a waste of good meat."

"Earth was a smorgasbord for you? How long have you been here? Are there more of your kind already here?" Stander found he couldn't tear himself away from the surreal conversation, or sight, of this alien being.

"I came here alone, lost among the faraway suns you see above each night. When my transport crash landed in what you now call South America, your kind was in a far different place than it is today. From my perspective, you were just directionless cattle, living only to eat and procreate. To survive, I too had to eat. And, as well known by my kind, the nerve center of intelligent beings provides the purest forms of nourishment. While it was hard to determine how vast your nerve centers might be, considering how simple your culture was, I soon discovered your brains held plenty of nourishment. But most surprisingly, the taste proved to be amazing. Indeed, your kind would be considered a delicacy among my worlds." As it spoke, Stander noticed a clear liquid began to seep and drip from the four-part moving beak. My god, he thought, this thing is drooling.

"So, I lingered. Slowly, I learned to tolerate the sickening sight and smell of your kind. And as I fed, I began to experiment on those I feasted on. Absorbing their limited knowledge, such as it was, along with their memories, fears, and faiths during every feeding. Eventually, I also discovered that, with a little practice, I could mold myself inside your inflexible bodies. Wear the leftover human flesh as a costume over my own advanced, more pliable form. Soon I began to walk among you and learned the many languages and customs of your individual tribes. It wasn't long before I understood your fears were my biggest advantage. Using all the different faiths you humans so blindly cling to, I began to pit man against man. It was simple once I learned how easily your kind hates one another over the pigmentation of skin tone, language, and most importantly, your silly beliefs and religions. Even today, the less enlightened among you still cling to these things as reasons to hate and kill one another." The black, nearly formless alien face began to laugh once again. The idea of hate and murder over something as inconsequential as race and religion a ridiculous notion among any truly intelligent life form. Stander couldn't help but picture in his mind beings from other worlds watching the futile politics of man on earth. If so, it seemed likely planet earth was considered a world of idiots.

The laughing stock of the cosmos, even.

"Using your own hate against you, I was always able to get what I wanted. What I needed. Sustenance. But I do think over time my diet changed me. I became slow witted, imbecilic even. Because, like all of humankind over the countless measure of time, I plundered this planet with little regard. Gorging myself until sated, then moving on to what you might call greener pastures. Finding the next group of man to taste. Donning a body, showing miracles of knowledge, math, and simple technologies. Often reigning as leader, but primarily using religion to influence your kind as simply as a shepherd might herd a flock of sheep. Finding over and over again that your kind values fanciful tales – what you call religion – over obvious truths. This, even though humanity moves from one dominant religious conviction to another, every couple thousand of your years."

"Couple thousand years?" Stander looked over to where Chris lay immobile on the ground. He'd been right along.

"Yes. Although your concept of time is particularly meaningless, I have made this place my home for most of my lifetime. Thousands and thousands of years, as you would trace it. Simply one lifetime as I trace it. For even a common housefly understands a lifetime. Though the fly may live merely days, and your kind lives perhaps decades or a hundred years, my kind lives thousands of your years. None of us escapes our lifetime alive. Measuring time is pointless beyond a lifetime. No matter where in the vastness of life you reside, a lifetime is the same. A great equalizer even. Though I know that concept is likely still beyond your ability to truly grasp."

"Why not call out for help? Return to where you came from? Don't you miss home?" Secrist shook his head as he asked the questions. Were they really conversing with an alien being? He discretely pinched himself on his arm, trying to wake himself. He had to be dreaming all this.

"Home? Again, a quaint concept once you understand we are all just energy. There is no home, no human or alien race, no religion and no ethnic differences. Those concepts are a sickness I could never get your kind to disregard. But I blame that on your maker."

"Maker? You mean God?" Secrist had lowered his weapon slightly, his upper arm resting against his chest, but with the barrel of the gun still pointed straight ahead.

The yipping laughter came again, though weaker and shorter this time. "God? You mean one like me? I've been a god on this planet since before you began to write down your pathetic beliefs. First, blending in with a tribe of people from the distant past your archeologists now refer to as the Norte Chico Civilization." At the mention of the now familiar name of Norte, Stander and Secrist exchanged a knowing glance.

The so-called Norte cult of Almore.

"Over the course of time, I became their God. They called me Viracocha. Later, I was transformed into a God named Itzamna by the Mayan people who followed after them. Before morphing into a God named Huitzilopochtli by their conquerors, the Aztecs. For that tribe, I decided I would play the role of a particularly brutal God. A god of war, the Aztec civilization would sacrifice their most precious, and most delicious, citizens too. It was a glorious time! Later, as that religion fell out of favor and a new people grew in power, I transformed myself once more. Ingratiating myself into Incan society before becoming a new God named Apu-punchau. There, I would have stayed forever had my own true body not begun to betray me."

"Betray you? In what way?" If what this thing was saying was true, its body had still lasted nearly another 1,000 years after the Incan civilization had disappeared.

"I was becoming what you would call elderly. A senior citizen that easily grew tired and restless, as is our way when nearing death. So, I left my little paradise and traveled north. Knowing my lifetime was nearing an end, I searched for lands not yet soiled by your kind. And here, as what you would consider an old man near death, I've spent the last of my lifetime. Living out my days on this continent, staying close to its mighty river and mixing with natives as I had in the past. Though I suppose I lost my ambition in old age, I still helped myself to a few tribes. Eating plenty, but not nearly as ferociously as I once had. Indeed, the ease of travel as man slowly began to understand technology made the need to convince large tribes of my divinity irrelevant. Rather than doing the work needed to convince and enslave entire nations and be looked at as their God, I instead played the part of a God's right-hand man, if you will. Often a priest or cleric of some sort. In that way, I could still sway the masses to provide me with human sacrifices for food as needed."

"If what you say is true, you have been the greatest enemy of mankind. A plague even. Worse than any monster or demon ever imagined." Stander thought back on what he'd experienced recently in France and back home in Michigan. Could this alien explain what he'd seen?

"Perhaps. Or perhaps your greatest gift. Much of the knowledge and what you now take for granted, I provided. Regardless, once I'd arrived at this place, I began using boats to move up and down the river you call the Mississippi. Using the ease of travel to put space between my feedings so as not to arise suspicions. Later, once the coal burning trains came and crisscrossed the lands, I used those to hop from small town to small town. Often riding the rails as a simple hobo, eating discriminately and sleeping much of the time. I've grown so weary, you see." The thing shifted, leaning back casually as it spewed the tale of its life on earth.

"More recently, once the automobile became prevalent, I switched to that for more timely transportation. Using a car, I could feed and be far away before anyone noticed. But it made me lazy. A fat cat even, if you will. Content to end my days here, of all places. Indeed, had I not risen to chase you and your friends for fun – your ripe young fears were so intoxicating – I might have lasted another few hundred of your years. But when you," the black thing motioned towards Stander, "unexpectedly hurt me, puncturing my insides with a mineral not of this planet, I knew my lifetime was nearly over. The last thing I decided I would do on this rock you call home, is taste the nerve center or brain of my killer. That's why I took over Dennis Reiner. I thought he would have knowledge of who and where you were. But to my surprise, as I melded with his mind before devouring it whole, I found he did not know where you'd gone. When he failed me, I tried to move over to Chris. Desperate and knowing my lifetime was at an end, I thought he was my last chance. But I found he was poisoned. Filled with chemicals I dared not tolerate in my old age.

Had I entered him, I likely would have immediately perished. So, I gave up and just waited for my death. And right as it came knocking, here you came, too. Calling me, practically inviting me to dine on you. How could I resist? Yet, for all I have accomplished during my exile here, once again you stand over me. Victorious over one who most on this planet have called a God. How could that be?"

"You're no god any more than I am. And we have nothing in common. You are simply a selfish and sick being. No different than a child burning ants with a magnifying glass. One that hides and cowers. Feeds off the unknowing, swallowing groups of people who gave you all they had." Stander felt his rage returning. How different would his life have been had this thing from another world never come here? Brian would have lived and his group of friends, the Wolf Pack, might still be together. Maybe live in houses close by each other, their wives and children the best of friends.

Just the way they'd planned.

"And how is that different from you? You are correct. I would devour your kind by the hundreds, by the thousands even. Sucking down your small, delicate brains just the same way you suck down chicken eggs and caviar. You see, we are not so very different, you and I. Which is not surprising since most of your precious knowledge is what I chose to share with you. I made most of your beliefs. Or made them up anyway..." The thing, the alien, the god or monster, whatever you believe, was mocking them. Stander felt the prickling sensation of fear churning in his stomach. Why was this thing sharing so much? Was it stalling?

"In that way, I suppose you are right. You on this planet were made by a god such as me." At this, the tube-like elongated eyes opened briefly and focused on Stander. "You... you'll meet him soon when he returns. He keeps bringing you back for some..."

WHOOSH!!

Flames engulfed the thing instantly. It was as much of an explosion as it was a fire. Out of the blaze, the shackled thing shrieked inhumanly. The billowing flames consuming the gasoline-soaked clothes and hair first. The bright fire so unexpected, both men instinctively turned away, shielding themselves with arms outstretched. Secrist could hear Stander screaming "no" over and over again, but he paid no mind.

Chris, still laid out on the ground, had one arm stretched in Jenny's direction. In the other was a cheap plastic lighter. His eyes were open again and, though clearly hurt and weakened, they blazed defiantly along with the fire. The torn shirt he'd borrowed from Stander gone, transformed into the torch he'd tossed and lit the thing inside of Jenny up with.

"God my ass! You're just an overgrown cockroach! Take that you pompous motherfucker!" Chris raised his middle finger weakly. "That," he gasped out, "is for Brian. And Denny...“

Stunned to silence, Stander slowly lowered his hands and stared at the mini-inferno. Some of the overgrown weeds, grass, and brush alongside where it had been cuffed was now burning as well. As were some of the assorted old rubber hoses and belts hanging from the tractor's rusted motor. The black smoke and rising heat made it hard to clearly make anything out. But something in the fire was still moving, growing bigger even.

Secrist spotted the movement as well. Out of the corner of his eye, Stander watched as Secrist raised his revolver. Taking aim at the abomination beginning to shred the remainder of its human disguise right before their eyes. As he prepared to pull the trigger for the second time that evening, the thing from another world suddenly tore itself from the rest of Jenny's body with frightening speed. Twisting and shaking, it quivered once before yanking entirely free of her figure. Pouring out from the top of what was left of Jenny's neck like a salamander wiggling out of a crack in a rotted log. Leaving behind a pool of bubbling and burning human flesh, the skin turned mostly inside out. The flesh suit left hanging limply from the still locked handcuff as the fire consumed it.

Secrist fired just as the enlarging black creature veered desperately to one side. Barely avoiding the bullet that punched a round hole in the metal behind it before flinging itself airborne towards the highest point in the overgrown field – the wrecked harvesting combine tractor with missing rear tires. The flaming thing landed awkwardly among the combine's damaged row dividers. Either miscalculating the jump or unable to land where intended, it was instantly skewered on the upturned, broken metal on the front of the implement. Bent and twisted pieces of steel gouged and tore the monster open along its soft underbelly as it struggled. The thing screeched. The unnatural cry echoing as the labored pitch wavered in and out of tones beyond human hearing. It was a sound Chris and Stander had heard once before. Something from their past they'd hoped to never hear again. But now, the reverberating tones were music to their ears.

The sound of hurt.

The black thing shuddered as it vainly tried to gain some measure of footing and leverage. It squirmed along the top of the combine tractor's twisted row dividers as it worked to free itself. But each frantic movement only seemed to sink the broken steel barbs deeper as it struggled. Underneath the thing, below the farm equipment's airborne and upturned frontend, a pool of white pasty fluid began to drip steadily. The smell of rot and decay, similar to rank or spoiled seafood, filled the night air. The thing was hung-up, trapped on the damaged front end of the tractor. It struggled futilely for a time, but despite the desperate ravings, the rusted metal only sunk deeper. Soon the thing's strength began to waver and fade; the white pool underneath grew larger.

It was dying.

Both Secrist and Stander robotically moved closer as the nearby flames began to wane and diminish. Equally enthralled and repulsed, unable to tear their eyes from the writhing mass before them. The black thing's whale-like skin began to ashen, slowly losing its dark shade and greying. Underneath it, the most severe cuts and injuries appeared brilliantly white, long bleached slashes from its poorly placed jump and ill-advised landing. Or from its struggles as it tried to free itself.

Behind them, Chris had managed to gain his feet. One hand pressed tightly to his chest, trying to slow the blood still seeping from the bullet wound near his shoulder. "Lived thousands of years, huh? And I killed it with a ninety-nine-cent lighter." He sputtered the words out as he leaned heavily against the piece of equipment he'd cuffed Jenny, or the thing in front of them that impersonated Jenny, to. "Some god..."

The white pool below the being continued to grow, and the black coloring of its skin or hide grew even lighter. Unmoving, ashy and grey all over, it lay draped over the front of the combine. The thing seemed to shrink and sag a little more with each passing moment. Something thick, like mucus or phlegm, or perhaps its blood, spilled from the four sharp corners of the mouth. Whatever energy, soul, or life the thing had was gone. Once jet black, the thing that had haunted Chris and Stander their entire lives became paler and paler. White flakes reminiscent of snow fell through the cracks of the farm implement. Like paper consumed by fire, once the light and heat left, the rest of the wispy remains withered and blew away. The slight summer's night breeze leaving only a pool of white mucus or blood behind. Even that slowly disappearing as it soaked into the ground of the deserted farmland.

Nothing left lingering behind.

ALMORE, ILLINOIS
AUGUST 10TH, 1900

NORTE WAITED IMPATIENTLY. TELLING himself he'd grown weary of the clingy ragtag group of loyal settlers who'd remained to service him. Some of whom he now feared might easily be swayed by the strange woman or witch who somehow had known all his secrets. Damnable mongrel! Tonight, he would be done with them all. He'd orchestrated a grand farewell feast in his honor before he abandoned the last of his followers. He could see from where he sat in the earthen tunnel that the line outside was forming. Like cattle in a shoot.

He wiped the drool off his chin.

He had decided, as he'd done occasionally in the past when suspicions rose among their kind, he would go into hiding. Forget all his previous plans of once more building his own little utopia along this grand river. Ah... he thought to himself, and he'd had such high hopes for this beautiful land. But it was time for him to disappear. The burgeoning village of Almore, a few miles away from their riverside settlement, had proven to be a thorn in his side. Only days before, a defiant woman had accosted him on the street. Marked in ink along her flesh was a symbol even he did not know the true origin of. But he knew enough to fear the wearer. Technology, he understood. But that mark was something entirely different. A sign any sentient life knew whether consciously aware of it or not.

What had she called herself? Madeleine? She'd stepped to him and whispered directly in his face. Spoke to him first in his own tongue, a language he'd not uttered nor heard in a millennium. The woman had known what he was and cooed in his ear all the awful things he'd done before arriving on this planet. Hissed at him, she'd soon expect his sacrifice in exchange for her leniency. Then chanted quietly in a language he did not recognize, yet somehow fully understood. Crooning a modulation of tones barely audible. It was then he'd fully understood his role and destiny. Quickly making plans for this one last feast.

Norte sat on his throne. The light from the nearby torches partially illuminating the short tunnel before him. The first of the remaining followers entered down into the chamber. A dazed look of rapture stupidly plastered across her face. She laid her head in his lap as she'd been taught, closing her eyes contently. Norte reached out his hand and caressed her hair.

"Time to be saved, my child." He spoke with the Spanish accent he'd inherited from his current human body. "Time to be one with my blood and flesh. Be not afraid, my child." He felt her trembling and could taste her fear in the air around them. The aroma intoxicating. But, meek as a little lamb, she remained kneeling at his feet. Even as a drop of drool dripped down from his own mouth, wetting the side of her cheek.

"Just have faith..."

ALSO BY DM GRITZMACHER

Book 1

Skulldiggery: The Relict

Book 2

Skulldiggery: The Quarry

Book 3

Skulldiggery: The Lingering

COMING SOON: Book 4

Skulldiggery: The Shroud

Gritzmonster.com